"Written with insight and humor, Sarah Smith's *Faker* is a charming, feminist, and diverse romance that will have you hooked until the very last page."

—Sonya Lalli, author of *A Holly Jolly Diwali*

Titles by Sarah Echavarre Smith

Faker
Simmer Down
On Location
The Boy with the Bookstore

The
Boy
with the
Bookstore

SARAH ECHAVARRE SMITH

BERKLEY ROMANCE

New York

BERKLEY ROMANCE
Published by Berkley
An imprint of Penguin Random House LLC
penguinrandomhouse.com

Library of Congress Cataloging-in-Publication Data

Names: Smith, Sarah, 1985- author.
Title: The boy with the bookstore / Sarah Echavarre Smith.
Description: First Edition. | New York: Berkley Romance, 2022.
Identifiers: LCCN 2022009305 (print) | LCCN 2022009306 (ebook) |
ISBN 9780593545980 (trade paperback) | ISBN 9780593545997 (ebook)
Classification: LCC PS3569.M5379758 B69 2022 (print) |
LCC PS3569.M5379758 (ebook) | DDC 813/.54—dc23
LC record available at https://lccn.loc.gov/2022009305
LC ebook record available at https://lccn.loc.gov/2022009306

First Edition: September 2022

Printed in the United States of America
1st Printing

Title page illustration by AIWD/Shutterstock.com

*For all the Joelles and Maxes out there.
You deserve all the happily ever afters in the world.*

The
Boy
with the
Bookstore

Chapter 1

Joelle

When Max Boyson walks into my bakery, I almost drop the tray of croissants I'm holding and try not to pass out.

It's a daily occurrence for me. Because this is what I have to contend with when he strolls in at seven forty-five on the dot: His six-foot-two frame clad in a black leather jacket, worn jeans covering his long, muscular legs. He wears a knit beanie over that mass of light brown hair, and there's a healthy amount of scruff sheeting along a jawline sharp enough to cut diamonds.

He's a cross between a ridiculously handsome Instagram model and a biker.

And that smile. Oh my freaking god, that smile. Always a half smile. Always the right corner of his mouth quirked up like he's hiding a secret that he's dying to tell. Always deliciously wolfish.

But it's not just his looks. It's his whole demeanor. The way he walks into a room, posture straight, gaze focused and unbothered at the same time. He looms large but is also aware of himself. As physically imposing as he is, he's careful not to crowd anyone when he steps into the tiny space of my bakery. He holds the door for people when he walks in and out. And he always moves out of the way when there's a line. It's an easy confidence he possesses—something I've always ached to have.

He is the epitome of everything I find attractive in a man. And that pinnacle of hotness walks into my world every single morning, setting fire to my skin and turning my brain to mush.

I wish I weren't such an utter cliché. But I am.

I am the physical representation of the phrase "mousy shy girl." If you were to search that on Google Images, my photo would be the first to pop up.

I've got it all: wild hair that hits all the way to the middle of my back and hides my face when it's not pulled into a ponytail, thick-rimmed glasses, a penchant for biting my lip and stammering when I'm nervous, and the inability to maintain prolonged eye contact when a handsome guy looks my way.

That's pretty much what I've done every other day when Max walks in here and places his usual order of an *ube* latte—iced in the spring and summer, hot in the fall and winter—and a plain croissant, just before he strolls next door and opens his bookshop, Stacked, which occupies the store space next to mine in this brick building we both lease in the Jade District of Portland, Oregon.

It all happens like some slow-motion scene out of a movie. Max half smiles. I instantly forget that I often have a store full of customers to help. He makes casual conversation, asking me about the morning rush, what new pastries I've got on the menu that day, if the pigeons in the dumpster behind our building have dive-bombed me when I took out the trash. And like the unsophisticated and painfully awkward human that I am, I burn hot all across my cheeks and neck and chest. I giggle, then stammer my way through the conversation, all the while trying not to stare unblinkingly at him so I don't come off like a psycho.

And then he leaves, my heart resumes a steady beat, and I will myself to act like a normal human being again.

It's all very embarrassing, the fact that I devolve into a flustered teen every time I'm in his presence.

But not today.

No, no, no. Today marks something new. Today, I'm going to actually do something about my crush on Max Boyson that kicked off when he started renting out the space next to me a year and a half ago. I'm going to ask him out.

It's a daunting prospect for sure. We're technically work acquaintances and if he shoots me down, that's going to be awkward as hell. But during our daily chats, I could swear I feel a flirty edge from him. Like, he's pulling back from obviously flirting with me because he doesn't want to come off like a creep who's hitting on the woman who works next door to him. And I definitely appreciate that.

Or maybe he's just being a cordial neighbor.

I deflate the slightest bit, then immediately straighten back up. No. None of that disparaging talk. I've done that enough my whole life. It's time to go against my play-it-safe personality and do something bold for a change.

Setting down the tray of croissants, I grip the edge of the metal countertop and flash a quick smile at Max when he strolls to the end of the line. I'm hyperfocused as I quickly transfer half of the croissants to the nearby display case before helping the next customer, who's a few people ahead of him. As I ring up orders and hand out pastries, I will myself to keep cool.

Breathe in for one, two, three . . . breathe out for four, five, six . . .

Yes, I'm aware of just how pathetic it is that I, a thirty-two-year-old woman, have to coach myself through a calming breathing exercise in preparation to ask a guy out. But it's no surprise given my dating history. I've only ever asked a guy out face-to-face once in my life . . . in high school. Yeah, I've asked men out since then, but it's only been a handful of times via dating app DMs. That's completely different from making direct eye contact with the ruggedly handsome and tatted-up bookstore owner I've been lusting after and saying the words "Hey, you wanna grab a drink sometime?"

Just the thought sends my nerves crackling, like a match falling into a box of fireworks. I swallow back the somersault in my stomach and greet the next customer, quietly counting down as Max inches closer and closer.

And then, finally, he's at the front of the line, just a foot away from me. I look past him and see that no one else is in line. That means I won't have to ask him out in front of an audience. Thank god.

Slowly, silently, I breathe in and take it as a sign that this moment was meant to happen. I muster every ounce of nerve I have and make eye contact with him while smiling.

"Joelle. Hey."

I will my eyes not to flutter. I love it when he says my name in that soft, low tone that's practically a growl.

"Hey, Max. How's your morning going?" If I could, I would high-five myself right now. My voice isn't one bit squeaky, like I assumed it would be. I sound cool and calm, not at all like the nerve-racked nerd that I actually am.

He tilts his head as he looks down at me, almost like he's intrigued. And there it is. That crooked half smile.

"Pretty damn good now that I've got your incredible coffee and pastries to power me through the day."

I bite back a humongous grin as I turn away to quickly prep his *ube* latte—hot, since it's almost the end of May and we haven't yet hit warm temperatures here in Stumptown.

"How's Pumpkin doing?"

I smile to myself at how almost every morning he comes in here he asks about my pet hamster, who I bring with me to work every day.

"She's good. Chilling on my desk right above the space heater, so she's pretty much in heaven."

His low chuckle makes me grin even wider.

I pluck a fresh croissant from the display case, tuck it into a paper wrapper, and slide both over the counter to him.

"How are Muffin and Doughnut?" I ask, trying my hardest not to squeal at the oh-so-cute names he picked out for his rescue pit bull mix and tuxedo cat. I would have never guessed that a guy who looks like a stereotypical bad boy would opt for such sweet pet names. But it's yet another endearing quality that lands in the column of "things that make Max Boyson insanely hot."

He thanks me as he hands over his credit card and I swipe it through the card reader. As he reaches his arm out, I get a glimpse of the black ink that peeks out from his jacket sleeve. It's a hint of that elaborate sleeve tattoo on his right arm, an intriguing mix of cursive script, several clusters of skulls, massive feather wings, and a stack of books.

I blink and recall just how delicious his tattoo looks when he's wearing a T-shirt or a tank top or a button-up shirt with the sleeves rolled up along his forearms . . .

I swallow and focus back on his face as he speaks.

"They're good. Doughnut is still picking on Muffin most days. He's been stealing that new bed I bought her almost every night."

"Aww, really? Poor Muffin."

"It's hilarious to see a fourteen-pound house cat bully a seventy-pound pit bull. It's like neither of them are aware of their sizes."

I glance up at the door, thankful that no customers have walked in yet so that I'd have to stop our conversation and help them. Our chitchat is easy and pleasant, the perfect segue into my big ask. The nerves inside me slowly dissipate and I'm feeling surprisingly light.

Now to wait for the right moment to actually ask him out.

He sips his latte, complimenting the yummy nutty-vanilla flavor of the *ube* before taking a giant bite of his croissant. His eyes roll to the back of his head as he moans, and I nearly choke. I'm one thousand percent certain that I've never heard a sexier sound in my life.

I whirl back around to the baking tray and start blindly stacking more croissants into the display case instead of fainting at the mere sound of Max eating.

"Christ, is that good." He frowns at the croissant like he can't believe the taste of it.

I laugh. "You say that almost every morning."

He shrugs and tugs at his beanie. "Best croissant in Portland, hands down. My death row meal would be a pile of these babies, no question."

I burst into giggles, which makes Max laugh between bites.

"That's a bit morbid," I say, wrinkling my nose.

His smile doesn't budge. "It's true. Best way to go out, death by carbs."

I cover my mouth, I'm laughing so hard.

He peers around the front space of my bakery, which holds a half-dozen small tables. All of them are full with customers chowing down on their own carb-laden goodies.

"So tell me." He leans over the counter, the expression on his face taking on a conspiratorial edge. "What's your death row meal?"

I gaze up at him, relishing how he towers over me since he's nearly ten inches taller. The heat from his body skims over me, and I have to look down for a moment.

"Um, well. I haven't given it much thought."

He wags his eyebrow at me before he sips his latte. "Come on. Play with me a bit."

This time that flutter hits straight at the center of my chest. Okay, that is unquestionably a flirty comment. Yay!

When Max first moved in next door and started dropping by and showering me in half smiles and pleasant conversation, I was giddy. But when I saw him acting the same way around my mom, auntie, and *apong*, I felt decidedly less special. Clearly that's just his personality—gotta charm the neighbors. We share a tiny brick building, after all.

But that eyebrow wag he's blessed me with just now combined with the growled delivery of "play with me a bit" is a game changer. It's the green flag I need to boost the last reserves of my confidence to ask him out.

"This is going to sound weird, but hear me out: a homemade, fresh-from-the-oven baguette with roasted bone marrow."

He frowns like he's unsure of what I've just said, but the look in his eyes remains playful. "Gotta say, I wasn't expecting that."

I shrug, and pull on the strap of my apron. "I'm full of surprises."

That earns me a full-on grin.

"What's bone marrow taste like?" he asks. "I've never had it."

He's leaning even closer now. Our bodies are less than a foot apart and before I answer, I take a second to just soak in the moment. I'm openly, unquestionably flirting with Max Boyson while we talk about food.

Way to go, Joelle! Look at you being an adorable and sexy flirt! Combining your two biggest passions: food and the hot bookstore owner next door! You're seriously doing it!

"It's rich. And smooth. And thick. And fatty, but in a good way. Like butter, but with a deeper, fuller, nuttier flavor."

Max's inky black pupils start to dilate as he gazes down at me, his mouth cracked open, like he's hypnotized and intrigued at once. I cease breathing.

He clears his throat. "Damn . . ."

I nod quickly. "On hot, crusty bread, it is divine. You need to try it."

He nods right back, like he's in a trance. I'm in a trance too. I can't seem to stop looking at him as I wax poetic about one of my favorite food combinations.

"How is it served?" he asks, his voice between a groan and a growl. "The marrow, I mean."

I watch, mesmerized at the slow movement along his stubbled throat.

I swear I can feel my skin tingling as my internal temperature rises. Who knew talking about bone marrow could get me this worked up?

"Sometimes they cut the bone lengthwise and you can just scrape your knife along the hollow part of the bone and out comes the marrow," I say. "And sometimes they cut it into chunks and the marrow's in the middle, so you scrape out as much as you can, but there's almost always some left, so the best way to get it out is to just put the bone in your mouth and suck it out, really get your tongue in the hole and lick and . . ."

I trail off when I realize what I've said.

A few heads pivot in our direction from the nearby tables. They've clearly overheard me. I notice too that Max's brow is at his hairline at what I've said.

"Oh my god." I let out a flustered laugh. "Did I really just say that? 'Put it in your mouth' and 'suck it out' and 'get your tongue in the hole and lick' . . . Wow. I, um, that's not what I meant to . . ."

When Max's eyes go wide, that's when a tidal wave of internal panic unleashes inside me. "I mean, that's absolutely what you *should* do if you eat marrow. Just, like, suck out the marrow and tongue it out—that's what you need to do to get as much off the bone as possible. Sorry, I just made it sound weirdly sexual and awkward talking about sucking and tonguing and licking. I swear, that's absolutely not what I meant to imply . . ."

And now the entire bakery is staring at me. And Max is gawking at me like I've grown another head.

On the inside, I've deflated like a stabbed balloon. That's it. My chance to ask out Max is officially blown to hell. I completely ruined the moment with my unintentional sexual innuendo.

I fight the invisible flames of embarrassment engulfing my cheeks and direct an apologetic smile at the tables.

"Um, our culinary chat got a bit impassioned. Apologies."

People slowly turn away from me. And then I muster the last morsels of my now fleeting dignity to face Max. He remains wide-eyed, his mouth partway open, shock clouding his entire expression.

"So um, yeah. Baguette and bone marrow would be my death row meal," I quickly mumble.

I clear my throat and pray that the floorboards suddenly open up and swallow me whole so I can escape the utter mortification of this moment.

Max nods once, a dazed expression on his face. "Okay . . ."

For a few seconds we say nothing. And then he backs slowly away and forces a polite smile. "Have a good day, then."

With a shaky hand, I wave good-bye, then dart straight through the kitchen doors and crumple to the floor, cradling my face in my hands. And then I groan.

"Real smooth, Joelle," I mutter.

My phone buzzing from the metal table in the middle of the kitchen pulls me out of my humiliation stupor. I lean up, snatch up my phone, and read the text from my best friend, Whitney.

Whitney: So? How'd it go? Did you ask him out??

Me: I almost did. And then I ruined it by talking about oral sex and bone marrow.

Whitney: ???

Me: I'll explain later.

Whitney: Hugs 🖤

I sigh, grateful for a best friend who for the past twenty years of our friendship has loved me unconditionally despite my near-constant awkwardness.

I force myself back out to the front of the shop, plaster on a fake yet polite smile, and continue with the workday, all too aware that in addition to mousy shy girl, I am officially the world's most cringe-y human being.

Chapter 2

Joelle

"You really said that? About the tonguing and the sucking and the licking?"

Whitney's hazel eyes sparkle with disbelief as she chows down on *pandesal* while perched on the edge of the metal table in the kitchen of my bakery.

I nod, frowning down at the slab of shortbread dough I've just whipped up. I punch it with my fist, then flip it over.

"Oh, Jojo. You didn't." Her defeated tone rings like a gong in my ears.

"Oh, but I did."

It's been one day since the most embarrassing attempt at asking someone out on a date in human history occurred. Just thinking about it sends me into a full-body cringe. I even asked Auntie Elba to come in early and run the register this morning while I hid in the kitchen and cooked and prepped so I could avoid Max. I can't handle seeing him right now.

I sigh just as Whitney hops off the metal table and pulls me into a side hug.

"It's okay, Jojo," she whispers with my head tucked under her chin.

I let out a chuckle, amused that she's coddling me like a baby. "I just . . . I don't know what's wrong with me. People ask people out on dates all the time. And the one time I do it, I screw it up in the most epic and humiliating way."

"You were nervous," Whitney says in that coaxing tone of hers that she always employs whenever she's trying to soothe me. She takes another bite of the pillowy, dinner-roll-sized, slightly sweet bread. "It happens."

"Not to you."

She steps back and out of our hug. When she tilts her head to the side, her cascade of fiery red hair falls across her shoulder. "Come on, Joelle."

I glance down at the flour coating nearly every inch of my pink apron. I'm used to this, but today it feels like a testament to my ability to make a mess. "It's true. I've seen you do it. Thousands of times. You make it look so easy. You just waltz up to whatever guy you set your sights on, flash that gorgeous smile, tilt your head to the side, and say, 'Hey, you.' They're down for anything—making out with you, getting kicked in the shin. They're putty in your hands."

She flashes a sympathetic smile. "I guess I just don't get nervous about that sort of thing. But there are a million things you're good at that I'm not."

"Like what?"

"Baking."

I laugh as I work the slab of *ube* shortbread dough along the cold metal surface until it's a light purple smoothish log shape, and then I wrap it in plastic film and stick it into the fridge to chill.

"I'm serious, Jojo." Whitney hops back up onto the table and sips the mocha I brewed for her when she dropped by this afternoon on her lunch break. "If I had to bake anything for anyone—let alone a store full of customers—I'd be hyperventilating. You know how bad I am at cooking. I'd go out of business after a single day."

When I look at her, I notice the furrow of her brow and the worry in her eyes. I soften instantly. Whitney is a disaster in the kitchen and it's one of her biggest insecurities. She's set the kitchen on fire in almost every apartment she's ever lived in. In the year she's lived in her new condo, she's had to put out one grease fire and replace her smoke detector. Twice.

"I live on sandwiches, salads, takeout, and leftovers from whatever you've cooked when you come over," she says. "And when I do have to cook for someone, I order from a restaurant, then lie and say I made it. How sad is that?"

I pull her into a hug. "Okay, okay. That's a worthy flaw. Slightly less embarrassing than my penchant for unintentionally alluding to oral sex while attempting to chat up my crush, but still. I'll give you that."

We share a laugh, and I start to feel the slightest bit lighter.

"At least you don't have to call the fire department every time your biggest weakness surfaces."

"Yeah. I just slowly die of embarrassment instead." I yank at the messy bun on top of my head and groan. "What was I even thinking, asking him out in the first place? I've seen the women he dates. They look nothing like me."

In the time that Max has had his bookstore next to my bakery, I've seen him attract attention from people constantly. But surprisingly, despite how handsome and charming he is, he doesn't appear to date much—or at least he doesn't bring them around his bookstore often. I recall a few times when dates have met him at the store. They greet him with a cheek kiss before leaving hand in hand. They all boast a similar effortlessly gorgeous look: flawless natural makeup, perfectly tousled hair, and stylish clothing.

Just thinking about how different I look from them sends a flash of insecurity through me. I'm the poster child for casual-wear. I'm average height and live in jeans, T-shirts, and sneakers. I'm always wearing an apron. And I'm always covered in flour.

"I'm definitely not his type. And I feel like a loser for even thinking I had a chance with him."

"Hey." Whitney's sharp tone and pointed look jolt me. "No talking shit about my best friend, got it?"

I can't help but crack a smile at how she wags her finger at me.

"Not only are you gorgeous, you're the most talented baker in all of Portland. And you're kind, sweet, loyal, and selfless. You put your dreams on hold to help your family. I'm lucky to know you, Joelle Prima. Never, ever, ever talk yourself down."

My chest aches, in part because of Whitney's fierce defensiveness over me. But the mention of my family and the tragedy that almost destroyed us fourteen years ago—and what I did to help keep my parents, my aunt, and my grandmother from falling into financial ruin—struck a chord.

The memory of my mother's pained tone echoes in my ears.

Joelle, anak, *we can't ask you to do this. This money was for your future—your dream.*

A lump forms in my throat instantly. Pain pulses as I attempt to swallow it away. Just like that day when I traded my dream for my family's financial security.

Mom. I want to help. More than I've ever wanted to do anything. Please let me do this for you guys. Just take the money, okay?

I shove aside the memory and force a smile at Whitney. "You're the best, Whit. Thanks."

Just then, Auntie Elba waltzes into the kitchen with Apong Celeste on her arm.

She beams at Whitney and pulls her into a hug, and then Apong Celeste hugs her. I smile at the sight of Auntie Elba and Apong stretching up to wrap their arms around statuesque Whitney. Then they pepper her with questions about her life and her job while she finishes her *pandesal* and coffee.

"Speaking of work, I gotta head back." She shoves the last bit of bread into her mouth, swipes her purse from the table, and blows a kiss at Pumpkin, who's snoozing away in the corner of her plastic portable cage that's propped on my desk. "Management finally approved my Chicks Who Code summer internship. Yay!"

We congratulate her with cheers. Whitney is a brilliant computer programmer at a local tech company who's passionate about getting young women to join the STEM field. She spearheaded a partnership between her company and a few local high schools to recruit students interested in STEM to apply for internships at her firm.

Whitney turns back to me. "I know you're slammed, but would you be able to prep baked goods for the official orientation in June? I know that's only a few weeks away, but I've got the company credit card at my disposal so I was hoping you could whip up some bougie pastries and charge top dollar."

She winks at me, and I'm reminded of how generous my best

friend is. She often uses my bakery, Lanie's, to cater company events for her firm because they've got deep pockets and she's always looking for ways to support my small business.

"Of course I'm on board. Whatever you want, I'll happily bake it for you."

She squeals and claps her hands. "I was hoping you'd say that. I was thinking in addition to pastries, you could maybe make cookies that look like computer screens? Maybe with some cute lines of coding in icing? I know that's probably so tedious . . ."

I can tell by the way her face twists in hesitation that she's shy to ask me this. But I know just how much this program means to her. Her interest in coding started when we were in middle school, and one of the things she despised was how so few girls were encouraged to pursue it as a career or even an interest. She's worked so hard to get this program off the ground at her workplace and to make STEM programs more accessible for girls. I'm so proud of her, and I want to help make sure the orientation for her internship program goes off without a hitch. If she wants a million sugar cookies with intricate icing designs, I'll happily do it for her.

"Anything you want, Whit. I'll make it happen."

She beams and pulls me into a hug. "Oh, thank you, Jojo! Can we meet up for a drink tonight at that bar on Glisan after work so we can go over the exact order?"

I tell her of course. We break apart, and she mentions that her boss and a couple of higher-ups at the company will be attending the orientation.

"I just want to blow them away from every angle, you know? Maybe it's silly to care so much about the food—"

I hold up a hand. "Not silly at all. I totally get it. I will make sure you have the most delicious pastries and the most beautifully decorated cookies your bosses have ever seen. They'll be so impressed that they'll green-light every idea you pitch to them."

Whitney pulls me into another hug before thanking me. I promise to meet her tonight and she leaves. I turn back to Auntie and Apong and refill their coffees.

"Thank you for coming early today," I tell them.

Auntie Elba pats my hand. "Of course, *anak*. You know how much we love helping out here."

I glance over at Apong Celeste, who sits at the stool draped in her favorite floral muumuu, her gray hair pinned back in a low bun, as she starts to work the dough with her slim fingers. Even at ninety-two years old, she's nimble with her hands and keeps up with everyone in the kitchen. She just has to sit while she works.

I pop over and give her a quick squeeze. Her floral perfume hits my nostrils and I close my eyes. It's the most comforting scent in the world. When I blink and breathe in, I recall a million memories of being cuddled next to her on the couch as we watched *The Price Is Right* and soap operas whenever she babysat me as a kid.

She kisses me on the cheek. "*Anakko*, you look so pretty today."

I tell her "Thanks" even though my instinct is to deflect the compliment. I look like I've fought my way out of a giant bag of flour. My hair is a mess and I've got white dust all over my jeans, shirt, and apron.

"Just trying to keep up with your gorgeousness, Apong," I say.

She laughs and I take a moment to soak in the joyful sound. Small exchanges like these are why I'm so thankful to be able to see my grandma every day. That's the best part of still living at home at my age. Sure, I sometimes endure judgmental comments and stares from people when they find out that I live in a small apartment above my parents' garage. But they can think whatever they want. We've always been a close-knit family, and ever since the day they almost lost everything, I vowed that I'd do whatever I could to always be nearby and help take care of them.

Auntie Elba gently grabs my hand, pulling me back to the moment. "You sure you don't want to leave early? It's only a couple of hours till you close. We can handle the rest of the shift and closing duties."

Sincerity and concern converge in her focused carob-brown eyes. No one else would detect that look in her gaze or the subtext in her words. But I do.

I smile at her. "I'm fine working the rest of the shift. Promise. You don't always have to offer to cover for me. You stopping by for a bit is help enough."

"Yes, but it's the least I can do."

"Auntie . . ."

I catch Apong nodding in agreement, her eyes shining with tenderness. They're the exact same shade as Auntie Elba's eyes, only her gaze turns pleading as she looks at me.

"It's just . . . I wish I could offer more, *anakko*. We all do. You've done so much and the least we can offer is to help out at the bakery more . . ."

Apong Celeste waves her slim hand in the air as she says something quickly in Ilocano. She's speaking so fast that I don't catch it all, except the mention of money. It jolts me like a bucket of cold water to the face.

"Auntie. Apong. Listen. You don't owe me any money. None of you do. Okay?"

Auntie shakes her head, like she doesn't want to believe me.

"I just . . . I'll never forget what you did for us. How foolish we were to believe that financial adviser."

Her eyes water as she recounts that day. And just like that, it all comes flooding back.

In an instant, I'm eighteen years old again. It's three months before my high school graduation, and I've just walked into the house after coming home from working my shift at the mall food court. I was so damn giddy. My boss had just promised me full-time hours that summer along with a week off so I could go on a summer road trip with my friends before heading to culinary school and kick-starting my lifelong dream: to become a pastry chef and move to Paris someday to work in a bakery.

But the minute I walked in, I stopped dead in my tracks at the scene unfolding in the kitchen.

Mom slumped at the kitchen island crying. Dad standing behind her, his hands resting on her shoulders, his face twisted in agony. Auntie Elba hunched at the kitchen table with Apong Celeste. They were crying too.

"Wh-what happened?" I asked them.

It took them a few seconds to answer. That was when I noticed the piles of papers and letters scattered across the counter and kitchen table. Numbers and dollar signs and red lettering covered the pages. None of it made sense to me as I quickly scanned them over. But I could feel that this was bad.

When Mom and Dad tearfully recounted to me what happened, I stood there, frozen with disbelief. I didn't understand everything, but I got the gist of it. Something about an investment that Dad's work friend told him about . . . something about how promising the presentation sounded . . . something about how over the prior two years, Mom, Dad, Auntie, and Apong diverted the bulk of their retirement and savings to be managed by that friend-of-a-friend financial planner . . . something about impressive returns . . . something about how over the last month the guy stopped communicating . . . something about how he ended up being a fraud. A liar. A thief.

And then the words I'll never, ever forget.

It's gone. All of our money. It's all gone.

I remember the strangest things from that moment. I remember the hum of the refrigerator in the background, how loud it was. I remember the smell of burnt fish sauce. I remember how stagnant the air in the room felt.

But what I remember most vividly was that feeling of resignation that washed over me. It didn't hit hard; it was slow-moving, like a cold, wet fog crawling across my skin.

In that moment, I knew I couldn't take the savings my parents put aside for me for college. I couldn't leave them, Auntie, and Apong in financial ruin while I lived my life like normal. I'd never be able to live with myself.

So I told them to take the money they had saved for culinary school and use it to replenish what they could of the savings they lost. It wasn't nearly enough, but it was better than nothing. And I promised them I would help dig them out of this hole. I promised them I'd work to help them earn money.

They refused at first—all of them did.

But your education, anak. *It's so important. It's your dream to go to culinary school. You can't give it up.*

Each one of them pleaded with me not to, that they would figure out a way to get through it without needing my help. But the longer we sat and scrambled together the facts of the situation, the more dire it was. The financial planner was a con artist who left zero trace of his whereabouts, and there was no way to get their money back. They didn't have money for lawyers or to hire a private investigator to try to track him down. That's what the police and investigators advised when my family went to them to file a police report. They were screwed.

I was the only one who could help.

And that's what I did. Instead of going to culinary school when I graduated, I started working full-time during the week and got an extra weekend job. For years, that's what we all did. Each of us worked and saved as much money as possible. Even Auntie Elba's two kids, who are older than me and grew up here in Portland, have jobs overseas and sent money over the years when they could to help. Auntie Elba and Apong Celeste sold their houses and moved in with my parents to save even more money and put the profit into their savings and retirement. Slowly but surely over the years, they rebuilt their savings. There's still a ways to go—Auntie Elba should be retired now, but she can't. There's not enough money saved, even with her kids helping, for her to quit working. And even though Apong Celeste is technically retired, she works as a babysitter for the neighborhood kids a few days a week to earn extra cash.

But we're better off than we were. And eventually I figured out a way to achieve some semblance of my dream. While working for a catering company a handful of years ago, I noticed the old bakery in this building was hiring. I started working here on my days off and when the owner retired, I approached the landlord, Ivan, and asked to take over the lease.

It was a hard sell. He was going to demo the interior of the building and build something new, then sell it. But I somehow talked him into scrapping all of those plans and giving me a shot at renting the space for my own bakery.

Maybe it was my enthusiasm. Maybe it was the number of times I called him and went to his office to convince him my bakery would be a success. When he finally said yes, I was over the moon.

I'll never forget what he said to me that day.

"You've got a lot of heart, Joelle. And even though I don't know you well, for some reason, I have faith in you."

I squealed, I was so thrilled. And then I jumped right into work mode. I renamed the bakery Lanie's, after my middle name, and made it my own: a cozy bakery serving Filipino and European baked goods—an homage to my heritage, my family, and my dream. I never was able to professionally train, but I'd amassed years of experience from a million catering and bakery jobs. And when my family's not busy at their own jobs, they drop by and work shifts here and there to help me out so I don't have to hire help.

It wasn't what I dreamed I'd be doing, but it's what I'm meant to be doing. I get to bake. I get to make people happy with my food. And I get to make sure my family is financially secure. That's more than enough.

I blink and refocus on the present, on Auntie Elba's teary stare. It makes my eyes burn with tears. I blink them away before they can tumble down my cheeks.

When I gently grab her shoulders, she shakes her head.

"You saved us, *anak*. We owe you everything."

My lips tremble as I smile. "That's not at all how I see it. You helped raise me, remember? You and Apong Celeste watched me ever since I was a baby so Mom and Dad could go to work and not have to pay for daycare."

I glance over at Apong, who's wiping away a tear from her face. The bright lighting in the kitchen illuminates the delicate wrinkles in the skin of her hands and face.

"You changed my diapers," I say to them both. "You walked me to and from school. You packed my lunches. You bathed me and put me to bed. And after all that, I wanted to do something for you. This is part of it."

She lets out a snotty chuckle and pats my cheek. "Oh, *anakko*. We did those things because we love you."

"Exactly. That's the same reason I did what I did. Because I love you too."

A tear escapes down my cheek at the same moment that one tumbles down Auntie Elba's face. She flashes a pained smile and shakes her head. "My Joelle. You are an angel, and we don't deserve you."

Apong Celeste mumbles her agreement.

Auntie cups my face with both hands and plants a kiss on my cheek before releasing me. Then she grabs a clean dishcloth from the table and dries my cheeks before drying her face.

"Okay. Time to finish those pork adobo croissants." She claps her hands.

I start to tell her that I wasn't planning on having them on tomorrow's menu, but she waves a hand. "I know, I know. I'm making them for Max."

"Oh."

Just the mention of his name has me sputtering. I clear my throat and pretend to fuss with a stack of metal bowls just so Auntie Elba doesn't notice.

"He gave my car a jump the other day when the battery died," she says as she pulls a small slab of chilled croissant dough from the massive metal refrigerator. "And he wouldn't take any money. Can you believe it?"

"Such a sweet boy," Apong says.

Auntie Elba nods. "I have to make him something to tell him thank you. It's the least I can do."

Despite the residual embarrassment I'm still nursing from yesterday, my insides turn gooey at the thought of Max helping my aunt and refusing money.

I leave her to finish baking while I head out to the front and run the register and lobby until it's time to close. When I spot Clarence, a local guy who collects cans for money, crossing the parking lot, I quickly pack up a handful of pastries and run them out to him.

"Oh, Miss Joelle. You spoil me." He peers into the bag and grins wide. "You sure you want me to have these?"

"I made too much today. You take them."

He starts to dig into his pocket, but I stop him.

"No charge."

He hesitates for a second, but I insist. I don't know Clarence well—he comes in from time to time to buy coffee from me, so we just make small talk. Because of that it feels wrong to ask him about his financial situation. But he mentioned being in between jobs before when I've chatted with him in the past. He looks to be in his seventies and diligently collects cans almost daily. The least I can do is offer him food when I see him.

He pats my hand. "Thank you. Really."

He heads down the street and I go back inside. When I slip back into the kitchen, the smell of soy sauce, vinegar, savory pork, and buttery dough hits my nostrils.

"Holy yum," I say as I gawk at the tray of croissants cooling on the metal rack against the wall. The phantom flavor of salty, vinegary, fatty pork with the buttery, flaky croissant has my mouth watering.

Auntie Elba beams up at me as she plucks the half-dozen pork adobo croissants from the tray, packs them into a paper bag, and hands it to me. "You can take these to Max, right? I have to take Apong to her eye appointment."

"Oh. Um, sure."

They both leave me with a hug and a kiss before heading out the back door. Bag of croissants in hand, I walk back out into the darkened empty lobby of the bakery. I peer across my glass storefront to Max's storefront several feet away and see him standing near the register, frowning at his laptop screen before he walks toward the back.

I take a second to deep-breathe, shoving aside the lingering embarrassment from yesterday. And then I walk into Stacked.

Chapter 3

Joelle

It's late afternoon, just a few hours before Max closes, and I count a handful of people perusing the stacks. I don't see him out here, so he must be in his office in the back.

As I walk in that direction, I admire the rustic style of his space. I've shopped at Max's bookshop more times than I can count to order books for myself and my family, and every time I'm in here I'm taken by the simple and cozy aesthetic. It's a small store, similar in square footage to my bakery with the same exposed brick walls and dingy hardwood floors.

His bookstore is more of a narrow space, and in the middle runs a single massive bookshelf stocked with a zillion books. The wall on the far side of the shop boasts a few narrow bookshelves. There's a duo of plush armchairs in the back near the floor-to-ceiling window. At the front is the register and checkout area. Behind it is a simple framed black-and-white photo of Haystack Rock at Cannon Beach.

Just before I turn the corner to his office, I take a breath, indulging in that distinct book smell. There's only one thing I love more than the smell of fresh-baked bread and that's the smell of books. Max's store is a combination of used and new books, and I find the scent intoxicating. There's something about the aroma of paper at every possible stage for a book: brand new, hot off the printing press, decades old, covered in dust and moisture. Yeah, it's probably a little weird. But I don't care. To me, it's divine.

The door of Max's office door is cracked open, and I spot him standing by his desk, his back to me. I lift my hand to knock, but then I freeze when I hear his angry voice.

When he pivots, I see him holding his phone to his ear.

"I don't really care . . . Seriously? That's all you think it takes to make things right between us? A single phone call? After everything you've done, after all these years . . . Well, I don't."

My shoulders jump back as his volume amps up. Crap. I shouldn't be eavesdropping.

I start to turn away, but then I hear him say my name.

"Joelle."

I start turning around and forcing what I'm certain is the most awkward smile in the world.

He hangs up his phone and shoves it in the back pocket of his tattered jeans. His brown-green eyes are wide for a split second. He's clearly dazed from the call. But then he shakes his head slightly and reins in his expression.

"Hey. Um, hi." He pulls the door all the way open.

"Sorry, I didn't mean to interrupt you. I was just leaving."

I start to walk away, but he says my name again, even more gently this time. I stop and turn around once more.

A sheepish smile quirks his lips. It makes the center of my chest squeeze.

"You weren't interrupting. That was just some family drama."

He chuckles softly, but a mix of pain and worry lingers behind his gaze.

"Ah. I know how that goes." I try to chuckle, but it comes off strangled. I clear my throat. "Sorry to hear it."

He waves a hand. "Did you need something?"

I hand him the paper bag. "From Elba. Pork adobo croissants. She made them earlier as a thank-you for helping jump-start her car the other day."

When he peers into the bag, he's full-on grinning. It takes most of the edge off that worried look in his eyes. "Holy shit, they look and smell incredible."

"Oh, they are," I say. "Seriously, thank you for helping her. And for refusing to accept her money. That was so kind of you. Are you sure I can't pay you at least a little—"

He narrows his gaze at me. "Don't you dare."

I flush at the growl in his voice. I mumble, "Okay, thank you," as I fight what I'm certain is the cheesiest smile on planet Earth.

"Just trying to be decent," he says. "You and your family are great neighbors. Always giving me extra pastries for free when you make too much. It's the least I could do."

He blesses me with that wolfish half smile. My cheeks start to heat at just how intoxicating it feels being on the receiving end of that look, especially after those sweet words.

"Well, um, have a good night, then." I bite the inside of my cheek, annoyed with myself that I couldn't think of a smooth way to make an exit.

"You don't want to stay and have a croissant with me? And maybe some whiskey?"

I glance over toward the front of the shop. "Aren't you worried about your customers?"

"Nah. There's a sign in front telling people to ring a bell if they need assistance. Besides, there aren't that many people here anyway right now."

I step out of the doorway and peer around. The handful of customers I saw earlier has dwindled to one: a guy who's sleeping in one of the plush armchairs, a book on his chest.

I glance back at Max, whose expression is shy.

"I could really use some company after that phone call," he says softly.

My heart thuds against my chest. "Okay. Sure."

He gestures for me to take his plush office chair before pouring two paper cups of whiskey. For the next ten minutes we chow down on croissants between sips of whiskey while exchanging ridiculous pet stories.

"Wow. So Muffin annihilated that entire loaf of bread?" I giggle as I brush the crumbs off my lap.

Max nods. "She's like her dad. Loves carbs."

I bite my lip and quietly swoon at the way he calls himself Muffin's dad.

"It was my fault, leaving food on the counter," he says. "Definitely learned my lesson after that."

He's leaning against the edge of his desk and we're less than a foot apart in the cramped space of his back office.

"Do you always keep a bottle of whiskey in your desk?" I ask as he tops off my paper cup.

"Always. In case of emergencies."

So far he hasn't elaborated on what his family drama issue is, and I haven't asked. It clearly upset him and I don't want to push it.

Plus, I'm having a blast sharing snack time with the guy I've been drooling over for the better part of the last year and a half. The funny part? I'm nowhere near as nervous as I was yesterday, and this is way, way more intimate. Sitting in this microscopic space, mere inches apart, laughing and chatting away. The whiskey buzz probably helps.

"So where do pork adobo croissants and whiskey land on your list of death row meals?"

Max grins as he chews. He wipes his mouth with the back of his hand before adjusting the gray beanie he's wearing. When he lifts his arms to stretch slightly and rolls his shoulders, my eyes go wide at the way his muscles flex under the light gray fabric of his T-shirt.

I lick my lips, then take another bite of croissant.

"This meal is up there," he says before taking another swig of whiskey.

"I'll relay the compliment to my aunt." I crumple a napkin, then toss it in the trash can nearby. "Are you sure you don't want to sit on the chair? I'm fine standing."

He shakes his head. "You stand all day for work. You take the chair."

I rub the back of my neck with my hand. "Honestly? My neck aches from having to look up at you. Can we please switch?"

He laughs, then nods yes. Because of how tight the space is, when I stand and move to swap places with him, I accidentally bump my boobs into his triceps. The start of a squeak slips out of my mouth, but I clear my throat, hoping that disguises the sound. Judging by the neutral expression on Max's face, the contact barely registered on his radar. Figures. He's handsome and charming. I bet that's not the first time someone has pressed their boobs against him.

Once he settles in his chair, he narrows his gaze at me. "I still gotta try bone marrow, though."

I groan. "Oh god. Please don't remind me of that conversation."

"What? I thought it was enlightening." He wags his eyebrow. My knees buckle.

"Yeah, right," I mutter, fighting back a smile. I yank off my glasses. "I still can't believe I said those words to you," I mutter as I clean my lenses with the hem of my ratty T-shirt.

"What words?"

I tilt my head at him. "You know exactly what I'm talking about."

"Refresh my memory."

Maybe it's the two glasses of whiskey playing tricks on my perception, but I could swear there's a teasing undercurrent to Max's softly growled request.

"Um, okay." I glance down at my scuffed white sneakers to buy myself an extra second to figure out how I want to play this.

But then I stop myself. Why overthink it? I've spent the past year and a half crushing on Max and being too freaked out to do anything about it. I need to just live in the moment and say exactly what I'm thinking.

"I still can't believe I went on and on about sucking and licking and tonguing in front of you yesterday morning."

I'm proud of the way I maintain unwavering eye contact with Max as I speak the words that sent me into a humiliation spiral yesterday. But today? Today those words earn me a sexy crooked grin. And right now I feel like a brazen badass for having the guts to say them again.

"I thought it was amusing. And funny. And really damn cute."

Those last three words send a jolt of electricity across my skin. He says them like there's a period after each one to drive home just how much he means it.

Inside I'm cheering. Max Boyson thinks I'm really. Damn. Cute.

I slide closer to him. Our knees bump, but I don't move. He pivots his chair to face me fully.

"Is that so?" I ask, my voice soft.

"Yeah. And actually." He drains the last of the whiskey in his cup, then roughly wipes his mouth with the back of his hand. "I'd be happy to listen to you talk about tonguing and licking and sucking again. If you wanted."

"Screw talking. What if I just do it?"

I cup my hand over my mouth the moment I finish speaking. Holy crap. Did I seriously just say that? Never have I ever said something so forward, so hot to any guy. Ever.

As my hand falls away from my face, I catch Max's expression. For a long second his eyes are wide, but then he grins.

"I was hoping you'd say that."

The rasp of his tone makes me salivate, and I know that I have nothing to worry about anymore, no reason to nurse that last lingering bit of doubt in the back of my mind. Max is totally into this—into me.

That's why I let go of the edge of his desk and walk the two steps to stand between his legs. I lean down, brace my hands on the back of his chair, just above his shoulders, and gently touch my mouth to his.

There's only so much I can blame on the whiskey. Yeah, it did the heroic job of lowering my inhibitions enough to flirt with Max in a bold way. But everything else—the way I'm touching his shoulders, the way I'm running my tongue along his deliciously plump bottom lip, the way I'm moaning softly into his mouth—is one thousand percent me.

Holy. Crap.

I'm not dreaming, this isn't some daytime fantasy—this is actually happening. I'm making out with Max Boyson.

When his hands grip my waist, I smile against his mouth. When he leads me to settle on his lap, I'm vibrating.

I close my eyes and lose myself completely in this slow, long, melt-in-your-mouth kiss. It's soft and teasing, just the way I like it. Almost like we're feeling each other out to decipher what rhythm and speed we both like.

It doesn't take long before things turn filthy, before I'm pawing at his shirt and sliding my hands underneath the fabric. My mouth waters at the hard mass that lies underneath.

His hands make their way from my waist to my hips to my ass. He gives me a squeeze that's just hard enough to have me moaning into his mouth and digging my fingers harder into his flesh.

"Mmm," he hums against my mouth. "Feisty. I like it."

I laugh against his mouth. "I can't help it. You're just so . . . hot. And your beard. Dear . . . god . . . your . . . beard," I say between kisses.

This time he chuckles against my mouth. Then he cups his hands over my cheeks and holds me still to look at me.

"What about my beard, Joelle?"

"It's just so sexy. And manly. And rough."

And I'm dying to know what it feels like between my thighs.

Just the thought of saying those words out loud has me vibrating.

He raises an eyebrow, like he can sense I'm thinking something very, very naughty.

I shake my head. Way, way too soon for dirty talking like that. Better to take things slowly and savor this kiss for exactly what it is: spontaneous and crazy hot.

"I can't believe this is actually happening," I muse.

That fiery gleam in his eyes softens. And then he smiles so sweetly, I almost pass out.

"I can't believe it either," he says. "Will you pinch me later? Just to prove that this is real?"

He pulls me back to his mouth to resume that dirty-as-hell kiss I'm growing quite fond of. But I don't miss the way my stomach jumps at what he's said. He's in disbelief just like me . . . and maybe that means he's liked me for a while too.

The thought sends shivers through my body strong enough to make my thighs quiver.

I settle lower onto his lap. When I feel the hard bulge between his legs, I have to will my jaw not to drop. Oh, damn. That is one impressive package—and it's not even out. I bite back a grin as I imagine the heft Max must be packing down there if I'm able to feel even this much of it while he's fully clothed.

I let my imagination run wild as he runs his hands all over my body. Through my hair, up and down the sides of my torso, to the tops of my thighs. His thick fingers slide slowly up my legs, like he's savoring the journey inch by inch. Like he's taking his time and loving every second of it.

I am too. It's sweet torture feeling his skin on me, wishing I could rip his clothes off and have him run his hands all over me without the pesky barrier of cotton and denim. But I remind myself we're in his bookstore office. There's a snoozing customer sitting just ten feet away from the closed door.

We can't get naked—yet.

Just then he stills his hands on my legs. As our tongues tangle and suck and lick, he presses his thumbs at the apex of my thighs, where I'm aching, throbbing, dying for him to touch.

I moan a curse word into his mouth, and he responds with a throaty chuckle.

I pull away from him for a second, my chest heaving as I catch my breath. I don't miss the way his pupils have turned into two giant pools of ink with the faintest ring of green-brown around them.

Before I can say anything, he runs his thumb along the seam of my jeans. My jaw drops as I inhale sharply. I cover my mouth with my hand, hoping that muffles the noise enough to keep from waking Sleeping Beauty on the armchair outside.

"I want . . . I need . . ."

Max nods like he understands perfectly. "Do you wanna maybe—"

My phone blares from my back pocket, jolting me.

"Hang on," I mutter, yanking my phone out. "Let me get rid of this."

I silence the call without even looking at the screen and go back to kissing Max, but then it blares once more. I growl.

The ringing fades, and I'm about to turn it off when I see that I've got two missed calls from Whitney. I attempt to focus through my arousal haze. I wonder what's going on that has her calling me nonstop.

Max presses a kiss to the exposed skin on my shoulder where

my shirt has slipped off in the midst of all our heavy petting. I press my eyes shut, relishing the feel until my phone sounds off once again. Whitney's name flashes across my screen. I swallow to get my out-of-control panting in check. Then when I'm certain I don't sound like I've sprinted a half marathon, I answer. "Whitney. Hey. What's up?"

I mouth "Sorry" down at Max as I straddle him. He mouths back "No worries," his eyes still dilated with arousal.

She starts to speak, but I don't hear a word. That's because Max is running his mouth and tongue along the side of my neck. My jaw unhinges completely and I have to cover my mouth yet again to muffle the sex noises I'm making.

". . . so are you coming?"

God, Whitney, you have no idea.

Max slides his arm up the back of my shirt, turning my brain to mush as his fingertips flirt with the band of my bra.

I press my eyes shut and try my hardest to concentrate on forming words. "Um, what? Coming where?"

"To that dive bar on Glisan. You were supposed to meet me here, remember? So we could go over the menu for my Chicks Who Code orientation."

My eyes fly open. "Oh. Right."

Every muscle in my body is screaming at me to stay right here in Max's lap. Whitney would understand. I wouldn't even have to go into the dirty details of what exactly I'm up to right now. She'd catch my drift right away and insist that I stay right where I am.

I'm about to do exactly that, but then she starts to tell me about some asshole in accounting who made a snide remark about her program in a meeting today.

"His exact words were, 'Why do we need to have a program

focused on solely girls? Isn't that a bit sexist in this day and age?'
God, can you believe that jerk?" She lets out an "ugh" noise. "But
honestly, it's made me even more fired up. All I want to do right
now is have a stiff drink, vent about that douchebag, and then
plan the orientation with you. That jerkoff is going to eat his
words when he sees just how successful Chicks Who Code is."

The last bit of my resolve evaporates. I can tell by the strain
in her voice she's stressed about this. I need to be there for her.

"I'm on my way, Whit."

I hang up, then scramble, phone in hand, and hop off Max's lap.

I wince down at Max as I attempt to straighten my shirt and
jeans. "I'm so, so sorry, but I have to go. I promised my best
friend, Whitney, I'd meet up with her to help plan a menu for a
big event at her work. She's kind of freaking out about it. It
means so much to her, she's been working so hard on it, and um,
and I can't ditch her."

Disappointment flashes across his face before he smiles up at
me. "It's okay. I get it."

I turn for the door, but then I stop myself. How the hell do I
end things now?

*Thanks for the heavy petting, see you tomorrow morning when
you stop in for your daily* ube *latte!*

When I observe Max adjusting his jeans, I can't help but feel
the slightest swell of pride. I did that to him. Hell yes.

"So, um . . . I don't really know what to say right now." I let
out an embarrassed laugh.

The expression on Max's face melts from flustered to amused.
And then he stands up, steps closer to me, cups his hand over
my cheeks, and presses a feathery kiss to my lips.

"I don't either, honestly," he says. "That was kind of . . ."

"Unexpected."

He nods once. "And fucking amazing."

"And hot."

"Definitely that."

I nuzzle into his hand slightly, which earns me a sexy smile.

"Can I still come in for my coffee order tomorrow?" he asks.

"Of course."

"And maybe after you close down the bakery you can stop by and we can get up to more fucking amazing and hot stuff?"

I'm full-on beaming. This definitely isn't what I had in mind when I was psyching myself out to ask Max out on a date; it's a million times better. And I'm down to see where it goes.

"I'd really, really like that."

I start to turn to leave, but then Max grabs me gently by the hand, pulls me back to him, then levels me with a kiss so hot, my panties are soaked all the way through.

I stay standing in that spot, my head spinning, as I struggle to find my bearings.

"See you tomorrow, Joelle."

I stumble out of his bookshop and back to my bakery, the taste of Max's kiss coating my tongue and lips, the memory of his wink and smirk flashing every time I blink. *Dear lord.*

As I fetch Pumpkin and hurry to meet Whitney, I'm floating. Not on cloud nine, but some higher, sexier cloud I didn't even know existed until I experienced the hottest, filthiest impromptu makeout session with Max Boyson.

Chapter 4

Joelle

The next morning flies by in a blur of flour, butter, sugar, and smiles as I prep for the day.

Mom asks me a half-dozen times while she helps me what's with the sudden lift in my mood. I tell her I'm just so happy for Whitney that she landed that STEM internship program for her company, which is true. But I'm not uttering a word of the other reason I'm buzzing since it has everything to do with grinding on Max's lap yesterday while making out with him. No way in hell I'm going to divulge that to my mother. I love my family more than anything, but nothing would creep me out more than to talk sexy times with them.

I did, however, gush about the impromptu makeout-slash-heavy-petting session with Whitney yesterday after we planned the orientation menu and she vented about that sexist jerk at her company. I thought her eyes were going to bulge out of her head as she demanded I give her all the details. She was irritated that I put a stop to things with Max to meet up with her, but I insisted that her work event was important to me and I wanted to do everything I could to make sure it's a success. And I told her that Max and I had plans to meet up tonight after work, so we'd definitely make up for what we missed out on last night. That earned me an excited squeal and hug, as well as the insistence that I call her afterward and tell her everything.

I silently tell myself to keep the cheesy smiles at bay so I don't have to keep brushing off Mom's comments and focus on taking customers' orders as the bakery picks up. I'm running the register while Mom handles prep in the kitchen when in strolls Max, like normal.

Only today is not normal, not even close.

Today is the day after the two of us set fire to our friendly and cordial work relationship in favor of heavy petting and making out.

He strolls up to me, my favorite half smile in the entire world on full display. As I scan my gaze over his tall, muscled form, I remind myself that I've run my bare hands over that rock-hard chest and stomach, I've tasted his mouth, I've felt his erection against my thighs.

My knees wobble. Okay, maybe I should save that memory for later. I need to function like a normal human being. I can't disintegrate into a puddle of hormones just yet; I have a full day of work to get through first.

I swallow back all the saliva pooling in my mouth and aim a smile at him.

"Hey, Max. Good morning."

"Morning."

The way his lip curls and that flash in his eyes give it away. He's thinking about what we got up to yesterday too. I bite my lip, grinning. It's a whole new kind of thrill to know that we're both replaying the same naughty memory while navigating this totally normal and wholly appropriate morning greeting.

"The usual?" I ask.

He nods, and I quickly prep his *ube* iced latte since it's already in the seventies this morning. I fetch a warm croissant from the display case, noticing as he glances around, seemingly relieved to see that there's a lull in the crowd at the moment. It's just him at the counter and a dad with a toddler standing off to the side, squinting up at the menu board.

"I don't mean to take up all your time here at the register, but . . ."

He rubs a hand along the side of his neck. I can tell by the slight hunch of his shoulders and the way he fiddles with the lid of his latte that he's nervous to talk to me. And something about that makes me want to squeal.

He pays for his breakfast, then pulls at the sleeve of his leather bomber jacket before making eye contact with me again. "Do you maybe want to get a drink tonight after I close up the bookshop?"

"I'd love that."

A wide smile blooms across his face. "Cool. It's a date, then."

His eyebrow ticks up as he sips his latte and heads for his bookshop, leaving me grinning like a cheeseball yet again.

Once I lock the doors to the bakery, I walk the dozen steps to the storefront of Stacked. I'm texting Mom to remind her to feed Pumpkin since I didn't bring her with me today, and then bump into someone.

"Oof."

I look up and see Ivan Mercer, the owner of the building that houses Stacked and Lanie's.

"Sorry!" I say quickly as I grip my glasses to keep them from sliding off my face.

Ivan shakes his head, chuckling. "Oh, it's okay. It's my fault. I wasn't paying attention."

He tugs at the sleeve of his crisp white dress shirt before glancing down at his watch and ruffling his wavy dark brown hair. He's the spitting image of ABC newscaster David Muir if David Muir wore wire-rimmed glasses and were a tad scrawnier.

I catch the beginning of a smile as he checks his phone.

That's a new one. Hyperfocused Ivan is the dictionary definition of a no-nonsense, always busy property manager. He owns a handful of commercial buildings in and around the Jade District of Portland. He operates in a perpetual state of hurry, always running from one building to the next, making repairs or checking on deliveries or collecting rent, usually while he's on the phone. When he's not at work, he's teaching spin classes at a local gym. In other words, he's constantly on the go. I'm so used to seeing him with a frown of concentration on his face. I can't remember the last time I observed a smile.

It's not that he's grumpy—far from it actually. I'll remember forever the tender look on his face three years ago when I convinced him to let me rent his space for my bakery and the words he spoke.

I have faith in you.

And ever since then he's been a supportive landlord. He's always polite and nonintrusive, and anytime there's a building repair that's needed, he runs over and fixes it within a couple of days.

I wonder what's got him grinning today.

"Doing okay?" I ask.

"Oh yes, yes. All very good." He looks up at me. "I've, um, actually got some exciting news. For you and Max."

Movement at the glass-door entrance makes us twist our heads. There stands a sixty-something guy waving at Ivan.

"Oh, just one sec," Ivan mutters before darting out the door. They have a quick chat and the man nods and walks off.

"Sorry, that was my dad," Ivan says when he walks back over to me. "I just hired him as a handyman so I'm showing him the ropes."

"Oh, nice."

Ivan turns toward the glass doors of the entrance to Stacked and waves at Max, who's standing at the register checking out a customer. Max nods at him, then turns slightly and smiles at me.

I wave at him, then turn back to Ivan. "Well, I think we'd both be up for some exciting news."

I move to follow Ivan as he walks into Stacked and trots to Max once he finishes with his customer.

"Hey, um, could we maybe have a chat in your office? You, Joelle, and me?" Ivan asks. "I've got some thrilling news to share."

"Sure."

The three of us walk to Max's tiny back office. He shuts the door, and Max and I stand in this microscopic space, waiting for what he's about to tell us.

Ivan beams wide, then quickly raises his arms and promptly smacks the brass light fixture hanging from the ceiling.

"Ow!"

Max and I wince.

"You okay?" Max asks as he reaches up to steady the light.

Ivan nods while wringing his hand, pained smile on his face.

"Oh yes, yes. I'm fine. Just got a bit excited." And then he takes a breath. "Big news, guys: I'm renovating the building!"

"Uh . . ."

"What?"

I'd laugh at my and Max's dual confused reactions if I weren't so shocked. Ever since I moved into this building, Ivan has scrapped the idea of renovating. And just last month I overheard him balking at the idea of remodeling another one of his buildings as he dropped by to fill a pothole in our parking lot. I remember vividly how he had his phone pinned between his chin and shoulder as he shoveled gravel and asphalt into the hole, explaining to whomever was on the other line what a waste of money that would be.

"My buildings are older, sure," he had said. "But they're in excellent condition as of now. No need for a remodel anytime soon. Completely unnecessary at this point."

At the time, I was relieved. Depending on how extensive a remodel is, there's always the potential that it could disrupt business. Sure, renovations are good in the long term to liven up the décor and add overall value to the property. But you have to contend with so many unknowns in the process. How much of the property will be out of use during construction? How much noise will there be? Will it deter customers from patronizing the business? Will all the contractors' vehicles and equipment take parking spaces from potential customers?

Those and a million other questions swirl in my brain as Ivan rambles on about his plan to update the electrical system, knock out some walls to make both the bakery and the bookstore more spacious, refinish the flooring, repaint the walls and ceiling, install central air to the building along with an updated security system and energy-efficient windows, and add a bunch of aesthetic touches to the overall design.

I don't miss the furrow of Max's brow. I'm guessing he's got concerns too.

Ivan's smile has turned into a purse. His brow lifts, as if he can sense the uncertainty emanating from Max and me.

"Now, I know what you're both thinking. How will this affect your respective businesses?"

We nod in unison.

That smile reappears on Ivan's face. "Well, I've got the perfect solution. Follow me!"

A minute later we're standing in an empty industrial space the size of a three-car garage at the back of the building, behind Lanie's and Stacked. I've never been in this space before. It looks like an abandoned warehouse that's been somehow tucked away into a quaint brick building. The floor looks like it belongs in a mechanic's workshop—it's bare concrete and littered with what look like paint and oil stains. Dirt, dust, and cobwebs cover the walls. Every surface is a shade of dingy gray. On one end of the space is a garage door. Christ. Maybe this is a garage after all.

The one thing that saves the space is the amount of natural light filtering in from the skylight above and the massive floor-to-ceiling window that takes up half of the far wall. "Ivan, what is this?" I ask.

When I take a breath, I inhale a cloud of dust and fall into a coughing fit. Max thumps me on the back. I mutter a thanks.

"I didn't even know this back room existed," Max says. "I never come here."

Ivan strolls around the space, still beaming. "I know it's a bit . . . run-down."

"A bit?" Max says.

Ivan nods sympathetically, then turns to face us. "Look, I know this isn't ideal and that I'm springing this on you both by total surprise. But an opportunity came up to renovate this building in a really exciting way. I can't pass it up."

The way his eyes glisten with hope dulls the irritation coursing through me.

"I'll make it worth your while," he says. "I promise. I won't charge you rent the entire time you're in the temporary space. And renovations will only take a month, so you'll be back in your spaces at the end of June—July at the latest."

I bite the inside of my cheek to keep from saying that's a laughably short timeline to do all the work he listed.

"And I'm gonna have a cleaning crew come and do a deep clean of this place before you move in," Ivan says. "And a moving crew will come help move your equipment from both of your stores into here."

Max and I lock eyes. I imagine that the look of shock on my face is identical to his.

"Wait, you want us to share this space?" Max practically barks.

As shocked and unhappy as I am about this, I'm blown away at how pissed he sounds.

Ivan's face twists slightly. "Yeah, I, um, I know it's not ideal . . ."

Max tugs off his beanie, crumpling it in his hand. He rests his fist on his hip, then glares at the floor, then kicks it with his boot.

"Not ideal? Ivan, this is a hell of a lot more than just not ideal. This space is smaller than the space I'm working with now. And we're supposed to share it? How the hell am I supposed to fit my giant single bookshelf in here? It runs the length of my shop.

And how is Joelle supposed to fit her oven and other kitchen equipment in here too? And don't you think that's a fire hazard, having a bunch of books next to an oven?"

I've never heard him sound this frustrated.

Ivan holds up a hand. "I understand your concern."

I almost laugh at his placating tone. He sounds like a therapist calming a disgruntled client.

He points out the gas hookup in the far corner where I'll be able to move one of my ovens and explains that it won't be a fire hazard as long as Max keeps his books and shelves on the other side of the space.

"And I know the sink is a bit smaller than what you're used to, Joelle." He gestures to the grimy sink nearby. "But the water pressure is great. I tested it out earlier."

He explains how we'll only be able to fit a fraction of our stuff in here for the time that we're occupying the temporary space.

"But it's only for a month! You'll be able to move back into your spaces at the end of June," he says with cheer in his voice. "I'll cover storage fees for whatever doesn't fit in here."

Max shakes his head, his jaw clenched so hard, I can see the muscle bulge through his short-trimmed beard.

"We'll figure out a way to make it all work, I promise." Ivan's gaze flits to Max, then me.

I rack my brain to think of some way to appeal to Ivan and convince him to reconsider. Clearly Max's anger isn't working. Maybe I need to bring a calmer, more rational point of view.

"Ivan," I say as calmly as I can. "I get that you're excited about this, but are you sure this is what you want to do? Yeah, I get this building is old, but it's still in great shape. The customer flow at Lanie's and Stacked has been impressive this past year especially. I'd hate to disrupt that with a renovation—and you know it will absolutely disrupt business."

Ivan frowns slightly. For a few seconds he's quiet as he looks down, as if he's seriously considering what I've said.

"I get that, I really do," he says when he looks back at me. "But I've run the numbers on this. It'll be tough for the month that we'll have to downsize, but in the long run, the renovation makes sense. It'll result in more parking space and more business space—that means more customers and more business for you both. And I'll put up signs in the parking lot to show customers how to get to the temporary space in the back."

I open my mouth to try again, but then I stop myself. Ivan went out on a limb for me three years ago. He gave me a chance, he gave me the space for my business when he didn't have to. Because he's a kind, supportive person who gives people chances. The least I can do is repay him that same kindness and support right now.

I close my mouth and nod. My shoulders slump in resignation that I'm losing my workspace for at least the next month, likely longer. But I owe it to Ivan.

"I'm sorry, you guys." He aims a sad look at both of us. "It'll be worth it, though, in the long run. I promise."

With those words, he leaves Max and me standing in the middle of this abandoned garage—our soon-to-be shared work space.

I look over at Max, whose arms are folded across his chest. He's glaring at the wall like he's about to start a fight with it.

"Well, fuck," he mutters.

"Yup."

When he finally looks over at me, his gaze softens. The corner of his mouth quirks up in a defeated not-quite-smile. "Still want that drink?"

Ivan's surprise renovation news is a bucket of ice water poured over our flirty vibe. We're definitely not picking up where we left off yesterday. I still want to see him, though.

"Yes. I'm gonna need all the alcohol."

Twenty minutes later we end up at a dive bar near the massive Fubonn Shopping Center in the Jade District, which boasts an Asian grocery market, a bakery, restaurants, and other stores.

"What a day, huh?" Max sips a whiskey on the rocks while I down an IPA.

"Yeah." I hiccup, which earns me a small smile from him.

As we sit side by side at the bar, I hazard a look at him. His expression is a cross between dazed and irritated. It unnerves me in the strangest way. Over the year and a half that I've worked next to him, I've never seen him this upset. Sure, I can recall a few times when he's been at Lanie's when I or one of my relatives has dealt with a rude customer—if Max happened to be there, he'd always step in and settle things with a stern look and firm words for that customer. And he's definitely vented to me once or twice the morning after a stressful day at his bookshop. But never like this. There's a part of him that reads so defeated. It's painful to see.

Part of me wants to lean over and hug him, but I don't. Despite what went down in his office chair a mere twenty-four hours ago, it doesn't feel like we're at the point where we can exchange impromptu hugs just yet.

"Hey," I say quietly. "I'm sorry about the remodel."

"Not like it's your fault," he mutters while staring at his glass.

"Yeah, but still. I'm sorry it's happening."

His eye cut to me. "You don't have to apologize for things that you didn't do, Joelle."

The edge in his tone makes me flinch. I stay quiet as he downs the rest of the hard liquor in his glass. Clearly what I'm saying isn't helping.

"We'll figure out a way to make this work," I say, determined to find some sort of silver lining.

His raised eyebrow conveys irritation when he looks at me. "You're weirdly chipper about this."

I fight another flinch. I know he doesn't mean to sound as harsh as he's coming off. He's still processing the shock and anger of everything that's happened. I search my brain for something else to say, for some other angle to highlight.

"God, this is gonna suck. Sharing that small space." He shakes his head and looks off to the side. "All this time I've spent building up my shop. And in the space of one conversation, it's gone just like that."

I feel the muscles in my torso harden as I sit up straighter on my barstool.

"It's just a month, Max. It's temporary."

The expression he flashes at me borders on incredulous. He looks at me like I'm being so naïve. "Tell me the last time you heard of a renovation that finished on time."

"Yeah, I know, but . . ." I'm fully aware of just how often renovations go past schedule. Still, though. He doesn't have to have such a bitter attitude about it, especially when there's nothing we can do about it. I take another sip of beer, hoping the cold liquid cools the frustration bursting inside me. It doesn't.

"Max, I know this isn't what either of us wants, but what choice do we have? Ivan owns the building. We can't do anything other than go along with it."

"It's just . . . never mind, Joelle."

My skin crawls at the bitterness in his mutter. He's never, ever said my name like that before, with such distaste.

I shove aside the feeling. Maybe a bit of playfulness and humor will help serve as a sort of reset. Too bad we're in public. If we weren't, I'd climb into his lap, grab his face, and plant the filthiest kiss on his mouth and remind him that sharing a space together means we'll get to do more of that.

Since I can't do that, I do the next best thing I can think of.

"At least we'll get to spend some time together. That could be a lot of fun." I let a small smile break free and wiggle my eyebrow at him, hoping it comes off as playful as I intend it to.

As soon as I say it, I regret it. Because Max's face immediately twists with near disgust, like he can't believe I had the nerve to mention that.

He scrubs a hand over his mouth before speaking. "Uh, yeah. About that."

Dread settles in the pit of my stomach. Even before he clears his throat, I know what's coming.

He is the picture of "I'm about to deliver some bad news": shoulders hunched, head hanging low, gaze glued to his empty glass, like he's avoiding making eye contact with me until the last possible second.

He takes a breath and then finally he looks at me. "Look, Joelle. Yesterday was fun, but . . ."

The small smile he forces when he trails off is tinged with pity. A phantom pain lands like a blow to the pit of my stomach. Somehow it hurts worse than a punch.

"Maybe we should cool things off between us." His eyebrows

pinch together, like he's bothered that he even has to speak the words to me. "We're gonna be working in a tight space together. It's probably not the brightest idea in the world to blur the lines."

"Blur the lines?"

He clears his throat. "I just mean that things should probably stay professional between us. It's gonna be chaotic enough as it is navigating this new setup."

The sip of beer I take turns sour on my tongue as I absorb the callous edge of his words. It's like I'm a stranger, not the girl he pulled onto his lap and kissed desperately just twenty-four hours ago.

"We probably shouldn't have kissed in the first place," he mumbles.

I make a quiet choking sound. Is he serious right now?

He pulls the beanie he's wearing farther down over his forehead, like he's trying to hide himself from me.

"I had a lot of whiskey. Too much, probably. And that phone call . . ." He sighs before he continues. "I just wasn't in a good headspace."

I bite down to keep my lip from trembling, then clear my throat and take a moment to process everything he's said.

Yesterday was a mistake—fooling around with me was a mistake. He couldn't have been more obvious about it.

"Got it. Loud and clear," I manage to say without my voice shaking too much.

I hop off the barstool and dig out cash from my pocket and toss it on the bar top.

"You don't have to pay for that. I'll cover it."

"Nope." I bark it so loud the bartender flips around to look in our direction. "I can pay for my own drink."

My tear ducts burn and my throat aches. I press my eyes shut for a second, willing my tears to wait just thirty seconds so I can make it to my car and cry there instead of in front of Max.

"Joelle, I'm sorry. I didn't mean to—"

He reaches for me, but I step out of his reach and frown down at my purse while I pretend to dig inside it.

"Let's just forget anything ever happened between us. Okay?"

I don't know why he looks so shocked when I say that. It's exactly what he said he wants.

Before he can respond, I dart out of the bar and to my car, quietly proud that I manage to make it a block before I burst into tears.

God, I'm so, so pathetic. I spent a year and a half crushing hard on a guy who, after one makeout session, discarded me faster than stale chewing gum.

I angrily wipe at my face, at the tears that fall down my cheeks. I'm thirty-two. I'm thirty-two years old and crying over yet another asshole guy. It's like I'm in high school . . . and in my twenties . . . and early thirties . . . all over again.

I stop crying after a minute, then focus back on the road as I make my way home. No more tears for a guy who's not one bit worth it. I've been through worse. Way, way worse. I survived. I thrived. And that's exactly what I'm going to do when next week we start sharing that tiny work space. I'll be professional. I'll be dedicated to my work, like always. And I sure as hell won't let Max Boyson distract me anymore.

Chapter 5

Max

Y ou are a fucking asshole.
       That's the silent mantra I've been repeating in my head for the past hour, ever since Joelle stormed out on me at that dive bar.

I could tell she was on the verge of crying as she slammed cash on the countertop and refused to look at me. A crushing sensation grips my chest, just like it did when I saw her lips start to tremble before she walked off. *God, I'm a bastard. I made her cry.*

When I walk through the front door of my house, I don't even smile as Muffin trots up to greet me, like I normally do. I bend down and give her a few pats and a kiss on the head, then lead her out to the front lawn so she can do her business.

As I stand there and wait, all I can think about is Joelle and that heartbroken look on her beautiful face. I see it every time I blink.

Maybe we should cool things off between us . . . We probably shouldn't have kissed in the first place.

I contemplate punching myself in the face. What the hell did I even say all that for? That's not even what I meant at all. I was so damn stressed from the surprise renovation that Ivan sprang on us that I could barely think straight. My brain instantly went into "oh shit" mode. I couldn't stop thinking about what stock I should put into the new temporary space versus what I should throw into storage, how much time it would take to pack and move everything, how to tell my customers about the temporary change in location, all the while worrying about the financial hit I'll likely take as a result of this mess.

Pressing my eyes shut, I shake my head. None of that should have been an excuse to say what I did—to hurt Joelle's feelings.

I was just so stressed and pissed and my brain was running nonstop and so for a split second I thought that maybe if we just cooled things off, it would make things easier. But as soon as I said it, I regretted it. I instantly realized that's not what I want at all. I don't want to stop things with Joelle. That's not even close to how I feel.

Muffin trots up to me for more pets. I crouch down and she falls to her side, then rolls to her back. I scratch her tummy. "Your dad is a grade A idiot, Muffin," I mumble. "What do you think about that?"

She sneezes, then yawns before rolling away from me and hopping up to sniff the grass along the edge of the lawn. I stand up after Muffin dismisses me and think about the million other ways I could have handled things between Joelle and me.

What I really wanted to do was take her out for a drink tonight and hear that melodic laugh, see that gorgeous smile. I wanted to run my fingers through that wild mass of black hair again, taste her lips again, feel her thighs on my lap as she worked herself all over me while kissing me breathless. I wanted to fog up those insanely sexy glasses she wears. I wanted to hear her moan again, hear her shout my name . . .

A grunt escapes as the memory of yesterday takes over my brain. My elderly neighbor, who's fetching his garbage bin from the curb, turns to me at the sound, and I immediately clear my throat and offer a friendly wave.

Get your shit together, Boyson.

It was nuts that after a year and a half of being casual work acquaintances, we'd ended up all over each other after a few whiskeys and croissants. But hey, I'm not complaining. I've always had a crush on Joelle. From the minute I met her when I opened Stacked next door to her bakery, I couldn't get her out of my head. She was so kind and welcoming. And so fucking pretty. I'm a sucker for a sexy and sweet girl in glasses, and that's exactly what she is. And for the past year and a half as we gradually got to know each other, I racked my brain to figure out a way to ask her out without jeopardizing our whole work setup. I didn't want to risk making her feel uncomfortable. We worked in the same building—that would have made things awkward as hell if she rejected me or we ended up not panning out. I even dated other women. But nothing ever stuck past a few dates. I could only think of Joelle.

I scoff at myself. Clearly, we would have been just fine, judging by what happened in my office yesterday.

For a moment I wonder if she's going to tell her family what happened between us. I have no idea if that's a normal thing to do. She and her family are a close-knit bunch, but even then, would she have told them that she made out with the bookseller next door?

You're the last person in the world who'd know anything about family stuff.

I silence the thought and instead think of Joelle's family. They've been nothing but kind, always dropping off extra baked goods at my store and going out of their way to order books from me. Always taking the time to chat with me, to ask me if I need help with anything. They made me feel welcome and wanted since the day they met me . . . a feeling I've never had.

I take an extra second to swallow the wave of emotion that thought unleashes inside me.

I catch Muffin chomping on a chunk of too-tall grass, a reminder that I need to mow the lawn. I yell at her to knock it off and she trots happily over to me. I give her a few more scratches behind her ears, and then we walk back inside. I drop my jacket on the couch, then scour the refrigerator for something to make for dinner, even though my stomach is churning so hard I'm not even hungry.

Instead I dish up dinner for Muffin and Doughnut. The sound of me breaking out their metal food dishes an hour earlier than normal causes a mild frenzy of excited barks and meows in the kitchen, which makes me chuckle. Damn, that feels good after that shit show earlier today.

But my mind still floats back to Joelle. I lean against the edge of my kitchen counter, wondering how the hell I'm going to make this right with her.

I glance down at Doughnut and Muffin, who are busy chomping away at their food.

"What would you two do? If you had a shot with your dream girl and you fucked it up, how would you make it right?"

Neither of them looks up at me. I shake my head, fully aware of just how ridiculous I sound talking out my personal problems with my pets. It's a habit, though. I'd rather chat with Muffin and Doughnut than just about any person.

My phone buzzes in my pocket, and for a second, I'm hopeful that it's Joelle. But when I see the familiar number flash across my screen—the number I've purposely never saved to my phone— anger rockets through me. I decline the call and toss my phone onto the counter.

Doughnut glances up at me while licking his lips, what he always does after he finishes a meal. The corner of my mouth quirks up at the hopeful look in his green eyes, silently asking for more food.

I lean down and scoop him up, then scratch under his chin. His eyes close slowly as he purrs, and I give his sizable middle an affectionate squeeze

"Sorry, buddy. That's all the food you're getting tonight. Vet's orders."

He slow-blinks at me while licking his lips.

"Give it to me straight, Doughnut. What about flowers and an apology? Is that too much? Not enough?"

Another slow blink is all I get in response. I set him down next to his water dish, then open the fridge. I spot that paper bag of pork adobo croissants Joelle's aunt made me yesterday. At the same time my mouth waters, my chest aches.

As I warm up a couple of croissants in the oven, I contemplate trying to call Joelle again, but I talk myself out of it. She didn't answer earlier when I tried to call her. Her feelings likely haven't changed in the past hour.

So instead I stand at the counter and eat the most delicious fucking croissants I've ever had while scrolling aimlessly on my phone, ignoring the sad eyes Muffin and Doughnut make at me as they wait for me to drop a bite for them.

"Sorry, guys. You know I can't."

Muffin lets out a whining noise that hits me right in the chest. I dig out a chunk of pork from the remaining bite of croissant and feed it to Doughnut, then give the rest to Muffin. I watch as they lick their lips when they finish eating.

"It was a moment of weakness," I say to them. "Won't happen again."

Muffin makes a snorting noise, as if to say "Yeah, right."

When I take her out for her evening walk, the gnawing feeling that I've screwed things up with Joelle in the worst way still hasn't subsided. I need to do something to fix this. I just don't know what.

I settle on a text. I know it's not even close to what I need to do to make everything better, but maybe if she knows I'm thinking about her, it'll make some sort of difference.

I'm in the middle of typing when I get a phone call from another unsaved number—this one I don't recognize. I ignore it. Probably some robocaller. But then a voice mail pops up. I pause from drafting and deleting and redrafting what is probably the shittiest text ever to check the message. And I stop in my tracks.

"Hello, this message is for Max Boyson. This is Dr. Givens calling on behalf of Sheila Holm . . ."

I almost drop Muffin's leash as the rest of the message plays. My hearing goes muffled after a few seconds, and I have to replay the message twice to make sure I've heard it all correctly.

And then I stand motionless on the pavement, Muffin whining beside me when I don't move for the next few minutes. But I can't. I'm frozen.

What the hell am I supposed to do now?

Chapter 6

Joelle

Whenever I look around the industrial space that's my new bakery for the next month, it takes every morsel of inner strength I possess not to scream.

Every surface is gray. Even after Ivan's cleaning crew spent two days scrubbing it down, the floor, walls, and counter remained that same shade of dull slate. Even after Max and I moved what little of our stuff we could fit in here, it did little to spruce the place up. Yeah, I'm glad the cobwebs and dust are gone, but the overall concrete-cave vibe remains. It's like we're operating out of a cement military compound.

Even though this is an open-concept space with no walls or dividers between my and Max's businesses, we're hell-bent on keeping invisible boundaries. I've taken over the right half since there's a counter on that side, which I use to set up my register and display case. I was able to fit one oven and my metal table in the back space of my side, along with a tiny seating area in the front.

Max has commandeered the left half with three tall and narrow bookshelves, which are packed to the brim. A rickety wooden console table and stool near the front door is where his makeshift register is, and there's an armchair near the window. That's it. This is our new combined space.

"God, this place sucks," I mutter to myself.

I bite my tongue and glance around, hoping that the customers who just walked in and are glancing at the menu above where I stand at the register didn't hear me.

And then I remind myself that I need to keep it together. This is just for a month. Thirty days. I can do this.

When I glance over at Mom working a slab of dough in the far corner near the refrigerator and oven, I force a smile.

She looks up and returns her own forced smile, then focuses back on the dough, dusting it with flour before letting it rest.

I recall the chipper tone I attempted when I told my family about our big move. They weren't happy about it either, but we were all resigned to the undeniable truth: there was nothing we could do other than go along with this temporary change.

We're just a handful of days into it, though, and already I can feel my resolve wearing thin. I've lost count of the number of things I've bumped into and knocked over. Since the space is so small, I can't have more than one person at a time helping me, which means we're putting in longer hours just to bake the same amount of pastries we used to. I'm so tired and irritated most days from putting on my customer service smile while fighting the urge to scream that it's a wonder I don't burst into tears.

And Max? He seems to be faring just as poorly.

I glance over to where he stands a dozen feet away from me. He's surveying a tall bookshelf with the most lethal scowl I've ever laid eyes on. Every once in a while, he scribbles something on a notepad.

Other than cordial greetings, he hasn't muttered a word to me since I stormed out on him at the dive bar last week, right after he told me he wanted to end things between us. We didn't even talk to each other when we moved into the shared space last weekend. That whole day all we exchanged was an awkward look when I first walked into the temporary space and saw he was already there. The rest of the day we kept our distance and focused on moving our own stuff, grunting and sweating along with the movers Ivan hired.

It's not that I expected him to block everything out and continue acting like his charming, sweet self from before. I figured there would be a hefty bit of awkwardness between us while we adjusted to this new normal.

But this perma-scowl he wears is a surprise. So is the cold shoulder he seems to prefer to show me in this new communal space. It's like he's so pissed about our situation, he can't even handle being in my presence.

That makes two of us. He's the one who wanted to end things between us before we even started up, yet *he's* the one acting so put off. What's this guy's problem?

Just thinking about it makes me want to rage and tear up at the same time. I'm like a stranger to him now. It's the worst feeling.

I close my eyes, force a quiet breath, then focus on the customers who have walked up to the register—the one silver lining in all of this. Our business hasn't stalled in these first few days, like I feared it would. Ivan made good on his promise to post signs about the new temporary location so that we wouldn't lose a single customer. And so far, we haven't. Even our regulars who always spent their mornings dining in the café on their favorite pastries have been so understanding about the change. I don't have enough room for the half-dozen small tables I had in my original space. Now all I have are two two-person tables crammed at the front. Despite that, customers still come in and pick up their orders and leave generous tips.

I ring up a few orders, then look up and see Merna, one of my regulars, walk in the door.

She beams and runs a hand through her dyed-pink hair before offering a sympathetic smile. "Hanging in there?"

"Always." I wrinkle my nose, which makes her chuckle. For a moment I feel relieved that I can be honest with Merna. She runs a floral shop down the street and has been a loyal customer ever since I opened Lanie's.

"For what it's worth, you're handling this like a champ," she says as I prep her regular order of an Americano and a half-dozen squares of *bibingka*. "If someone forced me to move my florist shop to an abandoned warehouse or garage or whatever this is, I'd rage."

"Oh believe me, I nearly did." I'm careful to keep my voice low in the hopes that Max doesn't hear me. I glance over and see that his broad back is to me. I bet he didn't hear a thing. He's probably tuning me out.

Merna pays me for her drink and pastries, then pats my hand. "You can count on me to show up wherever you want to put up your business. I live for your *bibingka*. I thought I was doomed when I found out that I had celiac disease and couldn't have gluten anymore. My life was pastries. But this ooey, gooey, coconutty rice flour cake saved me. All the sweetness and satisfaction I crave from a pastry, but without the gluten. I'll love you forever for introducing me to it."

The joy she radiates as she fawns over my *bibingka* recipe warms the center of my chest, especially after the difficulty of the last several days.

"Thanks, Merna. That means the world. Truly."

She hazards a glance over at Max, who's now helping the customer I served a few minutes ago find a book.

"I guess there are worse things in the world than being stuck in the same cramped space as a ruggedly handsome guy."

I purse my lips and try my hardest not to roll my eyes. Behind me I hear Mom chuckle. I twist around to see her smiling to herself before looking over at Merna.

"The view's not bad, I'll give you that."

Merna chuckles.

"Good lord, Mom," I huff through a breath, then dart my gaze over to Max, hoping he didn't hear.

"Oh, *anak*. He didn't hear me. I kept my voice low."

I roll my eyes, much to Merna's amusement. Then she gives my hand an encouraging pat before walking over to Max. I watch as he leads her to a nearby bookcase and points out a few books, observing that he's dialed back his scowl to an easy expression.

"Do you have any good steamy romances you can recommend to me?" Merna asks him. "I'm in a bit of a mood."

She wiggles her eyebrows and I have to pull my lips into my mouth so I don't laugh. I wipe down the counter and watch from the corner of my eye as the parts of Max's cheeks that aren't covered in that delicious short-trimmed beard turn pink.

"Absolutely." He moves a few feet to the side and points out an entire side of one of the bookshelves. "Here's the romance section. Sorry, I haven't gotten around to moving the sign over yet from my store."

"Yay." Merna smiles at him and gazes over the shelves. "Oh wow, this is great. What a diverse selection of authors and titles."

"I wanna be as inclusive as possible. If there are any titles you don't see, I can check and see if I have them in storage. If not, I'll order them for you no problem, and you can pick them up the next time you're here," Max says.

Merna thanks him and he leaves to let her continue browsing.

I soften the tiniest bit to him. Even though he's turned into a grump lately, it's great that he goes out of his way to accommodate his customers. Out of the corner of my eye, I see Merna pluck a couple of books from the shelf. Then she walks over to Max's register. She asks if she can order a few more, and he says, "Of course," before typing away on his laptop.

I turn back to the register to take a customer's order. As I prep her drip coffee with steamed oat milk, I turn back to her and notice that her gaze is locked on Max, who's standing by the front bookshelf, examining the spine of a book.

"So what's his story?" she asks.

"Sorry?"

"Bookstore hottie over there. Is he single? Taken?"

"Oh." I pop the lid onto her drink and hand it to her. "Um, single. I think."

She finally peers over at me and flashes a flawless smile so pearly white, I have to blink. "Yay."

She sips from her coffee cup and thanks me before pulling out a metal tin of lip balm from her designer purse. Once she shellacs her beautifully bee-stung lips with ruby gloss, she runs a hand through her ombre honey-blond locks and struts over to Max.

This isn't the first time a customer has inquired about Max's relationship status—it's happened almost weekly since he moved into the store space next door. And it happens even more often now that we share the same cramped work space.

And even though the prospect of Max and me being together is long gone, it still stings to watch someone else set their sights on him—even though I probably should be used to it. In our old storefronts, I often watched Max get approached by stunner after stunner, just like this woman.

But observing it now cuts deeper. When I was crushing on Max from afar, it was easy to brush aside those minor tinges of jealousy. We weren't a thing, so anyone had a right to chat him up. Even though we're not a thing now, I got a taste of just how hot things could be between us . . . until he decided I wasn't worth it anymore.

So now I get to stand back as this nearly six-foot-tall glamorous gazelle in a flowy, boho-chic maxi dress makes her move. I watch mesmerized at her confidence as she asks him about book recommendations. I don't catch all of their conversation, but it seems to be going well. She's laughing tons and touching his shoulder a lot. There's a strain in his smile at first, but it fades the longer she flirts with him.

Just then he looks over at me. I immediately dart my eyes to the display case and rearrange the remaining pastries, my face fiery. God, how pathetic that he busted me gawking at him as he gets chatted up.

"You sure you'll be okay the rest of the afternoon here on your own, *anak*?" Mom asks.

Grateful for the distraction, I turn to her.

"Yeah, I'll be fine. There are plenty of pastries in the display case and prepped dough in the fridge. With any luck we'll sell out just like we did yesterday and the day before."

She offers a gentle smile, then sheds her apron. Crow's-feet flank her earth-hued eyes, adding gentleness to her already tender expression.

"Thanks again for coming in on your day off to help," I say to her.

"Always." She wipes her hands on a kitchen towel, walks over to me, and pulls me into a hug. "It's the least I can do."

I press my eyes shut, wishing she wouldn't word things that way. I know the guilt she, Dad, Auntie Elba, and Apong Celeste feel even after all these years. They've done plenty for me, though—they still do given they spend most of their free time helping me at the bakery so I don't have to hire help.

"You do enough, Mom. More than enough. You always have," I say as she holds me by the arms.

"I don't know about that, Joelle." The sadness in her voice wrecks me.

I wish there were a way to convince her—to convince my whole family that as much as I appreciate them helping me, they don't need to view it as a way to pay me back for what happened all those years ago.

"Mom," I say gently. "It's enough. Promise."

She nods even though I know she's unconvinced. She heads for the door and says a quiet good-bye to Max, who manages a genuine smile as he waves at her. At least he's been sweet and cordial to my family when they stop in and help me, not letting his bad mood permeate every aspect of his demeanor.

The next few hours fly by in a blur as customers drop in.

When late afternoon hits, the display case is empty. All the dough I prepped is gone too. I smile to myself. That means I made some serious money today.

I finish closing and cleaning duties, then pop over to check on Pumpkin . . . and then I freeze. She's not in her cage.

"Oh no!" I gasp.

I notice that the door to her cage is open. I must have forgotten to latch it shut when I stopped to feed her a couple hours ago in between customers. Panic sends my heartbeat into a frenzy. My head nearly twists off my neck as I dart my gaze around the concrete space in search of her.

Max's head pops out from behind one of the nearby stacks. "What's wrong?"

"Pumpkin's missing. And I . . . I don't know where . . ."

I fall to the floor and search under the metal table where I prep dough, but nothing. I crawl around and look under every corner, behind the refrigerator and industrial mixer and the bags of flour in the corner. Still nothing.

Tears burn at my eyes as I sit up on my knees and tug both hands through my hair. "I—I can't find her. I don't know . . . could she have gotten outside?"

I choke on a sob at the thought. If she did, she's gone, no question. She could have been run over by a car or fallen into a sewer grate or . . .

"I can't . . . I can't lose her," I say in a shaky voice. "She's . . . I just can't . . ."

I shake my head and force myself back onto my feet and push away the thought.

"Hey."

Max's gentle, calming tone jolts me out of my panic. So does his stare. There's not one trace of the glare he's been sporting the past few days. Right now, as he stands in front of me, his massive hands cradling both of my shoulders, his stare is one thousand percent concern and compassion.

"It's gonna be okay. We'll find her. I promise."

I quickly nod and wipe away the tears that have trailed their way down my cheeks. Then I scour the counter on my side while Max darts over to his side of the space and looks around the bookcases.

Minutes pass and still nothing. I'm about to scream-cry when I hear a soft rustling noise from inside the bookshelves near me. I zero in on that, blocking out the muffled whirling of oven fans and hum of traffic from the street just outside of the building. I tiptoe quietly in the direction of the stacks like I'm imitating a cat burglar.

I catch Max frowning at me in confusion. He starts to open his mouth.

"Shhh!" I press my index finger against my lips and hold up my palm at him.

The rustling sound gets sharper. I turn slowly to the bookshelf on my left and squint slowly along each shelf. Movement in the corner of my eye captures my attention. I turn and see Pumpkin chomping and nuzzling her head inside the pages of some giant hardcover on a middle shelf.

"Pumpkin!" I squeal.

I leap over and scoop her into my hands. I can't help the cheesy-as-hell smile that makes my face ache or the tears brimming in my eyes as I gaze down at her.

Those deep brown bulbous eyes of hers glance around for a second before she settles in my palm. She runs her nose along my skin, the feather-light sensation tickling me.

"You're okay." My voice is a shaky whisper.

For several seconds I forget that it's not just me in this space. When I remember that Max is here too, I look up and see the softest, most tender expression on his face.

Then he walks the few steps over to me and gently pets the top of Pumpkin's head with his giant index finger.

"She's okay?" he asks in a soft voice.

I nod, my head dizzy from just how sweet and gentle he sounds. "I think so."

I sniffle, suddenly aware of how I must look in this moment: face swollen and tear soaked, covered in flour, hair in a messy ponytail, shaking as I cradle my pet hamster.

"Um, sorry for how I panicked." My face heats at how out of my mind I must have appeared. "I was just so worried."

He frowns slightly, shaking his head. "Hey. You don't have to be sorry, okay? I would have lost my shit too if Muffin or Dough-nut went missing." He bites his bottom lip, the look in his brown-green eyes sad. "I *did* actually lose my shit when I lost Muffin a while back."

My heart sinks. "You did?"

He nods, shoving his hands in the pockets of his jeans. "Yeah. She dug a hole under the fence in the yard at my old place. I didn't realize it until I came home from work and she was gone. I freaked the fuck out."

He shakes his head, like he's reliving the memory all over again. "I spent hours running around the neighborhood looking for her, but I couldn't find her. I had no idea what the hell to do, I was so racked with worry and panic. I finally gave up and went home. And cried."

"Oh, Max."

Carefully, I shift Pumpkin to one hand and then reach over to give his arm a squeeze. He smiles slightly.

"And then maybe ten minutes later my doorbell rang, and it was this little girl and her dad standing there with Muffin. They were on a walk when they happened to see her, read my address on her collar, and brought her back. I fell to my knees and hugged her. I was bawling like a baby in front of them, and I didn't care. I was just so happy to have her back."

He lets out a soft chuckle and runs a hand through his gold-brown hair. Then he gazes down at Pumpkin and runs his thumb along her pudgy middle.

"Don't be sorry, Joelle. These furry little bastards own our hearts. We can't help but cry over them when they give us a reason to."

I smile at his phrasing. For a minute we just stand there in silence together, looking at each other, then down at Pumpkin, then at each other again.

It's like the air in the room has shifted. The tension is long gone, leaving behind something else. Something warm and soft.

I happen to look over at the brass clock on the wall. "Crap. I should get going. I promised my grandma I'd drive her to the senior center tonight for bingo."

Max grins. "Duty calls."

I hurry to put Pumpkin back in her portable plastic cage and vow to be better about making sure the latch is secure from now on.

I grab my purse and hustle toward the door but stop myself before I reach for the handle.

"Hey, Max?"

He turns around to face me from where he's standing in front of the bookshelf by the opposite wall.

"Thank you."

That half smile appears and it feels like fireworks are exploding in my chest. I haven't seen that half smile in days. Holy hell, have I missed it.

"Anytime, Joelle."

When I leave, I catch myself smiling.

Chapter 7

Joelle

I'm at the bakery an hour earlier than normal, but it's worth it. Because I'm working on a surprise for Max.

As I put the finishing touches on this six-inch *ube* crème double-layer cake I've baked, I can't help but bite my lip in anticipation of his reaction. Max blew me away with how supportive he was yesterday when I panicked after realizing Pumpkin had gone missing. Maybe his attitude those past few days was just because he's been stressed with the move and consolidating so much of his inventory to fit into the cramped space.

But when shit hit the fan, he was his normal sweet and caring self—and it meant the world. And I want to tell him thanks.

Hopefully this two-tiered *ube* cake with buttercream frosting and passion fruit filling will brighten his morning.

I finish piping the perfect cursive "Thank you" in bright purple icing when the glass door squeaks open. Max is here earlier than normal, but this is perfect. I can give him his surprise cake before we start work. My back is to the door, so I take a second to set down the piping tool, grab the cake in my hands, and turn to face him.

"Hey! Surpri—"

I trail off when I spot that familiar scowl on his face.

"Hey," he practically bites.

"Is everything okay?" I set the cake stand down on the counter and watch as he yanks his arms out of his leather jacket.

"Not really," he mutters.

I open my mouth but shut it instantly, unsure of what to say or do. I spend a few seconds watching him angrily push open his laptop until I decide to say something.

"What happened, Max?"

His chest heaves with a sigh, and then he bites down, like he's irritated that I'm talking to him. And then he reaches over and grabs a stack of books set on the edge of the console table his laptop's propped on.

He walks over to me. "This happened."

He thumbs through what looks like a book that was bound and printed a century ago, revealing dozens upon dozens of tiny holes in the pages. My stomach sinks.

"Pumpkin did that," he says. "And that." He thumbs through another ancient-looking book with a million holes in the pages. "And that." He grabs another old book, and another.

"Oh . . ."

He turns away and drops the stack of books back on the table before turning to me. "Look, I don't mean to be a jerk, but she pretty much ruined those books."

I stammer for a second. "I'm really sorry. I can replace them."

He shakes his head, glaring down at the stack before walking back to his console table and plopping down on the stool. "You can't. They were part of my rare used-book collection. They cost a few hundred each. And they're ruined."

"Oh."

His angry stare cuts to me. "Yeah."

"I'm so sorry. I didn't mean for any of that to happen."

"That doesn't really matter," he mutters.

For a long moment I just stare at him, my head dizzy, fighting off the cringe that ripples through me. I haven't the slightest clue how to fix this.

I step out from behind the counter and walk over to him. "I want to pay you for them, it's only fair."

A bitter laugh falls from his lips. For a second, I just stand there, jolted.

"Look, I know that this is my fault, and I feel terrible," I finally say. "But if they were that valuable, why did you have them sitting on some random shelf? Shouldn't they have been tucked away somewhere?"

His head falls back as he groans. Then he braces his hands on the tops of his thighs and rolls his shoulders. For a second, I get lost in the movement of his muscles flexing under the thin fabric of the black T-shirt he's wearing, but then I catch myself. We're in the middle of an argument and I absolutely shouldn't be checking him out right now.

"God, Joelle." Another bitter laugh. "I know they should be put away somewhere safe—I *did* have them somewhere safe, in a display case. At my bookstore. But I can't do that anymore because my shop is currently torn to hell with the renovations. So I have to kind of just make do with the shitty space I have now."

I bite my tongue at the tone he employs, like I'm a moron. Yes, this is my fault. I've made it clear that I want to fix it and compensate him. He doesn't have to be so mean, though.

"Max, please don't talk to me like I'm an infant who doesn't understand the situation we're in. I'm fully aware of how much this sucks. And I'm so sorry for what Pumpkin did. But it's not like I meant for any of that to happen. Just tell me what it costs. I'll pay you back. I don't care if I have to make payments, it's the right thing to do and I want to do it."

My insistent tone doesn't seem to faze him. His bored expression and his lack of eye contact convey just how unaffected he is by my attempt to make amends.

He scrubs a hand along the side of his face. "Whatever. We'll work something out, I just . . . can you stop bringing Pumpkin in here at least?"

I nearly stumble back at his suggestion. "What?"

He purses his lips. "It's just, I don't want her to get out again and ruin more of my stuff."

My jaw falls to the floor. "Max, that was a onetime thing. It's not like this happens every day."

He presses a fist to his forehead, like talking to me is giving him a headache. "I just don't think it's the most professional thing in the world to bring your pet to work."

"Well, I disagree." I cross my arms over my chest. "I think it's perfectly fine to bring her here, seeing as she's a pretty nonintrusive presence as long as I remember to latch her cage—which I've only forgotten to do once the entire time I've had her."

He shakes his head and looks away as he rolls his eyes. "Look, I get it," he says after a moment. "I'm an animal lover too. I have a cat and a dog, but you don't see me dragging them in here every day, do you? There's a level of professionalism here that I think we should uphold. That's all I'm saying."

I stand there, stunned into silence. The bite of his tone hurts more than his actual words do. It's clear he thinks I'm an immature, unprofessional joke who can't function unless I bring my beloved hamster into work with me every day.

Frustration burns inside me. I swear I feel it across every inch of my skin. I spin around and march over to the counter where I left the cake, scoop it up, then walk it over to Max and set in in front of him.

"Here. I made this for you. Thank you for helping me with Pumpkin yesterday."

When he glances down at the cake, the sternness in his expression melts. A beat later his face and his neck flush red as a tinge of embarrassment seeps into his stare.

"After today, I'll be sure not to bring her with me as long as we're sharing this space together."

I swallow back the "and fuck you very much" I ache to spit, then walk back over to my side. I glance over at Pumpkin, who's snoozing in the corner of her cage, oblivious to the argument she's unintentionally caused.

"Joelle, wait. I—"

I whip my head up at Max. "I don't want to talk about this anymore. Understand?"

When his face twists, it looks a lot like regret. I don't care, though. I'm too upset to try to decipher any more of this weird dynamic of ours, where one moment we're good and the next we're bickering and the unspoken tension is so thick between us you could hack at it with a knife.

When he nods, I turn away. And then I tighten my apron around my waist, haul out a slab of dough from the fridge, and get to work, trying my hardest to ignore Max staring at me from the corner.

"Jesus. What the hell is that guy's problem?" Whitney whispers to me as we both assume a downward-dog position at our sunrise yoga class.

My hamstrings ache as I try like hell to touch my heels to the floor while keeping my palms flat. I squint, trying to focus on a random spot on the hardwood floor to take my mind off the discomfort, but without my glasses, I can barely see a thing. Not like it would make a difference if I were wearing them. The instructor prefers to keep the lights off during these predawn yoga sessions so that when the sun eventually rises and filters in through the window, we are then, as she says, "bathed in the purest light possible, giving us the most beautiful, holistic start to the day."

"No clue what his problem is," I mutter against the soft pan flute music playing in the background. "I mean, I kind of get it. Pumpkin *did* ruin those books when she got loose."

Whitney scoffs, then coughs. I glance over and see her sputter the end of her braid out of her mouth. She shoves her gold-red hair over her shoulder, then peers over to me.

"Yeah, but you didn't mean to, Joelle," Whitney says. "It was an accident. Accidents happen."

I think back on the humiliation that wrecked me as I struggled to get through the rest of the workday in the aftermath of our argument a couple days ago.

"I still owe him money for the books that Pumpkin ruined," I say quietly.

"The nerve of that—"

Whitney clams up when our instructor's feet pop into my view as she walks between the two of us.

"Feel the gentle pull in your muscles. That invigorating, cleansing stretch," she says, her voice a soft, melodic chant against the pan flute. "And breathe . . . and hold . . . for one . . . two . . . three . . ."

As the instructor counts us to eight, my muscles twitch. I grit my teeth, struggling to hold the pose. I'll never, ever be the kind of person who reaches the euphoria during yoga that some people talk about. I will always, always feel the burn in my muscles. The only reason I come to yoga is that Whitney drags me here about once a week; plus it's a great way to counteract the near-constant hunching I do when working at the bakery.

The instructor's soft voice releases us to cobra pose just as the sun starts to rise, and then we lie down flat on our backs with our eyes closed for the last few minutes of class.

"Feel the warmth of the sunlight as it washes over you. To restore your sense of peace after that challenging session, close your eyes and take a slow, cleansing breath. In through the nose, out through the mouth . . ."

Eyes closed, I hear Whitney's whispered tone once more. "You don't owe that jerk anything, Jojo."

I sigh, careful to keep my voice low. "Whitney, yes, I do. My pet damaged his property. I'm responsible for it, even if it wasn't intentional."

"You made him a cake!"

Whitney's shrill whisper earns a sharp throat-clear from the instructor.

"Let's all remember that this is a time for tranquility, peace, and centering ourselves, not gossiping." Her tone remains pleasant, but her pointed words get the message across loud and clear.

Whitney and I stay quiet for the last few minutes of class, and then when it ends, we roll up our yoga mats and walk out to the parking lot.

She unlocks her car, which is parked next to mine. "Like I was saying, you made him a cake. That is gift enough for what Pumpkin did."

I pull at the frizzy topknot on top of my head and groan. "It's not, though. Pumpkin chewed through some old editions of *Moby-Dick*, *The Scarlet Letter*, *A Moveable Feast*, *The Jungle Book*, and a couple other classics. They were pretty expensive. It'll probably be close to a thousand bucks total."

Whitney rolls her eyes. "You know, I am so sick of books written by wanky dead white guys a million years ago still being thought of as sacred, when in reality they're boring as hell to read."

I burst out laughing at her lethal yet dead-on assessment.

"Did any Bell Hooks or Yoko Ogawa or Louise Erdrich get damaged?"

"No."

"Then it's really not much of a loss. The world does not need more copies of dead white dudes' books. Pumpkin did everyone a favor."

I lean against the hood of her car as I double over with laughter. After a minute, I catch my breath and pull her into a hug.

"Thanks for that."

She nuzzles the top of my head as her nearly six-foot-tall frame holds me close. "Always."

We let go of each other.

"Don't let Max get you down, okay?"

I nod and try to smile, despite how heavy I feel. It's like I'm carrying an invisible anvil on my shoulders just being in his presence. Like I'm always expecting to do something wrong that will set him off or make him get mad at me.

"I mean it, Joelle," Whitney says. "I thought Max was a sweet guy the few times I've chatted with him. And I was pumped when you told me how you two finally hooked up after you spent so long crushing on him. I honestly thought you guys would work out. But clearly he's got a lot more to him than meets the eye."

I let Whitney's words roll over in my brain. It's true. Despite whatever geniality we've shared over the year and a half we've known each other and worked in adjacent spaces, it's a hell of a lot different to have to share the same cramped quarters and constantly get on each other's nerves.

"I think I spent a lot of time building him up in my head when I was pining after him," I admit in a quiet voice. "I guess my fantasy of Max didn't live up to the reality. That's my fault in a way too, I suppose. Unrealistic expectations, you know?"

"God, I hate how expecting to meet a decent man is seen as a fantasy," Whitney says. "Like, is it too much to ask for a sweet, thoughtful, respectful, well-groomed, and honest guy?"

I let out a sad chuckle. "I guess so."

Whitney shakes her head. "The bar is so damn low. All a dude has to do to be seen as a dream guy in this modern dating hellscape is to be halfway decent. But you know what he *should* have to be to be seen as actual 'dream guy' material?"

I nod, chuckling softly. We've had this discussion countless times when one of us has had a frustrating experience with a guy.

"Kind," I say.

"And smart."

"And attentive."

"And patient."

"And funny."

"And hot. Super hot. And dynamite in bed."

I snort at Whitney's embellishment. "Of course. Can't forget that."

"And willing to be open and honest about how much he cares about you," she says.

"Willing to say 'I love you,' no matter if you're blissfully happy or fighting like cats and dogs . . . and mean it just the same." I clear my throat, unable to hide the wistfulness in my tone. "That's a fantasy for sure."

I force a smile, but I still can't shake the disappointment of how things between Max and me took such a disappointing turn. I start to climb into my car, but then she calls after me.

"You're amazing, Joelle. No matter what Max says or does, you're amazing."

Her green eyes sparkle as she looks at me, and it feels like a bit of my spirit is restored.

"Thanks, Whit. Love you."

"Love you, Jojo."

When I pull into the parking lot at the bakery, I notice that a few of the contractor trucks are already there. As I grab my purse and bag with a change of clothes from the passenger seat, I hear a whistle behind me. Immediately I shrink into myself. Before, I'd never thought twice about wearing my sweaty yoga pants and tank top to the bakery after working out. I usually changed in the back before diving into prep and opening duties, but that was before the renovations. Now there's a dozen-strong crew of male contractors watching me crawl out of my car and make my way to the building, and it makes me wish I were invisible.

My cheeks burn as I pass by where a few of them stand as they smoke. I don't make eye contact, but it doesn't stop whomever's whistling.

"Look at you, sexy," a low voice bellows from several feet away. "You wanna come say hi? Don't be shy."

Out of the corner of my eye, I notice another guy elbow the guy who hollered at me. There's disgruntled murmuring for the next few seconds before I turn the corner to the back of the building where my and Max's temporary combined space is located.

It's not till I unlock the door that I notice my hands are shaking the slightest bit. I flex them and push the door open, then shut it quickly behind me, locking it.

God, I hate being a woman sometimes. Having to tiptoe around the space where I work—a place I should feel safe and welcome—just because there are men nearby who act like cavemen is a special kind of infuriating.

My heart thuds as I consider all the comebacks I could have hollered at him. But what good would that have done? He probably would have laughed or taken it as an invitation to keep hassling me. Or worse, it would have aggravated him, and things might have escalated.

I employ some of my yoga breathing to ease my racing heart. It's all fine. I'm in the building, and the door is locked. I'll get started on my to-do list. Everything will be okay now.

I flip on the lights and head to the back corner on Max's side behind one of the bookshelves to change. This temporary space doesn't have separate rooms for our offices, so this is the only semiprivate place I can change my clothes. I unzip my bag and quickly pull out a clean pair of jeans and a T-shirt to wear for the day. I'm shedding my sweaty tank top when I smell something burning.

I drop my top on the floor, then glance around the space, but I don't see any smoke. Is it coming from outside? For a moment, I think it might be the cigarette smoke from the contractors on the other side of the building, but then I hear a familiar beeping noise. I spin around and notice that the light on my oven is on.

What the hell?

I dart over and pull open the oven door and my jaw falls to the floor. There's a pile of dark fabric sitting on the middle rack.

I grab a nearby kitchen towel, yank the garment out, and throw it on the floor. I squint down at white lettering spelling out the band name "Mudhoney" on a black cotton T-shirt.

"Fucking Max," I mutter.

"Excuse me?"

When I look up, my jaw drops for a second time. Because there's Max standing at the entrance wearing nothing but jeans and a confused frown.

I stammer as I gawk at his sculpted chest. And his shoulders. And his arms. And his abs. My lizard brain counts the muscles.

One, two, three, four, five, six, s—holy shit, you can have eight ab muscles? What the hell, I never knew . . .

And oh damn, those V-lines along the sides of this stomach that I'm sure have a name, but I can't think of it right now. Because my brain is too busy taking in the flawless visual. It takes a second, but I manage to shake my head and refocus on the moment.

"What the hell is your T-shirt doing in my oven?"

That seems to jolt him. He throws his shoulders back and crosses his arms.

"I was, um, drying it."

"Why?" My pitchy tone bounces off every concrete surface.

He scrunches his face and for a fleeting second, I want to smile. Because holy crap, I've never seen him make such an adorable flustered face before.

"I got caught out in the rain this morning when I was jogging with Muffin, and then I had to take her to an early grooming appointment and didn't have time to change, so I thought I'd just dry it in the oven here."

My mouth hangs open as I stammer.

"What the . . . why the hell would you think that's okay? God, that's so unsanitary."

I don't miss the way Max flinches at my harsh words.

I bite my lip and look away for a second. God's honest truth? I find Max so insanely physically attractive that even if he had put his sweatiest item of clothing in my oven, it wouldn't have fazed *me* at all. But customers eat the food I'm baking in there, and I'm sure they would be grossed out by the thought of that same oven being used as a makeshift clothes dryer.

I pinch the bridge of my nose, close my eyes, and sigh. "Sorry, I didn't mean . . . I'm sure you're clean."

"Of course I'm clean." Max's eyebrows pinch together as he stands, ramrod-straight posture, arms still crossed against his chest. "I took a shower this morning. And I just washed that shirt."

"Good for you, but that doesn't mean you can use my oven to dry your clothes. God, what if a fire started? There was no one here—the whole building could have gone up in flames."

He rolls his eyes, which sends fury through my veins.

I step closer to him. "Are you seriously rolling your eyes at me? After using my oven as your personal laundromat and almost setting the building on fire? You have got to be kidding me."

He sighs. "Okay, yeah, I shouldn't have rolled my eyes. But I just stepped out for a few minutes to run and gas up my car. I was coming right back. There wasn't going to be a fire, Joelle. Don't be like that."

"Like what? Concerned with safety? Responsible?"

He shakes his head, his gaze off to the side, like he's sick of hearing me talk about this. It sends me to the edge of boiling over.

I walk up until we're almost toe-to-toe and point my finger up at him.

"And speaking of responsible, we live in Portland. It rains all the freaking time here. Pack an extra T-shirt for god's sake so you don't have to use my oven as a laundromat and set fire to our shared work space."

My chest heaves up and down as I spit the words out when I feel my pointer finger jab against something very hot and solid. And that's when I realize I'm poking Max in the chest with my finger. God, wow . . . that's . . . that's some firm bare flesh right there.

I remember just how exquisite his skin felt under my touch the one time we made out. But touching him like this, when our emotions are running high and his skin is hot and wet, it's a completely different sensory experience.

A second later I remember that I'm only wearing a sports bra. My cleavage and my stomach are on full display, mere inches from Max's body.

And that's when I notice that glazed-over look in his eyes . . . and where exactly he's looking.

It's not at my face. It's at my chest. My boobs specifically.

I step back and cross my arms over my torso. My cheeks heat

and I start to turn away instinctively. And then I see Max's hands fly to the waistband of his jeans. His fingers fumble and for a moment, I wonder what the hell he's so panicked about.

But then I see it. The bulge at the front of his jeans.

Max is turned on at the sight of me, sweaty and in a sports bra.

A whole new feeling consumes me. It feels a lot like satisfaction. Maybe a tad smug too.

I can't help it. Max Boyson is turned on by me again, but this time I barely even touched him.

Yeah, it's petty, but honestly? I don't care. This situation we're in is an utter mess. Each day we work in this shared space we're either ignoring each other amid a cloud of tension or bickering. Experiencing a moment of mutual attraction is a nice break from it all.

With a throat-clear, he scurries over to the oven and scoops his shirt from the floor. And that's when I see the massive tattoo taking up the entirety of his broad, muscled back. I almost choke as air escapes my lungs. Because I've never seen anything like it before.

It's huge, stretching from the top of his shoulders all the way down to his waist. The gray-black ink depicts what looks like a cross between a skull and a demon face in distorted detail. Kind of like a painting that was left out in the rain. The horns at the top of the head and the toothy smile are shaded in gray and black, but the rest of the image is without color. Just Max's lightly tanned skin.

For the several seconds that I stare at it while he picks up his shirt and shakes it out, I don't even blink. Some might call the tattoo scary, but to me it's not. More like arresting. My gaze glides to the cursive gothic lettering along the top of his shoulders.

Good Enough Alone

The words imprint on my brain even after they disappear when Max pulls his shirt over his head.

He darts over to his side of the space.

"Sorry I put my shirt in your oven," he mumbles as he starts up his computer. "Won't happen again."

"Okay. Thanks," I say quietly.

I throw on a shirt then run a clean cycle on the oven as I portion out the prepped dough from the refrigerator. For the rest of the day, all I can think about is Max's back tattoo. That demon skull face and that phrase must hold some meaning for him. I'm dying to know what it is.

I glance up at him as he strolls through the stacks, surveying the books, not once glancing up at me.

And then I realize it's not my business. I shouldn't want to know.

And so I look back at the slab of dough on my floured metal table and quietly get back to work.

Chapter 8

Max

I pull at the hem of my shirt and try not to think about just how badly I screwed things up with Joelle. Again.

What the hell was I thinking yesterday? I glance over at her side of the space and watch for a few seconds as she rolls out a giant slab of dough on the metal table. She stops to wring out her flour-covered hands and push up her glasses on her face with the back of her wrist. When she starts to look up, I quickly turn back to a random book on the shelf I'm standing next to and pretend like I'm engrossed in taking inventory.

I blink, and a visual of Joelle standing in front of me in just a sports bra and yoga pants as she tells me off flashes in my brain. Her black hair pulled back, the smooth curve of her hips, her glowing skin, the way her chest bounced every time she gestured . . .

"Damn it," I mutter to myself when I feel that familiar pressure below. I force myself to think of anything—baseball, long division, getting kicked in the shin, that pile of dirt in the parking lot—to avoid the same problem I had yesterday when my body decided to notice just how attractive I found Joelle as she verbally laid into me while wearing sexy yoga gear.

I internally scold myself for being such a shallow dipshit in this moment. Now that I've had a day to mull it all over in my head, I've realized that drying my soaked shirt in her oven was one of the worst ideas I've ever had, next to that time when I was sixteen and thought it would be funny to steal the cross-country running coach's car as a prank. And that time I mailed a nude Polaroid of myself to my high school girlfriend when she was visiting relatives for the summer . . . and her grandma opened her mail by mistake.

So yeah, file yesterday's massive lapse in judgment under "least intelligent things I've done."

I guess it's not all that surprising given that my ability to think clearly has been absolute trash ever since I got that call the other week while taking Muffin for a walk . . . the call I still haven't returned. Because that would mean contacting the one person I never thought I'd see again—the one person I never wanted to see again. It would mean rehashing one hell of a painful past, and I'm not even close to being ready to do that.

But it's making focusing on anything else—this weird new setup at work, how to undo this messy situation with Joelle—nearly impossible.

Being a moody jerkoff isn't helping things.

I silently scold myself for letting the tension between us get this bad. What would I even say at this point?

Hey, Joelle. Really sorry I've been acting like a dick lately. I'm having some serious personal problems that I've got no idea how to cope with and because I'm kind of a loner, I don't really have any-

one to talk to about it, so while I try to figure this all out on my own, my default is to act like a closed-off jackass.

No way in hell I'm saying that to her. Moody silence, as messed up as it is, is better than that. Because at least if I bottle it all up inside me, she won't know what an absolute dumpster fire my life—and my past—is.

The sound of someone clearing their throat pulls my attention to Joelle's side of the space. There's a woman standing at the counter with the deepest frown I've ever seen a human make.

"Excuse me." She waves an impatient hand at Joelle, even though Joelle is clearly looking at her and just taking a minute so she can wipe her hands on her apron before she helps her.

"This matcha latte is terrible," she trills before Joelle speaks a word. The way she wrinkles her nose, like she's smelling a pile of dog crap, makes me clench my jaw. What is this lady's problem?

"Oh. Um, I'm sorry about that. Can you tell me what's wrong with it?" Joelle asks in a polite tone despite how taken aback she looks.

The woman waves her hand, like she's annoyed to have to answer Joelle's question. "God, I don't know. It just tastes off."

"Okay, well, I apologize—"

My brow jumps to my hairline as I watch the woman hold up a hand to Joelle, cutting her off.

She brushes a lock of her light brown hair from her face. "I'd like a plain black coffee instead."

Joelle's shoulders slump the slightest bit. "Sure, I can get you that, no problem."

I swallow back the urge to make a smart-ass comment. If I happened to be in Joelle's bakery when a customer was rude to her or her family, I always called them out, which would result in a stammered apology. But now it feels wrong to even think about stepping in because of the tension between us. I doubt she'd want me waltzing over there and interfering now that we're barely speaking to each other.

So I stay put while she handles this bullshit complaint much better than I ever could. I'd probably tell that lady tough shit and that if she wants something else to drink, she can pay for it.

But Joelle isn't a grumpy asshole like me. She's an angel and gives the woman a free coffee, that polite smile still on her face, before going back to prepping more pastries. Just then a high-school-aged kid walks in and heads for my side of the space. I nod at him, but he barely makes eye contact with me.

I head over to my laptop and work on my inventory spreadsheet until a shrill voice cuts through my focus.

"You little thief!"

I look up and see the annoying lady pointing at the high school kid, who's standing between the bookshelves. She hops up from the small table where she's sitting and marches over to him. I stand up too and start to walk over to figure out what the hell is going on, but the woman kicks off before I can even open my mouth.

"I saw you swipe that book from the shelf and slip it into your backpack! Oh my god, I can't believe you did that! You little—"

"Hey." My hard tone cuts off the woman's tirade. I look over at the kid. "What's going on here?"

When the woman starts firing off again, I hold up my hand at her. "I wasn't talking to you."

Out of the corner of my eye I see the kid's eyes go wide. The woman purses her lips and crosses her arms. "Look, I'm just trying to help you out. You run this bookstore, right? Do you really want little delinquents like this cutting into your profits—"

"I said, I wasn't talking to you." My tone is a hair under a shout. Normally the thought of yelling at a total stranger makes me cringe, but that seems to be the only way to get through to this lady.

She mutters something I can't understand under her breath, but I ignore it and turn back to the kid.

"What's going on? Did you do what she's claiming?"

The kid's face scrunches, and his eyes dart everywhere but me. He hesitates, then clamps his mouth shut.

"Hey." I rein in my tone so that I sound less pissed and more concerned. Even if this kid tried to steal a book, something in the way that he's acting doesn't sit right with me. He's behaving less like a guilty shoplifter and more like a desperate kid who's terrified that I'm going to go off on him for breathing wrong.

And something about that hits deep inside me—because I can relate to that. I remember feeling that way a lot when I was his age.

He stammers for a few seconds before his eyes start to water.

"It's okay," I say after a few seconds. "Tell me the truth and I promise I won't get mad. We'll work something out."

The kid stares at me with those gigantic brown eyes. "Okay, yeah, I—I, um, I took a book. I'm so sorry." He unzips his backpack and pulls out a paperback copy of *The Joy Luck Club*. "But I . . . I just didn't know what else to do . . ."

"Are you kidding me? You didn't know what else to do? How about you pay for it?" The lady scoffs. I press my eyes shut as I draw on the last of my patience so I don't lose my shit on her.

"I don't have any money," the kid mumbles, his gaze glued to the floor. "And I . . . I need that book for school and I just didn't know what other way to get it—"

The lady wags her finger near the kid's face. "How about you go to the library and borrow the book instead of acting like a little hoodlum and stealing? Did that ever occur to you?"

"I did go to the library—I took the bus to three different branches in the city, but every copy is checked out. Even the ebook copies." The kid wipes the tears streaking his face. "I have a book report due next week and I haven't even started reading it. I—I know it was wrong, but I'll fail my book report if I don't—"

"Oh boo-hoo, cry me a river. You think that makes stealing okay?"

I huff out a breath. Jesus, she's a piece of work. Her personality reminds me of those people who call the police on kids selling lemonade because they're doing it without a permit.

"Will you please be quiet?" I bark at her.

She rolls her shoulders back and crosses her arms. "I most certainly will not be quiet. And I will not just stand back and let some junior criminal ruin a small business."

I roll my eyes in full view of her. "Lady, as the owner of this small business, I'm more concerned with the way your incessant interrupting and vigilante bullshit is ruining my will to breathe. Now would you give it a rest and back the hell off so I can handle this?"

Her jaw drops. At least now she's quiet.

I turn back to the kid, but before I can say anything, Joelle speaks.

"I'll pay for your book." She walks over, wallet in hand, and digs out three twenties. "Here."

The kid stares at the cash in her hands. "Um, no, that's okay."

"I insist." She presses the cash into his palm, then smiles at him, like it's no big deal.

"That's, um, more than the book costs," the kid mumbles as he tugs on the strap of his backpack.

"It's fine," she says. "Save the rest in case you need to buy something else for school."

It's clear the kid is so taken aback by Joelle's gesture that he doesn't know what to say. Neither do I, honestly. I mean, I've witnessed Joelle's generosity multiple times. I've seen her give free pastries to Clarence and let customers pay her later on when they've forgotten their wallets. But something about this gesture is different. Her kindness is a welcome interruption to the tension in the room.

"Well, this is just astounding." Out of the corner of my eye I spot the self-righteous lady throwing her hands up in the air. "Are you honestly rewarding this little criminal for stealing?"

The tender expression melts from Joelle's face as she turns to the lady. "No. I'm helping a new friend."

Joelle turns back to him. The lady laughs like she can't believe it. "Wow. Just, wow. Society really is going straight to hell now that we're rewarding criminals. You should be ashamed of yourself."

I don't miss Joelle's eye roll, the way her chest heaves as she inhales and pivots back to the woman. "Actually, I think this is the sign of a good society, helping people who need it. And the only person here who should be ashamed is you. I make the best damn matcha latte in all of Portland and you didn't like it. That means your taste buds are crap."

The start of a chuckle falls from my lips before I clear my throat.

"And on top of that, you went out of your way to make a kid cry. Pretty damn shameful all around."

The lady's jaw plummets all the way to the floor at what Joelle's said. "That's it. I'm out of here."

"Thank god," Joelle mutters. I hold back a laugh.

As the lady marches out the door, we turn back to the kid.

"You know that stealing is wrong, right?" Joelle says gently.

The kid nods. "I'm sorry. I swear, I've never done it before and I'll never do it again. I just . . . didn't know what else to do."

"I get it. I was there once too," I say.

Joelle turns to look at me for a brief moment, but then focuses back on the kid.

"You don't need to pay for that book," I say. "You can have it for free."

He stammers, then thanks me, then starts to hand Joelle her cash back.

"No, you keep it."

"If you have trouble getting a book for school, you can come here and I'll help you," I tell him. "I can't promise that every book will be free, but I'll get the price down as much as I can."

He sniffles and the hint of a smile appears. "Okay. Thank you."

"What's your name?" Joelle asks.

"Henry."

"You hungry, Henry?"

"Um, yeah, actually."

She gestures for him to follow her to her counter, where she fishes a ham and cheese croissant from the display case. He tries to pay for it, but she tells him no. She sits with him at one of the small café tables and they chat as he eats. I overhear bits and pieces of their conversation as I work on my side of the space, mostly about what books he likes.

"I love Amy Tan too," Joelle says. "I read her a lot when I was your age. Have you read Gail Tsukiyama?"

The kid shakes his head. She grabs a small pad of paper from her apron pocket and scribbles on it before sliding it over to him. "Those are some of my favorite titles of hers. Most libraries should have them."

His face lights up. "Thanks. Seriously, this is so nice of you."

She hops up from the table and heads back to the metal table in her space. Henry finishes his food and thanks Joelle again before he walks over to me.

"Hey, um, I'm sorry again. For trying to steal from you. Thank you for not calling the cops."

He can barely make eye contact with me, he's so embarrassed.

"It's all right, man. Like I said, I've been there."

He nods. "Promise I won't do it again."

I tell him it's all good, water under the bridge.

When he leaves, I walk over to Joelle's counter. "That was pretty great what you did."

She turns around to look at me, her eyebrows nearly to her hairline. "What?" I hate how shocked she looks when I speak to her—it's such a far cry from how we used to be, when we'd joke and chat and laugh almost every day before this shared-space mess.

"How you stood up for Henry. How you helped him."

I hate how I'm mumbling. I sound so insecure and unsure. But that's exactly how I feel. Because I don't know how to smooth over this divide between us and it's making things awkward as hell.

But I want to say something. I want to make it clear just how much I admire her. I want her to know in this moment, no matter how messed up things are right now, that's she's an incredible human being.

"Oh. Thanks." She purses her lips and the corners of her mouth turn up. Not quite a smile, but better than a blank stare or a glare.

"I forgot you liked Gail Tsukiyama and Amy Tan," I say, inwardly cursing myself for the abrupt transition. "I, um, I remember now, how you've ordered their books from me before."

The confused frown melts from her face. Her scrunch-smile appears. "I've been a fan ever since I was a kid."

"You were a brilliant kid."

That earns me a smile. It's slight and small, but the joy is there, and it floors me. How easily she shifted from bold when she told off that woman to kind and sweet when she helped put Henry at ease by feeding him and chatting about books. Witnessing that makes my heart beat faster. All the bones in my rib cage shake.

"Hardly brilliant," she says. "Just a bookworm, especially when I was a kid."

"Bookworms are brilliant. I'm one myself. I would know."

The sound of her chuckle is so light and easy. I haven't heard it in a while and it makes me grin till my cheeks ache.

Just then a group of older folks walk in. Half of them mill around my book stacks while the other half peruse Joelle's menu board.

I glance over at her as she helps her customers, in awe of how she's kindness and grit in equal measure—how she stands up for what's right, no matter what. How despite all our conflict lately, she was gracious enough to chat with me just now and let things be pleasant between us, even for just a few minutes.

My phone buzzes, and I recognize Dr. Givens's unsaved number right away.

I freeze, just like I did the first time he called. As I watch the number illuminate my screen, my thumb hovers between the decline and accept buttons. I wonder if I've got it in me to be kind. Maybe even to forgive.

I hit the decline button. It happens so quickly, almost like a reflex. I shouldn't be surprised. I don't possess that type of kindness; I haven't in years. When it comes to this, I'm all grit now. I don't know how to be anything else.

Chapter 9

Joelle

"You're a lifesaver!" Whitney says as she hops out of her car and follows me around the corner of the building to the back.

I glance up at the storefront where the remodeling is taking place, relieved that none of the workers are outside right now. It's the middle of the day, so they must be busy inside. They were definitely around this morning, judging by the near-constant jackhammering and drilling that persisted for hours.

If they weren't inside working, I'm sure they'd be in a catcalling frenzy after seeing tall and stunning Whitney with her ruby-red hair, porcelain skin, and supermodel figure.

I lead her inside and glance over at Max, who's on the phone on his side of the space, frowning down at his computer as a half-dozen customers mill around the bookstore. A few days ago when that kid Henry broke down after trying to take the book from Max's store, we seemed to have a reprieve from our tension and conflict. It's like we were willing to put aside our baggage and come together to help him. We didn't even speak directly to each other during that interaction, but we had a short and pleasant chat afterward. I swore I could feel a shift from hostility to kindness then . . . like we were inching back to what we were before the remodel threw everything out of whack.

But that didn't last long. Later that day I noticed he was back to scowling and saying next to nothing. He's been in that mood ever since. I try not to think about just how disappointed I am that things between Max and me aren't magically good again. Instead I focus on Whitney's order. I point out the covered trays of freshly made *pandesal*, *bibingka*, croissants dipped in a rich purple *ube* glaze, *haupia* hand pies, and *biko*. There's also a basket of individually wrapped sugar cookies in the shape of computer screens with lines of coding in delicate white icing.

"Oh my god!" Whitney gasps, her hand cupping her mouth. "Joelle! You didn't have to go all out like this!"

I lightly smack her arm. "Of course I did. This is a special event—the orientation for the kickoff of Chicks Who Code. I want them to know that they're experiencing the best of the best, and that includes the baked goods you're serving them."

She pulls me into a hug as she squeals.

"Are you sure this didn't cost more than what you quoted my company? This looks like something out of a gourmet magazine spread."

"Positive. I'm just that good."

I wink at her, and she giggles. Then we start loading the pastries into her car.

"You sure it's okay for me to take all of this? You don't need any of them for the bakery?" She slowly shuts the door to her SUV, careful not to hit the trays of pastries.

"Yup! I've got an hour left until I close, but the display case is packed with plenty of stuff. I'll be good."

She hugs me one last time. We pull apart and I hold her by the shoulders. "I'm so proud of you for creating this program. I know you won't need it because you're amazing, but good luck. The girls are gonna love you."

She beams back at me. "Aww, Jojo. You always know how to bring out my happy tears."

She smooths a hand down the front of her blouse, then hops into her car. I wave her off, then head back inside.

When I walk through the door to my side of the space, I do a double take at the display case. It's empty save for one croissant, a square of *bibingka*, and an empanada.

"What the . . ." How in the world did that happen? Just minutes ago, the display case was half-full with pastries I spent the entire morning baking and now they're all nearly gone?

A crunching noise from across the room catches my ear. I turn to see Max chowing down, a half-eaten empanada in his hand.

"What are you doing?"

In the two seconds it takes me to walk over to him, he's devoured the rest of the empanada. As he chews, I survey the damage. On the console table he's sitting at, there's an empty paper plate littered in crumbs.

"What?" He has the audacity to sound annoyed and it's enough to make me scream.

"Don't you 'what' me. Did you seriously just help yourself to all the pastries in my display case? The pastries that are meant for my customers and not you?"

My voice echoes in the space, but I don't care. I'm irate that Max would do something so inconsiderate.

He holds up his hand. "Relax, I paid. I left you plenty of cash on the counter."

"That's not the point!"

A woman standing with her elementary-school-aged kid shoots a wide-eyed stare in our direction before ushering her kiddo out the door.

"You can't just grab whatever food you want from my bakery and leave money on the counter, Max. That's not how this works."

He shakes his head, like he's utterly confused. "Hey, I'm just doing what your family said."

I grip the edge of the console table. "What the hell are you talking about?"

He braces his hands on the tops of his thighs like this conversation is physically taxing and lets out the most exasperated sigh. "Your dad told me yesterday when he was working that I was welcome to whatever pastries I wanted. Whenever." He shrugs, then rubs the back of his neck. "I figured it was fine."

His nonchalant tone makes my head throb.

"You should have asked me—I'm the one working today! And oh my god, did you eat, like, ten pastries when I was gone these last five minutes?"

He crosses his arms in a defensive stance. "I was hungry. I was on the phone for the past two hours sorting out a shipping issue. I hadn't eaten all day."

I shove a hand through my hair. "That's so not the point," I groan. "Max, I'm open for another hour. I have regulars coming in who were expecting to be able to order those pastries you just inhaled. It's not like I don't track inventory with my usual sales each week. Merna comes in here every Wednesday for beef and raisin empanadas to take home to her partner. And Walter gets *bibingka* to take home to his wife and grandson after his daily walk in the nature reserve. And I wanted to set aside some stuff for Clarence too just in case he drops by. And there's this cute high school couple who always come in after school gets out and they order coffee and *pandasal* . . ."

I trail off when I recognize the glazed-over look in Max's eyes.

And then he shrugs. "Maybe you should figure out a way to communicate with your parents better. You're close, right? Talk it out or whatever it is you guys do."

I stand there, stunned. All I can do is blink. It takes a second to process just how callous his tone is. And when I do, it sends my rage through the roof.

"You can't be serious," I snap.

He throws his hands up. "What do you want me to say, Joelle? What's done is done. I paid for the food. I'm sorry I did it. It won't happen again."

And then he mutters "Jesus," slams his laptop shut, and turns his attention to a stack of books on the edge of the table, clearly ignoring me. His blatant apathy stuns me into silence. Max is about as concerned about this as he would be about a scuff on the sole of his shoe.

He clearly doesn't give one shit about me or my hurt feelings. "Screw you, Max."

I stomp back over to my side and glance at the nearly empty display case once more. And then I open the fridge and see if there's any dough left that I can quickly prep for the rest of the day. But there's nothing.

I slam the door shut and slump on the nearby stool, preparing myself to tell Merna and Walter and Clarence and the cute high school couple that sorry, I don't have their favorite pastries like I normally do because the bookstore owner with whom I'm forced to share a work space has the appetite of a puma and apparently doesn't know how to meal plan properly.

Yeah, it's technically all fine because Max paid for what he ate. And I know my customers will understand. But it's just one more thing to add to the list of things that aren't working out like they should be. And I'm sick of having to just roll with the punches.

For years, I've had to play the cards that life dealt my family and me. And I did. Because I didn't have a choice. I couldn't control that a morally bankrupt financial planner swindled my family out of their savings, but I could control how I helped them. I couldn't control that Ivan decided on a whim to remodel this building, throwing my business into disarray, but I could control how I treated my customers, like always making sure I had their favorites in stock so they could have them when they came in to see me, just like before.

But I can't even do that anymore—not with Max Boyson invading my space and throwing a wrench into almost everything I try to do.

I lean over and rest my head on the cold metal tabletop and groan softly since I can't scream. I don't know how much more of this I can take.

"Sweetie, I just wanna say that I'm sorry," Dad says as he helps me prep a tray of *pandesal* before it goes into the oven.

"For what?" I turn around and check the temperature of the oven.

"For telling Max that he could help himself to the display case the other day." He straightens to his full height and rests a hand on his hip. "I didn't realize that was going to screw up your inventory for the day. And I didn't realize just how much he was going to eat. I should have known, though. He's a big guy."

I glance in the direction of Max's side of the space to make sure he can't hear our conversation, but I don't see him. He must have stepped out for a second.

I smile weakly at Dad. Mom must have told him that I vented to her when I came home from work. As annoyed as I was, I told her that I understood he meant well, but that I always want to prioritize making enough food for our customers.

"It's okay, Dad. I know you didn't mean to. It was an honest mistake."

He lets out a sigh that sounds a million times heavier than usual. "It's just that I like that Max fella. I didn't want him to go hungry."

Max walks out from behind one of the bookcases, followed by a couple of high-school-aged kids. He pulls a book from a shelf, then hands it to them. After they pay, he walks out the door.

"I know the situation's not ideal right now," Dad says. "And I know you two have been squabbling a bit. I thought offering some baked goodies was a way to extend an olive branch, so to speak."

I can feel myself turning red at the thought of my dad knowing anything about the complicated relationship Max and I are currently navigating. I'm thirty-two years old, I shouldn't have to have my parents try to smooth over disagreements for me.

Dad's eyes shine with embarrassment as he smiles slightly. The crow's-feet that frame his pale face send the tiniest bolt of worry through me. He works full-time as a mechanic in a garage, often putting in overtime for the extra money to replenish his and Mom's savings.

You'd think more than ten years of working would be enough to replenish the money my family lost, but it takes a long time to build up multiple retirement savings that took decades to build. And maybe by now the money would have been replenished had there not been various incidentals along the way, like medical bills, repairs for the house, new cars, and every other expense that could possibly pop up.

That's the cost of living life, sweetie, Dad's always said. *There's always something to pay for, and it's always more expensive than you think.*

I look at him. "I appreciate you trying, Dad. But at this point, I think it's best if Max and I just try to stay out of each other's way as much as we can until the renovation is over."

The faint sound of a drill echoes from the other side of the building, reminding me that we still have two weeks to go of this disastrous setup—at the very least. I need to message Ivan for an update to see if things are on schedule. But as eager as I am for this to all be over so Max and I can return to our respective spaces and work separately, part of me is scared to even ask about it. Because there's a very real chance that things are behind schedule, and knowing that I'll have to endure even more time in the shared space from hell with Max would send my brain and my nerves into a stress panic.

Max walks back in, small paper bag and coffee cup in hand. He sets them on the console table, then walks over to help a customer. I quietly fight the sting at the sight of that coffee chain logo on the paper cup. Ever since our spat about him eating almost all the pastries in the display case, he hasn't bothered to order anything from me.

I'd be lying if I said it didn't cut deep. Even though I understand why he's avoiding me, there's a pain that lands square in the center of my chest whenever I think about how in just the span of a few weeks he's gone from craving my coffee and cooking on a daily basis to no longer needing it.

A sliver of doubt creeps inside my head. Did he ever like the food from my bakery? Or was he just trying to be neighborly?

The skin on my neck and chest flush from embarrassment. If he's been pretending this whole time, he did a hell of a job making me believe him.

I bite the inside of my cheek, focusing on the pain of that just to distract myself from the humiliation engulfing me.

"Hey there, Max. How's it going?"

Dad's cheery holler seems to stun Max as much as it does me, judging by the wide-eyed glance he gives Dad. Sandwich in hand, Max quickly chews, swallows, and smiles at Dad.

"I'm good, Bill. You?"

"Oh, you know. Same old, same old. Feeling good and looking good—most days. Can't complain." Dad chuckles at his standard response to that question.

A more natural smile tugs at Max's lips. "Well, you're definitely looking good today, sir."

I almost scoff at how flustered Dad gets at Max's compliment. I guess no one is immune to his charm.

"Well, I'm out of here, sweetie." Dad whips off his apron and presses a kiss to my forehead. "See you tonight at home."

I tell him thanks again for stopping by to help, then start to tidy up in the kitchen. As I'm wiping down the counter by the register, I overhear a guy perusing the bookshelves at Stacked in conversation with Max.

"Well, I'm starving," he says, patting his belly. "Anyplace good you can recommend?"

I quickly wipe my hands, ready to head to the register and take the guy's order.

"Try that deli up the street. They've got good subs," Max mutters.

My head whips up to see Max not even looking at the guy when he speaks to him. Is he kidding me with this crap? Fine if he doesn't want to order food from me anymore, but to sabotage my business by telling people to dine elsewhere? That's all sorts of messed up.

Anger flattens my insides. Just this morning I pointed a couple who stopped in for pastries and coffee to Max's bookstore because they mentioned having an hour to kill before heading out to their next destination. I didn't even hesitate when I did it.

What exactly does that say about me?

That I'm painfully naïve . . . and too nice for my own good.

Shame levels me as I stand there and gawk at Max.

"Hmm, really?" the guy asks him. "There's a pretty nice-looking bakery right here—"

"Go to the deli," Max barks. He's looking at the guy this time . . . only "looking" is a kind way of putting it. More like Max is leveling him with a brutal glower.

Once again I'm so frozen with embarrassment and anger that I can't do anything other than stand there and gawk in disbelief at what is happening.

"Wow. Okay then." The guy leaves.

My gaze flits to Max, who pays me barely two seconds of eye contact before walking off toward the stacks, where an older woman has waved him over to ask a question.

I grit my teeth until my temples start to ache. My dentist is going to scold me yet again for all the abuse I've been bestowing on my poor mouth. Whatever, I'll deal with that later. I can't yell at Max, I can't storm out, I can't change the situation.

I grab the nearest spray bottle and start rage-cleaning every surface I can get my hands on. I'm wiping down the register when I overhear the woman's voice.

"Oh you have a book club? How fun!"

"Yes, ma'am. We're reading *East of Eden*. Next meeting is next Thursday afternoon if you'd like to join," Max says.

I think back to all the times in our old setup where I saw Max hosting his monthly book club. I always swooned seeing him flash that sexy smile as he welcomed patrons into his bookshop to chat about whatever book they were reading that month. Every meeting, he'd order pastries and coffee from Lanie's for his members. I'm certain he's not planning on doing that this time.

"It's a laid-back discussion. Everyone's welcome," he says. "And you don't even have to finish the book if you don't like it. It's just nice to have a group of people stop in and chat once a month."

"Count me in!"

He offers to add her to the email list, which she happily accepts . . . and then I pause right there in the middle of my kitchen as the most deliciously evil idea pops into my head.

Yeah, it's underhanded. It's all sorts of wrong. And it is very, very unlike me.

But I'm done going along with this madness, just letting everything slide—things that end up screwing me over. Look what it's gotten me: a hostile work environment with the most infuriating man.

Maybe it's time to pay him back a little for that hostility.

Chapter 10

Joelle

It's middle of the afternoon on Thursday, the day of Max's book club, and I'm buzzing to see how it all plays out.

I'll admit, this isn't the most mature thing that I've ever done. It's downright petty.

But it was also petty when Max told his customer to avoid patronizing my bakery in favor of some random deli right in front of me.

And now it's time he has a taste of his own medicine.

It took a couple days to figure out how to access Max's book club email list and mail out new books to everyone, but with Whitney's computer expertise, I did it.

As I serve a cluster of customers, I look over at his side of the space, to the makeshift book club meeting spot where he's set up a small table and chairs. Max is going to be in for the surprise of his life and I get a front-row seat to it.

I bite back the smile aching to let loose on my face, then focus back on the customers. While I ring up orders and dispense food, people filter into the book club and sit down. Merna waves at me as she joins them. I wave back, giddy at what her reaction will be once the discussion starts. She's not in on my plan, but she's been to a few of Max's book clubs before and mentioned to me in passing wanting to read a romance for book club—she's finally getting her wish.

A few other people I recognize from Max's past book club meetings appear and settle in. They start murmuring to each other the minute they sit down. I can tell by their inquisitive expressions that this is going to be one hell of a chat.

Max appears from wherever he was hiding behind the stacks and gestures for the stragglers to sit down. He seems distracted as he keeps looking at his phone, which is probably for the best—the fact that he hasn't noticed the book that people are holding isn't *East of Eden* will make the reveal even more shocking.

About a dozen people are present for this meeting. Max, nose still buried in his phone, sits down at the table and looks up at them. His clouded stare makes it seem like his brain is a million miles away.

"So." He sighs and rests his hands on the tops of his jean-clad thighs. "What did everyone think of the book?"

"Well, I for one was shocked," says a fifty-something man whose name I think is Chester. He's a regular customer of Max's and comes to Lanie's from time to time. "I mean, I don't normally read such . . . salacious books. And I'll admit, I was a bit put off at the premise initially." He scrunches his face, like he's trying to find the right words. "But I told myself to give it a fair chance. After I read the first chapter, I couldn't put it down."

Max frowns and thumbs through his paperback copy of *East of Eden*. "I guess that makes sense. We all get taken by different parts of a story." He squints at the text on the page. "I wouldn't have thought to describe this book as 'salacious,' though . . ."

"Oh, but that's the perfect word for it, Chester!" Merna pipes up. "I thought it was brilliant. So very progressive of you to have this as a book club choice, Max."

Max's head whips up toward Merna. "Oh. Um, thanks."

While she speaks, she twirls a strand of her dyed-pink hair, which is styled in soft waves today. "And I just have to say, I always thought the book choices prior to this one were a bit stale," she says with a slight wince. "And truthfully, I was getting a bit tired of all the literary fiction you had us reading. I kind of assumed you were one of those boring guys who only preferred heteronormative fiction written by dead white guys. But! You sure proved me wrong with this one, kiddo."

Max's frown deepens. He shakes his head. "Sorry, Merna, I'm not quite sure what you mean—"

"I think what Merna means is that those threesome love scenes were quite descriptive. And fascinating. And aspirational in a way," the woman sitting next to Merna says thoughtfully. She pinches the frames of her glasses as she squints to an open page in the book.

Max's eyes bulge. "What?"

I cup my mouth with my hand to keep from howling in laughter. I quickly turn away, pretending to check on something in the display.

"Lisa, what are you talking about? There aren't any threesome scenes in . . ."

I hazard a peek back over in time to see Max finally noticing the book in everyone's hands.

"That's not *East of Eden*," he mutters. "What the . . ."

Chester's eyebrows fly up to his white-gray hairline as he snaps his fingers and points to Lisa. "Aspirational! Brilliantly said, Lisa. That's exactly what I was thinking when I was reading those parts, but I couldn't find the words to describe it just right."

Merna nods, flipping through the pages. "Refreshing, don't you think? To read such descriptive sex scenes. And that it's not glossed over, like so many other books do. Like, really, we're all adults here. I think we could all stand to have a bit of open-door sex in our reading."

"And how great that it was a relationship that involved three people," a guy at the far end of the table says. "It's not often you see polyamorous relationships highlighted in such a positive light in literature."

Max holds his hands up, his glance darting between everyone. "Okay, what book did you all read?"

Merna's eyebrows furrow as she shows Max the cover of the book. "What do you mean, 'What did we all read?' You know what we read. You emailed us and told us you were changing the selection last week. And you mailed us all the new books."

"What? I absolutely did not do that." Max runs his hand through his hair, which looks more disheveled than normal. The skull tattooed on the edge of his biceps bulges with the movement.

A flurry of conversation follows, but his expression waffles between bewildered and confused.

After a minute, he holds both hands up. "Okay, okay, wait. I don't know what you all are talking about, but this must have been some kind of mistake because I never emailed you to change the book or sent out new books . . ."

Just then his eyes cut to me before I can avert my gaze. I turn and instantly scrunch my lips, hoping that hides my smile. But it doesn't. My lips are trembling with the urge to burst out laughing, and I know beyond a shadow of a doubt that Max can see it.

Even though I'm now focused on straightening this stack of napkins, I can see Max in my peripheral vision as he stands up from the table.

"Gimme a second, everyone."

He's at my counter before I can even move. He plants both of his palms on the countertop and hunches over so he's eye level with me. "Hey. Wanna explain why the hell you screwed up my book club?"

All giddiness and amusement has gone up in smoke. All that's left is my fight response. Because yeah, what I did was immature, but man, he deserved it.

I cross my arms over my chest. "I don't know what you're talking about," I say calmly.

"Like hell you don't," he bites. "How dare you, Joelle."

His tone unleashes the anger and frustration brewing inside me ever since we moved into this shared space and he started acting like a closed-off jerk.

"How dare I? How dare you!" My voice is so loud, he flinches. "You screwed me first, Max. This is just a tiny taste of what you deserve."

Normally the thought of lashing out at someone has me cringing. It's so not in line with my personality. But with everything— that woman who berated Henry last week, the slow-moving renovations, and especially Max—I've had enough. I can't take Max treating me like I'm a nuisance he lives to ignore while actively diverting business away from me. Even a shy introvert like me has limits, and he just pushed them.

"And you know what, I'm not sure that I screwed up anything—it sounds like I did you a favor actually," I say. "It sounds like everyone in your club was tired of reading your list of boring book choices and was thrilled to have something steamy and exciting to read for a change."

Half of the book club crew murmurs affirmations and nods along. Max whips his head around and scowls at them.

"What are you—how the hell did I screw you over?" he snaps when he turns back to me.

His green-brown eyes look almost like earthy-hued geodes. They sparkle with the heat in his voice. It's as arresting as it is hot—*stop*.

I press my eyes shut for a moment and concentrate. "You screwed me over when you ate all my pastries and gave me the most half-assed, insincere apology."

His jaw clenches, like he's about to argue with me, but I speak before he can say anything.

"And then when you told one of your customers to go to that deli down the street instead of eating here when he asked for a recommendation. Right in front of me. God, you just . . . I can't believe you could be so mean." My voice chokes up for just a moment.

I look past the broad spread of Max's shoulders and see the entire book club crew gawking at us with wide, fascinated eyes. Adrenaline rockets through me.

I drop my hands to my sides and shake my head. "You think I was just going to stand there and do nothing while you trashed me like that?"

I ball my hands into loose fists to keep them from shaking.

All the anger from that day resurfaces, like soda bursting from a bottle.

I expect Max to fire back, to level me with a scowl before verbally laying into me. But he doesn't. Instead he leans back up, creating space between us. And as he rests his hands at his sides, the scowl on his face melts away. His shoulders relax and he clears his throat.

And then he aims a gentle stare at me. "I told that guy to go to that deli because he was being a creep. Toward you," he says in a low tone, probably so that only I can hear him. "He walked in while you were working with your dad and kept looking at you. I watched him as he stood in the stacks and kept staring over at you."

He pauses to swallow, like he's not sure if he should say the rest.

"When I noticed what he was doing, I asked if he needed help finding a book or something, but he shook his head and then said . . ."

Max grimaces, like he's just tasted something rotten.

"What did he say?" I ask in a firm voice.

He aims a stare at me that's somehow pointed and kind all at once. "He said, 'Just enjoying the eye candy,' while looking at you."

Dread settles in the pit of my stomach. I don't miss the way that muscle at the side of his jaw bulges. Max is fucking pissed— at the thought of that guy being a creep to me.

"That's why I told him to leave," he says. "And that's why I was so pissed."

"Oh."

For a few seconds I just stand there, my head heavy with the realization that Max was actually helping me in that moment.

He rubs the back of his neck. "I know I probably should have told you, but I didn't want to creep you out. And, um, we've been fighting a lot too, so I figured it was best if I just didn't bother you."

I nod. "Right, well . . . that's . . . that's, um . . . I appreciate . . ."

It's a struggle to process what's going on in my brain. Gratitude for Max standing up for me and prioritizing my safety. Embarrassment for how I ruined his book club.

"I need some air."

I dart out the entrance and head around the building. My head is spinning with new information. I just need to be in a quiet spot and gather my thoughts for a few minutes before I go back in there and apologize to Max for being the biggest jerk on the planet. Maybe I should sit in my car for a bit to clear my head.

I unlock my car, hop in the front seat, and shut the door. For a minute I sit there staring straight ahead at nothing in particular, processing what just happened. I've spent more than half my life enduring harassment, and when it happened in front of other people, no one has ever intervened before. Not once. But last week Max went out of his way to do something about it—to help me.

The flurry of thoughts whirring through my brain finally halts. I hop out of my car. I want to go to Max and tell him just how much what he did means.

I jog back toward the building. When I turn the corner, I bump into him.

I make an "oof" sound as he reaches for me, steadying me with my arms in his massive hands. Concern radiates in his eyes as he looks down at me.

"Crap. Are you okay? I'm sorry, I should have watched where I was going."

He's breathless, his gaze shifting from worried to watchful as he holds on to me. Inside I go gooey.

"Yeah. I'm fine."

His hands fall away from me. "I, um, just wanted to make sure you were all right." His gentle tone sends warmth through me.

"I'm okay. Thanks."

The tiniest smile tugs at his lips. He looks so relieved. Then he nods once and starts to move toward the entrance to the shared space, but I catch him by the wrist. "Wait."

He turns to me, eyebrows lifted in surprise. I let go of him, feeling a bit foolish for grabbing him.

"Thank you," I say quietly. "For what you did to get rid of that guy."

"You don't need to thank me, Joelle," he says gently.

"It was really kind, though."

"I was just being decent. Decency shouldn't be thanked. It should be baseline."

I go quiet as I mull over his words. He's right.

For a second, we just stand there and look at each other.

"I'm sorry for ruining your book club," I say. "That was really awful of me."

He flashes the softest smile. "It's okay. They clearly liked your book better."

His smile fades and he clears his throat. "I owe you an apology too. For how I've been acting lately. I, um, I haven't been myself. I've been sorting out some family stuff lately and it's been getting to me. I'm sorry for taking it out on you."

Behind the sincerity in his eyes, there's a tinge of pain. It hits something deep inside me. There's just something about seeing this tough and tatted-up guy show vulnerability that melts me.

I grab his hand in mine. It happens so quickly, like a reflex. "I'm so sorry, Max."

He gives my hand a squeeze, and for a second we just stand there, hand in hand, gazing at each other.

"I'm here for you."

I'm not prepared for the look on his face after I speak those words. It's soft but intense. Like he can't quite believe what I've said, but he's so, so happy to hear it.

"Thank you," he rasps.

And then he gives my hand one more squeeze before letting go. When we head back inside, my head is spinning for a totally different reason this time.

Chapter 11

Max

When I walk into work the morning after book club, Joelle's already there. She looks up at me from the giant slab of dough she's working on the metal table in her kitchen space. I instantly grin.

That tension I saw in her yesterday when I explained how that creep harassed her seems long gone. Her shoulders aren't hunched and her expression is relaxed. Just seeing her look comfortable again eases the knot inside me. I can't imagine what it must be like to be a woman and have to deal with that bullshit day after day. How demoralizing and even terrifying it must feel to have men repeatedly violate your sense of security.

I think back to the other day when I saw one of the construction guys catcalling Joelle as she hurried to her car, clearly trying to ignore him. I just happened to see because I was taking out the trash. One phone call to Ivan got that prick fired from the remodeling crew. Still, though. Who knows how long he had been creeping her out before then.

I grit my teeth. God, a lot of men fucking suck.

I push aside that thought and focus on the moment. How happy and energized she looks when it's barely six in the morning. Her hair is tied up in the messiest, sexiest bun, and she's sprinkled in flour. All over her apron, on her arms, her jeans, and the tip of her nose.

My heart slingshots around my chest as I take in the sight of her.

She's so goddamn cute. And sexy. And stunning. And every other word that exists to describe just how amazing a person can look.

"You're here early," she says.

"I had a coffee craving."

She smiles so wide, the tops of her cheeks bump her glasses.

I swallow back that pulse in my chest and walk over to her counter. "Would you hate me if I ordered this early before you opened?"

She tilts her head at me and lifts her eyebrow. "I was hoping you would, actually."

Some part deep inside of me bursts. Holy shit. She is fucking adorable.

As she wipes her hands and walks over to me to start prepping coffee, the air in the room feels different. Like something between us has shifted. I can tell by the way her gaze lingers on me for an extra second and that warmth in her eyes that she feels a shift too.

It makes sense given what happened yesterday with the book club and when I told her about that sack of shit who was harassing her. But that's not the only reason why things feel different today. It's also because I mentioned the family crap I'm sorting out. Yeah, I didn't give any detail—I couldn't. I can barely make sense of it myself—I don't even know how I'd begin to explain this situation to someone else.

But Joelle understood. And she said the one thing I didn't even know I needed to hear.

I'm here for you.

Those four simple words probably shouldn't have felt like such instant comfort, like some sort of phantom hug. But they did.

If anyone else had said them, I'd know better than to feel that way. I'd know that they were just trying to be nice.

But Joelle doesn't do "nice." Nice is too passive for what she is, which is a genuinely sweet and kind and thoughtful person— one of the best I know. I've watched her for over a year and a half pouring her heart and soul into her bakery, treating her customers like members of her own family. She remembers their names, the names of their kids and pets, birthdays, first days of school and work, graduations and weddings.

I've seen her give out pastries and drinks to people on the street near our building. I've seen her offer up her bakery as a hangout for local high school students who want to host some club meetup and elderly folks who want a place to play cards and dominoes. I've seen her give cash out of her pocket to a kid in need.

All because she cares. She doesn't do a single thing that isn't rooted in sincerity.

That's why what she said to me yesterday meant so much. Because despite the stress of our current work setup and how it's caused countless fights between us, she still cares about me. And that means everything—more than she'll ever know.

I watch as she moves swiftly behind the counter.

"Black coffee is fine," I tell her when I notice her reach for the bottle of homemade *ube* syrup.

She turns to me. "You sure? I didn't know you liked drinking black coffee."

My gaze falls to the counter as I bite back a smile. "I, uh, it's my preferred way to drink coffee."

When I look back up at her, her mouth is open slightly.

"Seriously?"

I pull at the collar of my T-shirt. "Yeah, actually."

She laughs. "Then why have you never ordered one?"

My cheeks feel like they're on fire as the truth dances on the tip of my tongue. I'm gonna sound pretty fucking pathetic when I admit this. Too late now, though.

"Because it takes longer to make an *ube* latte than a regular black coffee. And when I stood in line the first time I came into your bakery, I noticed how you chatted with customers if their drink took a bit of time to make, and I, um . . . well, I thought you were really pretty and sweet, and I wanted a reason to talk to you for longer than it would take for you to pour a black coffee."

Her mouth falls open. "Wait, you—you were interested in me? Ever since then?"

The look of utter shock on her face throws me. I mean, I went out of my way to play it cool. I definitely thought Joelle was insanely hot when I met her and started to get to know her, but I didn't want it to be obvious. So I just tried to be as casual and friendly as possible.

But come on, she's gorgeous. She has to know that every guy who ever comes in contact with her is unquestionably struck by her looks and how sweet she is.

"Um, yeah. I've liked you since I met you, Joelle," I say with a chuckle, hoping it softens just how much of a weirdo I must come off like in this moment. "I had a pretty big crush on you."

That makes me sound like I'm in high school. Jesus.

Just then she holds up a hand. "Wait. Do you even like *ube* lattes?"

"Not at first. It was a lot more sugar than I'm used to. But I kind of love them now."

She bursts out laughing, which makes me laugh too. After a minute, she turns to check on the drip coffee.

"Here." She hands me a paper cup filled with steamy black liquid. "And don't worry. You don't have to order *ube* lattes anymore if you don't want to."

She winks at me and I swear to god my heart flutters. Then she sighs and plants her hands on the edges of the countertop. "Well, I guess now's as good a time as any to tell you."

She straightens up to her full height and looks me square in the eye. "I've had a huge crush on you since you moved in next door."

"No way."

My head falls back as I let out a groan that turns into a laugh. Her giggles echo off the surface of the concrete slab. And then we look at each other and shrug.

"What a twist, huh? Didn't even see it coming."

I smile at her remark, then blow on my coffee before taking a sip.

"So this whole time we had a thing for each other?" I say after I swallow.

"Yup." She lets out a frustrated laugh. "God, we really went about things in a strange way, didn't we? Spending a year and a half crushing on each other, not saying a word, and then making out in your office one random day."

She looks off to the side and shakes her head like she can't believe it either.

"Why did you say you wanted to cool things off between us the day that Ivan told us about the renovation? Have your feelings changed?"

The directness of her question catches me off guard. She has every right to ask, though. It's a pretty mixed bag of signals I was sending.

I shake my head. "Not at all. I still really like you, Joelle."

The uncertainty in her gaze fades.

"Honestly, I was so thrown off and upset about the renovation that for a split second, I thought it might be easier if we didn't go further with each other. Everything felt like such a mess and I didn't want to complicate things even more," I say. "But pretty much as soon as I said that to you, I regretted it. I realized it was just a fleeting thought. It wasn't how I really felt. But then you stormed out before I could take it back and didn't answer my calls. I felt like the biggest asshole for hurting your feelings. And I figured after that massive screwup, you'd want nothing to do with me."

She glances off to the side, like she's thinking carefully about what I've said. For a few seconds, we're both silent.

She turns back to me. "That really hurt my feelings how you went back and forth like that," she says.

"I'm so sorry I hurt you."

A soft smile tugs at her lips. "But I still really like you too, Max."

My face stretches into the biggest grin.

When she turns back to look at me, the light catches her face and I notice that dusting of flour on the tip of her button nose again.

I reach over and brush it off with my thumb. A lip bite is her response, which makes my blood pump hot.

"You had a little flour on your nose," I rasp.

"Thanks," she whispers back, then clears her throat. "Funny story. I actually was going to ask you out. The day before we made out in your office."

"Wait, you were?" I ask.

She nods, her full cheeks turning pink. I notice her neck and chest flush too. A hard swallow moves through my throat. Something about discovering that so much of Joelle's body turns red when she blushes is sexy as fuck.

"Yeah, um, all that talk about sucking and licking bone marrow kind of derailed things. But um, my plan was to ask you out for a drink that day."

I think back to that morning, recalling how adorably flustered she was.

"For the record, I would have said yes. Obviously."

We both go quiet for a few moments before exchanging a knowing smile.

And then my brain finally catches up.

She couldn't have dropped a bigger hint. Ask her out now!

"Let's go out," I finally say.

Confusion mars her angelic face.

"What, now?"

"Yeah. Why not?"

"Um, because we both have to work a full day."

I shrug. "So? Let's close for the day. I think we both deserve a break after all the hours we've put in lately in this concrete box."

That smile I love so much appears as she considers it.

"Okay. Let's go."

I swipe my coffee, and she unties her apron, tosses it onto the table, and then grabs her purse from behind the counter.

She starts to ask me what I've got planned this early in the morning but abruptly stops talking. When I turn to her, she's staring wide-eyed at her phone.

"What is it?"

When she looks up at me and I see her eyes brimming with tears, something weird twists inside me. I haven't experienced this in years. It takes a second, but I finally recognize it. It's the fear of seeing someone I care about in pain.

I swallow back the dread as it burns up my throat and focus on helping Joelle.

"Joelle," I say softly. "What's wrong?"

Her faces twists in pain as she looks up at me. "My aunt. She—I just got a text from my dad . . . I missed so many calls . . ."

I reach out and touch her arm.

"My aunt fell. She's hurt. I—I need to . . ." She steps out of my hold and stumbles toward the door, but I catch her wrist, gently turning her back to me.

"Let me drive you to her. You can't drive like this. You're too upset."

She opens her mouth to object, but I shake my head.

"Joelle. Let me help you."

My words don't register right away. But when they do, a memory I buried deep from years ago resurfaces.

I'm walking into a stranger's apartment and see my mother collapsed on the floor, a pool of her own vomit under her face.

Panic washes through me, then fear, then dread, then anger.

Mom. Let me help you. Please.

I blink and the memory fades, and I refocus on the moment. I look at Joelle once more, at the tears pooling in her deep umber eyes that are as big as saucers, at her quivering lip, at the worry that's etched in her entire expression.

"Please let me drive you."

She nods. "Okay. Thank you."

Chapter 12

Joelle

We make it to the Adventist Health emergency room in record time thanks to Max's driving. I didn't think it was possible to cover that stretch of 92nd Avenue and Market Street in less than five minutes, but given the early time and the fact that Max drives like a Formula One racer, it was doable.

After he drops me off at the hospital entrance, he goes to park his car. I dart through the halls, my heart pounding. When I see Auntie Elba resting in a hospital bed, her left leg in a cast but otherwise looking well with Mom sitting next to her, I release the breath I've been holding ever since I got the message from Dad.

"Auntie." I run over and hug her. "Are you okay?"

"Oh yes, *anak*. I'm fine."

"*Manang*, I told you to be careful on that stepladder. You never listen," Mom mutters, arms folded. Disappointment radiates from the frown she trains on Auntie.

Auntie shakes her hand. "Ay, *adingko*, I heard you already. You said it a million times. You don't need to keep saying it."

"I just don't understand why you don't listen to me. You don't need to clean the cabinets at the crack of dawn."

Auntie Elba shakes her head and rolls her eyes. "Because the tops of those cabinets are filthy. Do you know how much grease is caked on them? It's so bad for the wood."

Mom scolds Auntie for daring to question how she takes care of her own kitchen. I sigh as the two of them bicker. Normally I'd laugh and roll my eyes. As much as they love each other, they argue about the most random things. They've always been like that, even before Auntie and Apong moved in with Mom and Dad.

"I was just trying to be helpful," Auntie Elba mutters as Max walks in.

"Hi." He stands in the doorway, his eyes darting between me, Mom, and Auntie, like he's unsure of where to stand and what else to say.

"Oh, hi, Max!" Both Mom and Auntie beam at him, clearly surprised yet thrilled to see him.

"Come in, come in!" Auntie gestures.

He walks over to stand next to me. Even though we're not touching, I can sense his unease. It radiates off him like static energy. He must hate hospitals. I don't blame him. I don't have an extreme aversion to them, but I've never been a fan. That weird sanitizer smell and the sterile, confusing layout they all seem to have where all the floors and hallways look the same, making it so easy to get lost.

"What a surprise seeing you here," Mom says to Max.

My mind races through the morning's developments as I try to explain why Max is here, but he speaks first.

"I offered to bring Joelle here when she found out about your injury. I didn't want her to drive when she was worried about you." He nods to Elba.

Both she and Mom go "aww."

"You holding up okay, Elba?" he asks.

"Oh yes, yes. I'll be just fine. Just have to rest for the next few weeks so this bruise on the bone in my ankle can heal."

"Well, at least you'll finally listen to me about leaving my kitchen alone," Mom mutters.

"I was just trying to help," Auntie huffs. "Joelle usually cleans the tops of the cabinets because she's taller than me, but poor thing's been working so hard lately at the bakery, she hasn't been home much. I was just trying to pitch in more."

Mom and Auntie's bickering continues in Ilocano. Soon they're speaking so quickly that it's hard for me to understand what they're saying. It's just as well because I'm gutted by Auntie's words.

Even though I know she didn't mean for her comment about my absence at home to come off so harshly, that's exactly how it hit. These past couple of weeks working in a cramped new space all the while feuding with Max has sucked up all my time and energy. I realize now that all I pretty much do when I'm home is sleep and shower. I try to go into the house and chat a bit with my family if they happen to be around after my work shift, but I haven't even done that in a while. The only time I see them for any stretch of time is when they come to help out at the bakery— and lately, I haven't been giving them much attention there either since I've been so distracted by arguing with Max.

I'm absent from my family in a whole new way . . . in a way I vowed I never would be. And now it's hurting them.

Guilt takes hold of me. It lands so heavy that my shoulders hunch forward.

Max seems to notice because he asks me if I'm okay.

"Um, yeah. I'm just . . . thinking about some things."

He nods like he knows exactly what I mean, even though I know he can't possibly.

And then he looks between Mom and Auntie, his expression unsure. "I don't understand what they're saying, but I'm guessing they're arguing judging by their tone? And how they're frowning at each other."

I sigh and turn to them. "Mom. Auntie."

They stop and look up at me. "Auntie, I'm so sorry for forgetting about the cabinets. It's my fault you got hurt."

"It's not your fault your auntie doesn't know how to listen to me," Mom says.

"I listen just fine," Auntie says sharply before turning a tender gaze on me. "*Anak*, you are so busy with your business. I just wanted to give you a bit of a break. It's not your fault."

I nod, even though I know deep down that this never would have happened, she never would have hurt herself, if I had been more present at home.

I contemplate pressing the issue but decide not to. Now's not the time or the place to talk about my failings as a daughter, niece, and granddaughter, especially now when Auntie's recovery should be the focus.

I ask Auntie and Mom about going home once Auntie's discharged, but Mom reassures me she can handle it on her own.

"You sure about that, Ramona?" Auntie says sarcastically.

I wince. She only ever uses Mom's actual name when she's

annoyed with her, normally preferring to call her *ading* or *ad-ingko*, the Filipino term of endearment for a younger sibling.

"I still think I should go home with you and help take care of Auntie," I say.

"Oh, don't be silly, *anak*," Mom says. "You don't need to do that. Once we finish up with the paperwork here, I'm just going to help Auntie get settled at home. Then I'm running errands with Apong."

Auntie Elba shakes her head. "No need to fuss over me. I'll be set up on the sofa just in time to watch my favorite morning soap operas."

I'm slightly heartened that they're agreeing and getting along in this moment, but the guilt still bites at me. "Are you sure?"

"Positive," they say in unison.

I glance over at Max, who's looking at me. The corner of his mouth quirks up slightly. "Still up for taking the day off?"

"You were going to take the day off?" Mom asks.

"Yeah, um, we were thinking . . . I mean, Max and I were chatting before I noticed all the missed messages on my phone about Auntie. He mentioned maybe closing the store and taking the day off. But I don't have to do that if you need—"

"Actually," Mom interrupts. "I think Max is right. Why don't you take today and rest?"

"Oh yes, I think that's a great idea. You've been working so hard, *anakko*. You deserve a break." Auntie Elba smiles and nods along with Mom.

My head spins at just how quickly they went from fighting to agreeing with each other.

"You never take a day off normally," Mom says. "You work every day usually. Why not play hooky just this once?"

I catch Max smiling at her phrasing.

"Yes. You had a family emergency, so you should take full advantage and not show up to work."

"Auntie, it's clearly not an emergency anymore."

She winks. "No one has to know that. You kids go and have some fun."

"I have to agree with your mom and aunt," Max says. "I've worked next to you almost every day for over a year and a half. You deserve one day off. I think we both do."

I don't miss that glimmer of mischief that dances in his eyes.

I turn to Mom. "Are you sure you're okay taking Auntie home by yourself?"

She frowns at me. "Of course. I've been taking care of my sister ever since we were kids."

Auntie scoffs. "You've got that mixed up, *ading*. I'm older than you, so it's me who's been taking care of you."

"Ha. I don't know about that," Mom mutters, which makes Max laugh.

Mom assures me that the hospital staff are discharging her soon and will help her out to the car.

"Dad's home right now so he'll help me bring her into the house and get settled."

I mull over Mom's words. "Okay." I turn to Max. "Let's play hooky."

"Where are we going?" I ask Max as he drives through North Portland.

"It's a surprise."

I don't miss the way the right corner of his mouth hooks up.

Instead of peppering him with more questions, I settle deeper into the passenger seat of his hatchback and check my phone again to make sure no one has called or messaged me.

"I think your family's fine, Joelle," he says gently.

I shove my phone back in my purse. "I know. It's just a habit."

He pulls into a neighborhood with older Craftsman homes lining the blocks.

"I think it's really cool how close you are with your family," he says after a minute.

That tiny bit of worry festering inside me after saying goodbye to my mom and aunt in the hospital dissipates, leaving something warm behind.

"Thanks for saying that."

He pulls into a narrow driveway of a small Craftsman house with light blue siding, then turns off the car.

"You wanna see Muffin and Doughnut?" he asks.

I practically squeal the word "Yes." It's been ages since I've seen Muffin. He's brought her by the shop a few times over the past year and a half when he's had to take her to the vet or groomer and didn't have time to run home and get her. But I've never seen Doughnut in person, only in the framed photo on his desk in his office.

I hop out of the car and follow him up the porch steps to the solid oak front door. Before he can even open the door all the way, Muffin sticks her head out and shoves her muzzle right between my legs.

"Oh my gosh." I squeal out a laugh.

"God, Muffin," Max mutters. He quickly grabs her by the collar and leads her away, then tells her to sit.

She obeys, but she looks up expectantly at both of us, her tail thumping against the hardwood floor.

Max closes the door behind us as I lean down to pet her short, light brown fur. "Hey, pretty girl. It's been a while."

She nuzzles into the palms of my hands, then licks me. Max leans down behind her and gives her haunches a pat.

"The muzzle-in-the-crotch move is her standard greeting for strangers. Sorry about that."

I giggle, then spot Doughnut slinking out from the kitchen.

"Aww, look at how fat he is!"

Laughter rumbles from Max as I walk over to Doughnut and scoop him up. When I scratch his chin, he closes his eyes and purrs.

I glance up at Max, who's still petting Muffin with an amused look on his face.

"Sorry, I guess I should have asked if I could pick up your cat. I know a lot of them don't like to be handled."

"He loves it. And he clearly loves you."

When I stop petting Doughnut, he immediately nuzzles my hand. I let out an "aww" as I laugh.

"Doughnut, you traitor," Max teases. "He never lets me hold him for that long."

I turn my gaze to Max. "This was the best surprise. Cuddling a sweet dog and cat is exactly what I needed today."

Doughnut starts licking the palm of my hand.

I chuckle. "He probably smells Pumpkin on me."

I notice that Max winces slightly. "Hey, I'm sorry I told you that you shouldn't bring her with you to work anymore. That was such a dickhead thing to say."

"I get why you did it." I give Doughnut more scratches under his chin. "You never told me how much I owe you for the damaged books. You need to so I can pay you."

"You don't owe me anything."

"Max, come on. Those books were expensive and my pet damaged them. I'm responsible for compensating you."

His expression softens. "It's fine. I filed an insurance claim. They're covering it."

"What?"

"That's what insurance is for, to cover stuff like that. So you don't need to pay me anything." He glances down at Muffin for a moment. "And you should start bringing Pumpkin in to work with you again. If you want. I had no right to tell you not to."

He sounds so regretful when he speaks, the urge to hug him hits once more, but I hold back. Definitely not at the point where I can give Max a spontaneous hug.

"You're okay with that?"

He smiles. "Absolutely."

"She's just really special to me. I got her when I was having a rough time." Instantly after I say it, I regret it. God, that probably comes off like a massive overshare. Why did I bring that up?

"What happened?" he asks. The look in his eyes reads curious. And caring. It softens me right up.

"Nothing major, really. Just . . . I had a bad breakup at the beginning of this year and I was so sad about it."

I still can't believe how heartbroken I was over Bryce. We only dated six months, but it was one of those whirlwind relationships. The kind where you spend all your dates on fun nights out or hooking up at each other's places. You're so wrapped up in all the good times that you don't stop to figure out if you're actually compatible with each other long-term. And we definitely weren't compatible, seeing as I wanted to be exclusive while Bryce was more interested in screwing anything that moved.

"He cheated on me. A lot."

Max's face twists at my softly spoken admission. "That's messed up, Joelle. I'm sorry."

"He was a dirtbag. I see that now. Not at the time, though, of course," I say. "I wandered into a pet store one day just to make myself do something other than go to work and then go home and cry my eyes out. I saw Pumpkin in a hamster display and thought she was the cutest thing ever. The store employee let me hold her for a bit, and I realized that was the first time I had smiled in two weeks. So I adopted her right then and there. She was this little ray of sunshine when I was down in the dumps."

The softest smile lights up Max's face. "I'm happy you have her."

"Me too."

"I think you should start bringing her to work again," he says softly.

"Okay. I will."

For a moment we just look at each other, and then he walks over to the kitchen. He fills a glass of water, then hands it to me. I down it all the while cradling Doughnut in one hand. Muffin scurries over to him, and he fishes a treat from a ceramic jar sitting on his granite countertop, tells her to sit, and tosses it in her mouth.

"Nice work, Muffin," I say before strolling through the open-concept space.

The décor is no-fuss with a clean, minimalist aesthetic. The house has clearly been remodeled. The chestnut-finished hardwood floors shine in the sunlight that streams through the nearby windows. There's a plush gray couch and a flat-screen TV hanging on the wall. The brick fireplace is the focal point of the space, which sets a rustic tone. Unsurprisingly there are multiple bookshelves packed to the brim with books.

"This space is so you."

Max shoves his hands in his pockets and raises an eyebrow. "Is that good or bad?"

"Very good. It's no-nonsense, only what you need: someplace to lounge, TV, and books. Lots and lots of books."

A wide grin stretches his face. "So in other words, I'm simple?"

"In the best kind of way."

It's a short and silly exchange, but there's a playfulness that hangs between us that's making me all sorts of giddy. It's probably because we've officially given in to the tension that we've spent the past year and a half building. It kicked off that day in his office when we made out like two hormonal teenagers. It amped up the day we saw each other topless while arguing. And it culminated early this morning when we both admitted that we've been crushing on each other ever since we met.

And even though I'm not sure how exactly to proceed, one thing's for sure: there's really no way to go back to being the friendly colleagues we once were—and that thought excites me.

Doughnut starts to squirm, so I set him gently on the floor. He heads for the kitchen, and Muffin makes a whining noise, then quickly moves to hide behind Max's legs.

"Aww."

"Wanna go with me to take her for a walk?" Max asks.

"Absolutely."

A minute later we're out the door, Muffin pulling Max as he holds her leash. I follow them through the neighborhood lined with a million impossibly green trees. We end up in Cathedral City Park and walk toward the massive St. Johns Bridge, a steel suspension bridge that spans the nearby Willamette River. Under the now-overcast sky, the steel beams appear robin's-egg blue.

When we stop to let Muffin sniff the grass for a bit, I stand there and take it all in. The vivid shade of each grass blade, the majestic spread of the bridge, how the endless hillside of evergreens on the opposite side of the river swallows up the far end of the bridge.

"It's been so long since I've done this," I say after a minute.

"What? Walked a dog?" Max asks.

I chuckle. "Yeah, that too. I just mean, it's been a while since I've taken a day to do something fun and leisurely. Like head to the park or go for a walk."

Max glances down at me. "I'm glad you're letting yourself relax. You should do it more often."

"Yeah, but . . ."

When I trail off, I notice he doesn't push me to say more. Instead we continue walking along the perimeter of the park, along the path of the river.

"I don't think I realized until my mom and aunt mentioned it back at the hospital, but I haven't really done a whole lot other than focus on work for a really long time. And I feel pretty shitty about it. My family needs me, and I need to be better about helping them."

Max looks thoughtfully down at the grass. "I know I'm an outsider to this situation, but I've been working beside you for a while, and to me it seems like you help your family a lot, Joelle."

"They're the ones helping me at the bakery."

"That's not true. I mean, yeah, of course they're helping you at the bakery, but you help them constantly. I hear your parents and your aunt and grandma tell you all the time how nice it is to have you close and all the things you do at their house. I've seen you take your grandma to appointments. I've watched you run errands for your parents and your aunt," Max says. "So yeah, they help, but you do a lot more than I think you realize."

There's a gentle conviction in his tone that hits somewhere deep within me.

"Thanks," I finally say. "I just wish it could be more."

I wish I could wave a magic wand and restore my entire family's savings along with their sense of security. I wish I could get back at the fraud financial planner who conned them out of nearly everything they had.

And I wish I could have had the chance to go to culinary school and travel Europe, to have a go at the life I once dreamed of.

I press my lips shut so I don't accidentally spill the thoughts swirling inside me. Max doesn't need to hear my family's sob story.

"Oh my god! Joelle Prima, is that you?"

A cheery, pitchy voice pulls my attention across the park. I squint behind my glasses, and after a few seconds, I recognize the smiling and beautifully made-up face walking toward me. My stomach drops to my knees.

"Shit."

"What?" Max asks. "What's wrong?"

I grab his hand that's not holding the leash. "Can you, um, do me a favor?"

"Yeah, sure."

"God, I can't believe I'm about to do this." I swallow as I work up the nerve. "Pretend to be my boyfriend."

He chuckles. "Um, what?"

"Please? I'll explain later, I just—I really, really need you to do this for me, Max. Please."

His face softens. "Okay. I'm your boyfriend."

"Mindy. Hey."

Before she can even say "hi" back, Max steps closer to me and laces his fingers in mine. I look up at him and flash a grateful smile. This is gonna be the catch-up from hell with Mindy, a mean girl from my high school who pretended to be my friend. She's also the reigning queen of one-upmanship. The few times I've run into her since we graduated, I've always felt like absolute shit after talking to her. She's always throwing thinly veiled insults at me and making condescending comments about my mediocre life, which usually pales in comparison to hers.

But at least this time I have a sexy boyfriend to soften the blow, albeit a fake one.

Mindy jogs up to me, clad in head-to-toe designer activewear, and pulls me into a hug. I stiffen for a second, then slowly wrap my arm loosely around her in what is probably the least convincing hug ever. But she doesn't notice—or care. She's too busy squeezing me and squealing over and over how nice it is to see me after all these years.

"How long's it been?" she asks in that cheery, singsong tone that makes me want to gouge my own eyes out. "Five? Six years?"

I shrug, shaking my head, an awkward chuckle falling from my lips. I straighten my glasses, which were bumped askew when Mindy yanked me to her chest.

She shakes her head and gazes down at me, like she can't quite believe it's me standing there in front of her. Then she scoops her long, barrel-curled, chestnut hair over her shoulder. I briefly wonder how the hell she's able to maintain such glamorous curls when it's been drizzling on and off this entire morning.

"Look at you! You haven't changed one bit," she says. "Still looking so . . . youthful!"

The pause before the word "youthful" jolts me back to that

day in high school when I overheard her talking about me behind
my back.

"God, she looks like a child. So small and mousy," Mindy had
said around the corner while standing at her locker. "I mean, no
wonder no guy wants to go out with her. Who the hell wants to
date someone who looks like an elementary schooler?"

"Yeah, well. I can't really help the way I look," I mutter.

She flinches, almost like she's surprised at what I've said.
Then her gaze hooks onto Max, who's standing to my side.

She reaches out her hand. "Mindy Beckinsale. I'm an old
friend of Joelle's."

I almost snort, then clear my throat. "Friend" is putting it
generously. I *thought* she was my friend all through high school
until I found out she constantly shit-talked me behind my back,
then went after the guy I was crushing on.

"Good to meet you. I'm Max, Joelle's boyfriend." He leans
over to kiss my cheek, and in that moment, I could fucking fly. I
don't miss the way Mindy's eyes go wide for a split second. Yeah,
it's petty, but I adore him for that little bit of PDA.

When I catch her eyeing him up and down, I grit my teeth.

*Are you seriously jealous right now? He's not even your real
boyfriend.*

I refocus. "What are you doing here, Mindy? I thought you
were in Europe."

"Oh, I still am. I'm in Milan now. Still doing the hospitality
thing for the family business. Just visiting friends for a few
months."

She giggles and I try not to roll my eyes in full view of her. By
"hospitality thing," she means her megarich parents secured a
job for her after college at some luxury hotel that they own in

Italy. She gets to travel on their dime all over Europe and show up to work whenever she feels like it.

With her perfectly manicured hand on my arm, she flashes a sad face at me that's somehow tinged with both pity and insincerity at once. "I'm still so bummed you never got to go to Europe after high school like you wanted. It would have been so fun traveling with you."

I bite my tongue, annoyed that she's indirectly bringing up my family's worst moment.

"Yeah, well, sometimes plans don't turn out."

"Aww, I know." God, even her sympathy noises are tinged with condescension. "Well, how are things now? Still working at the catering company?"

"I quit a few years ago to open up my own bakery. It's a cute little brick building in the Jade District."

"Oh gosh! Like you always wanted! Your dream come true!"

She grasps my forearm so hard, I wince. I wiggle away and rub my hand.

"Well, I mean, sort of." She chuckles. "After all you've been through, you and your family—and what you did for them. You deserve that little bakery, Joelle Prima."

Little bakery.

I bite the inside of my cheek and tell myself not to smack her . . . even though she knows how annoying I've always thought it is that she insists on calling me by my first and last name randomly, for no reason at all. Like she's trying to be weirdly formal but also cute. The whole thing just comes off as obnoxious and fake.

"Yeah, well. It's not Paris, but . . . it is what it is."

I fight the urge to slap myself for how pathetic I sound.

Mindy tilts her head to the side, her brow furrowed in an exaggerated sad frown while she nods, like she's an actress being told to emote for the camera.

"Exactly, if life were fair you would have gone to culinary school like you planned, then traveled Europe. Oh well! You're making do."

Inside my blood boils, but I tell myself to keep calm. I'll never have to see Mindy after this.

I start to wonder if Max is picking up on these little digs of hers . . . and I wonder if he's curious as to what exactly Mindy is talking about when she mentions my family and my scrapped plans for culinary school and Europe.

"She's actually more than making do," he says. "People come from all over the city for her pastries. The things she does with sugar, butter, and flour are fucking genius."

The pointed way Max speaks has my heart soaring.

"Oh. Well." Mindy's tone goes a tad more pitchy than usual, a sign she's thrown off. "That's nice."

"More than nice. Pretty damn impressive," Max says.

"Of course," Mindy says curtly.

Her gaze flits between the two of us, almost like she's studying us. It's confusing for the briefest second, but then it dawns on me why: she thinks we're an odd coupling. Max is clearly a mega hottie and I'm the former quiet nerdy girl she used to make fun of in school.

"So how long have you two been together?" she asks.

I glance up at Max, hoping she can't read the worry in my eyes. "Oh, um, wow. It's hard to pinpoint an exact date." I play it off with a laugh, secretly scolding myself for freezing up when it was my idea to lie about this in the first place. I didn't even think our conversation would get this far.

"Technically it's been just over six months," Max says confidently. "But if I'm being honest, I've been trying to get her to go out with me since the day I opened my bookstore next door to her bakery." He gazes down at me.

Mindy makes a genuine "aww" sound. I'm shocked into silence for several seconds.

"I'm head over heels for her. Someone who's as hardworking as she is stunning, who runs a successful business on her own, which she built from the ground up, no help from anyone. That's rare to find, you know?"

The way he narrows his stare at Mindy has her pursing her lips.

"Well. That's just great," she practically mutters. "I should get going. Lovely to run into you, Joelle."

"Likewise." This time when I'm smiling, it's one thousand percent genuine.

She spins around and jogs away, her pace noticeably faster than when she made her way over.

"She can't get away from us fast enough," Max says. "I'd call that a win."

My head falls back as I laugh. I start to let go of his hand, but he keeps a gentle hold. "Let's sell it for a bit longer. Just in case she turns around and looks back at us."

He winks down at me, and I'm sold. While we walk hand in hand, Max clears his throat.

"Hey, can I ask you something?"

"Sure."

"Mindy mentioned something about you giving up culinary school and traveling Europe to help your family. What was that about?"

I stop and let go of his hand, then cross my arms. It's been years since I've told this story. I can feel the muscles in my chest pull tight at just the prospect of doing it.

"Sorry, I didn't mean to pry," he says quickly. "If you don't want to talk about it . . ."

I shake my head. "No, it's okay. It's just a long story."

"I'm happy to listen," he says gently. "But only if you want to talk about it."

The sincerity in his tone and his gaze eases me. My muscles relax.

As we continue walking, I tell him about the fraudulent investor who conned my family out of everything they had and how I convinced them to use the money my parents had saved for my college to replenish their savings. I tell him that I gave up my college plans to work and help them—I'd dreamed about traveling to Paris after I graduated, but I gave that up so I could work and help my family recover financially. When I finish, we've done almost two passes around the perimeter of the park.

When I peek over at him, his expression is dazed.

He stops walking and scrubs a hand over his face. "God, Joelle. I'm so . . . I don't even know what to say. 'I'm so sorry' isn't enough, not by a long shot."

"It's okay. There's really nothing to say. It was just an awful situation."

I start walking again, but Max stops me with a hand on my arm. "You know you're incredible for what you did, right?"

I stammer a refusal, but he cuts me off. "No, Joelle. Seriously.

You are without a doubt the most selfless person for helping your family the way you did."

He says it with conviction, like he needs me to believe, right here, right now, the words he speaks.

Part of me wants to. But the other part of me won't allow it. Because that other part of me knows that as noble as that gesture was, I sometimes wish I had never done it so I could have lived my dream.

But I don't say that. Because I know how heartless that would sound—and I can't bear for Max to think I'm heartless.

"Thank you," I quietly say to him.

We walk in silence for a few seconds before Max speaks. "Mindy seems like a piece of work. What was it like going to school with her?"

I chuckle, appreciating how he changed the subject.

"Interesting to say the least. She's just a really fake person. Pretended to be my friend and was nice to my face, only to talk behind my back for the entirety of high school. And she knew I liked a guy and went out of her way to go out with him."

"Damn. That's really shitty."

"I mean, it's not like I had a claim on him."

"Yeah, but that's still a hurtful thing for a friend to do—go after someone that she knows you like."

I shrug. "Other people go through worse things in high school."

"That doesn't make what you went through any less bad."

I pause. "I guess you're right."

We continue walking until we reach the edge of the park again, near where we'd entered.

Max suddenly turns to me. "How about a Bloody Mary?"

I let out a laugh, mystified but grateful for the change of subject. "That's gotta be the most random proposition I've ever heard." The sly smile he wears doesn't budge. "Max, it's barely nine in the morning."

"Morning is the exact time of day you're supposed to drink a Bloody Mary."

I laugh. "Okay. Let's do it."

Chapter 13

Joelle

Half an hour later we're sitting at a table in the outdoor dining area of a pub overlooking the Willamette River, the name of which I can't remember because I'm already two Bloody Marys deep.

"This was a brilliant idea." I slurp the last of my drink, then hiccup.

"Told you."

Max is finished with his second drink too, but given he's ten inches taller than me and close to two hundred pounds, he's likely not feeling it the way my five-foot-four self is.

He signals the waiter and asks for a serving of hash browns.

"To soak up all that alcohol," he says to me before glancing down at Muffin, who's snoozing under the table by our feet.

"Thanks for this," I tell him, head slightly dizzy. "This has been the most random morning, but it's been a blast. I really, really needed this."

"You should listen to your family more often when they tell you to take a break," he teases.

I wag my finger at him. "Oh no. No way. They bestow their unsolicited advice on me constantly, without asking. Not all of it great, mind you."

Max flashes an amused smile. "What kind of advice?"

I groan. "Like, *anak*, you should wear your hair down more often. You look so pretty with it down," I say, imitating Mom's voice. "Or, *anak*, you need to go out and meet someone and have some babies. Don't you feel your biological clock ticking? We want grandbabies."

Max laughs as I shake my head.

"Glad you think it's funny," I mock-whine. "I bet you don't think it's as funny when it's *your* family giving you a hard time."

I notice that his smile twitches. Then he scrubs a hand over his beard and clears his throat. "I, uh, don't really have family. That I'm close to, I mean."

"Oh."

His gaze fixes down at Muffin.

"Sorry. I didn't mean to bring it up."

"It's all right."

I shake my head. "My whole life is pretty much family, so it's kind of my default to talk about them a lot."

"You don't have to feel bad about that, Joelle."

Just then the server drops off a giant plate of hash browns. The smell of butter and fried potatoes hits my nostrils, and my stomach instantly growls.

Max's eyes widen. "Damn."

"You heard that?"

He nods, then chuckles. "Better eat up."

I do exactly that. When I finish, I push the empty plate aside and gulp down my glass of water.

"Better?" Max asks.

"Much." I squint at him. "I want more, though."

"Hash browns?"

"No. Alcohol."

The corner of his mouth crooks up. "What are you in the mood for?"

When I lick my lips, I swear his eyes widen the slightest bit. "Whiskey."

"I can make that happen."

"Wow. That's a lot of whiskey."

I gawk at the drink cart sitting in the corner of Max's kitchen that I somehow didn't notice when I first walked into his house.

"I've gotten really into whiskey over the past year. God, I sound like a douche."

I giggle, then ask him to pour me a glass of whatever is good. Then I dart to the couch and snuggle up with Muffin, who happily rests her head in my lap.

"Room for one more?" Max asks as he stands with two glasses of whiskey on the rocks in his hands.

"Always." I scoot over to give Max room to sit.

He hands me a glass, and together we sip.

"God, what a day," I muse as I lean my head against the back of his couch. "Never in a million years did I think I'd ever end up on your couch sipping whiskey."

He chuckles into his glass. "You say that like I'm a celebrity or something."

I shrug. "When you have a crush on a person, that's kind of what it feels like. To me at least." After a second I cover my face with my free hand. "Wow, I sound like such a loser."

Max rolls his eyes at me as he sips through his smile.

"It's just that I think I spent so much time building you up in my head," I say. "Here you are, this insanely handsome guy who looks like a bad-boy Instagram model with your tattoos and your leather jacket and your beanie, and it kind of made me nervous to be around you sometimes."

He squints at me, like he's confused by what I've said.

I point at him. "It's true."

Sober me would never, ever speak a word of this to Max. But thanks to those two Bloody Marys I had this morning and the whiskey I'm sipping now, I'm tipsy and very comfortable divulging all of this.

It's freeing in a way. I spent so much time over the last year and a half freaking out about how I acted around him. But now that our relationship has progressed so much in the last few weeks—a hot makeout, seeing each other half-naked, and admitting a mutual crush—it's like we're suddenly putting everything out in the open. And because of that I feel uninhibited around him in a whole new way.

Max ruffles his gold-brown hair, leaving it deliciously messy when his hand falls away. "I always thought 'bad boy' was synonymous with 'dickhead.'"

"A lot of times it is. Not for you, though. And really, it's more about how you look. You're a total sweetie on the inside."

He lets out a laugh. "Well, thanks."

I down more whiskey and gaze at him for a long moment. "I really can't believe it."

"Believe what?"

"That you had a crush on me."

I drain the rest of my glass, hop up from the couch, then stroll to the drink cart and pluck a random bottle from it and pour myself more. I take a long sip as I walk back and plop down on his couch.

"Easy there." Max juts his chin to my glass.

"I'm good. A little buzzed. Like, I definitely shouldn't drive, but I've got my wits about me. Promise."

He aims his furrowed brow at me, then opens his mouth before closing it.

"What?"

"Why is it so hard to believe that I like you, Joelle?"

I shrug. "I just didn't think I was your type. I didn't think you'd go for a girl like me."

I sip some more and give Muffin a pat on the tummy when she stretches. When I turn back to look at Max, the look in his eyes throws me for a loop. Like he's hungry and curious all at once.

"A girl like you?" His thick eyebrows furrow. "What do you mean by that?"

Shaking my head, I look away. It's funny, of all the things I've said so far, *this* is the one that sends a wave of nerves crackling through me. But I need to say it. I'm the one who brought all of this up anyway—I need to be honest with him.

I can't keep eye contact with him if I'm actually going to say these words out loud—the words that have been implanted inside my head ever since I saw Max. Ever since I started dating actually.

I stare at the bottom of my glass. "I'm just . . . I'm not the kind of girl that a guy who looks like you normally dates."

As soon as the last word leaves my lips, my cheeks warm. It's weird to admit out loud how out of my league Max is. But it's true. We both have eyes. We both own mirrors. And we both are well aware of the kind of attention the other receives since we've spent the past year and a half working next door to each other.

I gesture at myself. "I mean, with my nerdy glasses and unruly, messy hair, not to mention the fact that I'm pretty much covered in flour twenty-four-seven. It's not really the picture of hot and sexy, you know?"

Instead of the chuckle I expect him to make, there's silence. When I look back at his face, I'm shocked. His expression is twisted into a disapproving scowl. He almost looks angry.

"Hang on a sec." He presses his eyes shut, then shakes his head, like he's trying to make sense of this all. "What?"

I swallow, choosing my words carefully. "You don't have to play clueless, Max. I've seen the women who chat you up at work. I've seen who you've dated in the past. I saw them at the bookstore when they'd visit you. That one woman you were with when you moved in next door looked like an actual runway model. So did the woman after that. And the woman after that, the one who would come to my bakery and request that I prepare more gluten-free options."

He doesn't say anything in response. He just looks at me with this hard expression, like he's attempting to burn a hole through my head with that laser stare of his.

I almost laugh at how seriously he's taking this. I wonder if this is the first time anyone has ever spelled out his exact type right in front of his face.

"Actually, Mindy too. She has a similar look to the gluten-free girl."

Max grimaces at me. "I'd rather hack off my own arm with a dull axe than ever see Mindy again."

I snort out a laugh. Soon I'm cackling so hard that I double over. After I catch my breath, I sit up and take another pull of whiskey.

"Okay, yeah, maybe the Mindy comparison was a bit off. But it's okay to have a type. And your typical kind of woman is hot. Tall. Sophisticated. Pretty much the exact opposite of me."

Still nothing from him. Just more silence and that hard look.

"Guys like you don't normally go for mousy, unassuming girls. I get it. It's why Mindy looked at us weird when we pretended to be together at the park earlier today. It throws people like her for a loop when they see us as a couple. We don't really match."

I try to hide the wince I make at my assessment. Because even though it's true, even though I'm the one who's said it, it's still brutal. Shy, introverted women like me don't nab hotties like Max. We sit quietly in the corner and watch as everyone around us pairs off. And then if we get lucky—or we get drunk or desperate enough to approach some random guy or DM him—we score a date that maybe sometimes goes somewhere for a while. But then it ends. Eventually. It always does. And then we're left to quietly go back to our corner.

The silence between us grows, except for the steady rhythm of Max's shallow breathing. When I start to twist around to check on Muffin, I hear him scoff. The sudden sound makes me jerk my head to him.

"Joelle." The whispered growl he lets out when he says my name makes my stomach do a triple flip. "Are you fucking kidding me right now?"

I let out a surprised chuckle at his response. "Um, what?"

When he stands suddenly, I jolt and my back hits the couch. I wasn't expecting him to react so . . . physically to what I've said. But then he steps in front of me and lowers himself to rest that gorgeously sculpted rump on the edge of the coffee table. We're sitting across from each other now, our faces just a handful of inches apart now, his stare fixed on mine. It's so determined and intense, like he'll lose a bet if he stops looking at me for even one second.

"You really have no idea what you are, do you?" he says. His warm breath hits me as he speaks. It's the most deliciously unnerving feeling in the world.

"Wh-what's that supposed to mean?"

His chest heaves with a sigh. "You're goddamn stunning, Joelle."

I let out a laugh of pure shock. If there's one thing I'm sure of, it's that I look the exact opposite of what is considered stunning. I'm the disheveled, curvy, small foil to the tall, perfectly made-up beauties who I've seen society hold up as the ultimate standard of beauty. And not once in my life has anyone ever called me stunning. At best, when I put on the right makeup and throw on the right flattering outfit, I look cute and pretty. Sometimes even a little bit sexy if I really go for it. But not stunning. Never, ever stunning.

I roll my eyes, still smiling to play off this out-of-the-blue determination Max suddenly has to make me think of myself as anything but ordinary.

"You don't have to butter me up, Max. It's really—"

In an instant his hand is over my mouth, muffling my words. I stop talking, shocked at the sudden feel of his skin against my lips. All I can process is how Max's palm is so warm and calloused yet also soft at the same time. How is that possible? He's like the sexiest, most delicious muzzle ever.

No guy has ever been ballsy enough to cover my mouth to force me to stop talking—I'd probably try to smack any other man who tried. But Max is so gentle and assertive, and I think . . . I think I love it?

He shakes his head. "Don't. Enough of your self-deprecating bullshit."

My brows jump up at his words. They're not harsh, though. Just honest. And I can tell by the tenderness shining in his eyes that he means what he's saying in the sincerest way possible.

"No more making jokes about yourself or putting yourself down I'm sick of it. You're going to sit here and listen to every single wonderful thing I have to say about you."

I nod slowly, his hand moving in tandem with my head

"You, Joelle, are fucking goddamn mind-blowingly beautiful. I have no idea how you don't see it. Those glasses that you think made you look nerdy? If they're nerdy, then nerdy is so incredibly hot. Because when you wear your glasses, you look smart *and* sexy. Your hair that you think is unruly and messy? It's not. It's wild. And wild is so fucking hot, I can't even begin to tell you." He presses his eyes shut and shakes his head, like he can barely contain the thought. "I can't take my eyes off it. Every time you brush past me and I feel your hair on my skin, I get goose bumps. And your skin is so soft that every time I've touched you, I've almost lost my damn mind. Like when you were on my lap kissing me, I honest to god thought I was going to pass out. I mean, did you not feel my boner against you? You felt so fucking good I could barely take it."

My eyes are wide as I soak in every word he says.

"When we started working in the same space together, I over-heard you mention how big your ass is when you were joking with your mom and aunt. Why? Your ass is a fucking national treasure. Why do you think I spent so much time grabbing it while we were fooling around?"

Against his palm, I let out a muffled "oh" sound. It's the sound I make when I've figured out an especially challenging crossword puzzle clue. These are some damn good points he's making.

Shaking his head, he looks away for a split second, like he's so frustrated, so hell-bent on getting these words out that he needs a moment to collect himself.

His eyes cut back to me. "Do you have any idea the way people look at you? Everywhere you go, people can't take their eyes off you. Nonstop. And you don't even notice it because you're too focused on others. Do you have any clue how sexy that is? Everyone else is so concerned with their image and what people think of them. But you don't give it a second thought. Even if you don't realize it, you come off so sure of yourself. It's the hottest thing ever."

I huff a breath against his hand in response to his words.

"I hate that you compare yourself to other people." A pained expression crosses his face. "Don't do that. Please. You are so above and beyond any person I know, any ex I've ever had. You care about more important things than your Instagram follower count, how much money you make, what kind of car you drive—all of that bullshit. You care about people. You sacrificed your dream to help your family. Do you know how amazing that is? Do you know what an incredible person that makes you?"

I shake my head no.

Max's stare turns even more determined. "Believe it, Joelle. You're the whole package. Beautiful, smart, hardworking, kind, and a genuinely good person. Forget Mindy. Who cares if she did or didn't buy us as a couple? Clearly she's too self-involved and vapid to care about anyone other than herself."

He pauses to swallow and take a breath. For a second my gaze falls to his neck and on the luscious way his Adam's apple bobs when he swallows. Then my eyes dart below to watch the slow rise and fall of that beautifully broad chest of his.

"But just for the record? If anyone were to ever see us together and had a hard time believing that we're a couple, it's not because of you. It's because of me. Because most days I look like a moody biker punk who woke up on the wrong side of the bed, and you look like a sweet, beautiful angel. They'd just assume you're too good for me. They wouldn't buy that a woman like you would ever care for someone like me."

The way his voice dips at the end, the way the fire in his eyes dies down as he admonishes himself sends an unfamiliar squeeze to my chest.

Part of that is the shock of hearing him praise me so highly. I never knew he thought any of that about me. No one has ever made me feel so confident, so wanted in less than three minutes. And to hear it from a guy who I considered so far out of my league for so long is even more mind-blowing.

"But I'd be the luckiest guy in the world if you did."

The squeeze dissipates, sending heat from my chest across my body.

And even more of a mind-fuck is that Max genuinely thinks that he'd be the lucky one if we ever officially got together.

It's not even close to true. Sure, we've had our squabbles, but even counting those, he's one of the most genuine and kind people I have in my life currently. He defended me when I was being harassed. He comforted me at work when I was crying and distraught. He's made me feel safe and comfortable and wanted all at once. That is head and shoulders above anything my exes ever gave to me.

That ache inside me turns frenzied. And my body reacts on its own.

When he finally pulls his hand away from my mouth, I don't say a word, even though I probably should. I don't hug him.

Instead I grab his face with both of my hands and kiss him.

Chapter 14

Joelle

When I tease Max's lips open with my tongue, he smiles against my mouth. A low grunt rips from his throat as he cups his hands over my cheeks. His fingers thread slowly, gently through my hair.

His tongue gets firmer and filthier as the seconds pass. And then he backs off, going smooth and teasing and slow once more. It's a slow build of sensation and damn, do I like it. No one's ever touched me like this before. The change in rhythm makes my chest and thighs tingle, it sends the most delicious ache to my core and builds and builds and builds until I'm panting even harder.

And we're just kissing.

My head spins, and I tug my hands through his thick hair. He grunts against my lips.

I pull away, breaking the kiss. "Oh! Sorry! Was that too hard?"

His pupils are bigger than I've ever seen, even bigger than

when I was grinding on his lap and kissing him like it was the end of the world.

"Not at all. I love it when you pull my hair."

We both smile and I tug his hair harder before pulling his mouth to mine once more.

Soon I'm clawing at his shirt, desperate to see once again what's underneath.

I'm slipping my hands underneath the fabric and up his muscled stomach when he gently wraps his hands around my wrists and stills me.

"What's wrong?" I ask.

He shakes his head, smiling slightly. "Nothing, I just . . . I don't want to do this in front of an audience, you know?"

He nods to Muffin, who's snoozing next to me. And then I see Doughnut perched on the arm of the nearby armchair, aiming a sleepy yet also judgmental stare at us.

I laugh. "Oh, right. Agreed." I turn back to Max. "Can we move this somewhere more private? Like, a room with a door?"

I bite my lip at how dopey I sound. But judging by the grin on Max's face, he's not one bit bothered by my phrasing.

"You're insanely cute, you know that?"

I scrunch my nose before unleashing a relieved smile as Max stands and reaches his hand out to me. He leads me down the hallway to what I assume is his bedroom.

"Cozy," I say as I take in the king-size bed covered in a plush white comforter.

"Sorry the bed's not made. I wasn't really expecting company."

I turn to face him, press my palms against his midsection, and try not to moan at how divinely hard his body feels.

"It's okay," I say. "If everything goes to plan, your bed will be a lot messier than this."

My eyes bulge the slightest bit when I hear what I've said.

Thanks, whiskey, for lowering my inhibitions enough to say something I'd never say sober.

But Max doesn't seem fazed. In fact, judging by his wide grin and the way he scoops me into his arms, he's totally into it. I squeal, instinctively wrapping my legs around his waist and my arms around his neck. The squeaky noise I make is cut off by his mouth on mine.

"That was such . . . a hot move . . . you just pulled," I say between kisses.

He chuckles against my lips and pulls away slightly to look at me. "I like having you in my arms and your legs wrapped around my waist."

Maybe it's the gleam in his eyes or the way he squeezes my ass with his hands. Maybe it's the feral register of his voice. Maybe it's that half smile I like so much. Maybe it's all of them combined.

Whatever the reason, it compels me to leave my inner shy girl behind and embrace every desire surging through me. It's like a match dropped into a vat of lighter fluid. Every inch of me is vibrating. I need Max undressed; I need his skin on my skin, now.

My chest heaves up and down as I gaze down at him. "Let's get naked."

A low laugh rumbles from his throat. "Yes, ma'am."

He presses one more kiss to my mouth, then drops me onto his bed. A giggle bursts from my throat as I bounce around on the plush mattress. But I lose the ability to make any sound as I watch

Max take off his T-shirt. It's something I've seen a million guys do—that ultra-sexy move where they grab the collar of their shirt from the back of their neck and yank the fabric from their body.

But when Max does it just inches in front of me, giving me a front-row, unobscured view, it's downright hypnotizing.

"Wow, um . . . you're really good at that."

Another chuckle falls from that beautiful mouth of his. "Good at taking off my clothes?"

I bite my lip, nodding quickly. "Yup. Just thought you should know. Positive reinforcement and all that."

His head falls back as he booms out a laugh, and then I'm hypnotized for a whole new reason as I watch the muscles in his chest, shoulders, and stomach flex with the movement.

After several seconds of my shameless gawking, he holds his arms out at his sides and spins around. Clearly he noticed that I can't stop staring at him.

"I'm pretty good at spinning while I'm nearly naked too."

"You most definitely are."

He grabs the belt of his jeans. "Help me with this part?"

I shoot up into a sitting position to the sound of his chuckling. And then I loosen his belt, unbutton his jeans, and push them onto the floor.

"Oh . . . wow . . ."

My face is inches away from the sizable bulge of Max's crotch and it's just as epic as I assumed it would be. To see it in person is something else entirely.

"You don't want to help me with that last bit?" Max asks. The grin on his face turns wicked.

"I just wanted to enjoy the visual here for a sec."

His cheeks turn rosy at my compliment, and then I finally,

slowly pull his boxer briefs down his toned thighs. And that's when my jaw drops. Not just because of how well-endowed he is, but also because right now for the first time ever, I'm getting to see Max Boyson totally, completely, utterly nude.

He. Is. Exquisite.

If there ever was a perfect male form, I'm certain it's him. It's clear he works out, given the cut of his body and the hard lines that drag across his light-tan skin. But it's more than that. It's the ruggedness that his body exudes. The gold-brown hair that runs along the center of his chest and down his stomach, the curly hair dotting his tree-trunk thighs and calves, the spicy smell of his cologne.

My gaze fixes on his right arm, and I study the sleeve of tattoos I love so much. I've never seen them this close before. There's a cluster of skulls adorning his forearm. They rest against a spread of intricately drawn feather wings, which run all the way up the side of his upper arm. A larger skull stretches across his biceps. Along his triceps is a colorful stack of books.

I can barely allow myself to blink, I'm so enamored with the sight of him. He is literal perfection. It tests my heart rate, my blood pressure, my ability to introduce air into and out of my lungs.

I do a scan from head to toe, then back up again. My eyes are likely glittering in awe. I bet I look like one of those cartoon characters whose eyeballs bulge out of their head.

"You're pretty quiet there, Joelle," he says.

"Well, you're a lot to take in."

He tilts his head at what I've said, and we both laugh.

"I guess we'll find out," he says with a wink. And then he leans down and leads me in yet another long, teasing, and crazy sexy kiss. With his fingers resting along the line of my jaw, he bites gently along my lower lip.

"Joelle. I thought you said, '*Let's* get naked.'"

I claw at his shoulders. "I did. I did, I did."

I sound feverish. But I can't help it. It's like my body has gone into some kissing frenzy. I can't get enough of Max's tongue and lips and skin.

Grabbing my hands, he stands me up with him. "Well, come on, then."

I laugh as he pulls my T-shirt over my head. I reach behind me to unhook my bra as his fingers fall to the button of my jeans, but then I stop when his hands still.

I look at him, noticing that his eyes have glazed over as he stares at my boobs.

"Wow. Those are nice."

I laugh. "You haven't even seen them properly yet."

He tugs at the strap, which makes me actually laugh this time. And so I shed my bra along with my jeans, and I'm left standing in just the worn blue cotton panties I threw on this morning because I didn't have the forethought to put on anything sexier since I never imagined that I'd be having sex today.

"Holy shit," he mutters as he gazes at my bare chest. It's a few seconds before he blinks.

The chuckle I let out seems to break him out of his trance. He runs his thumb along the waistband of my panties, and my midsection aches with pleasure. He's barely touching me and already lust is taking hold of me.

"Can I take these off?"

I nod so quickly that I start to get dizzy. I expect him to swipe them off in one swift move. But oh, am I so wrong.

Instead, Max hooks his thumbs around the top of the fabric

and does nothing for a few seconds. He stays holding me there, gazing down at me, hovering his lips over mine.

And then he runs his tongue along my bottom lip before closing his mouth. I nearly scream, the ache in my body winding tighter and tighter the longer I stand here and wait for Max to take off this tiny bit of fabric so we can finally be naked together.

God, what a tease.

But then he slowly lowers himself down to his knees and positions his face in front of the apex of my thighs. He exhales, the wet air coating the insides of my thighs and the already damp crotch of my panties.

And then he presses the lightest kiss against my stomach, right below my belly button. My knees buckle.

"You look fucking incredible, Joelle."

With that same slow rhythm that he employed as he glided down my body, he pulls off my panties. A crazed energy unleashes inside me. It's so powerful, my knees wobble, my hands tremble, and my skin tingles. I run my fingers through his hair to ground myself.

Steady, firm hands glide up my legs, resting just under my ass cheeks. Then he kisses me where I want it—where I *need* it most.

My jaw plummets to the floor. It happens completely involuntarily, like a reflex triggered by ecstasy. His tongue works slowly, steadily, in the most divinely torturous rhythm.

I tug his hair tighter as the ache of pleasure flashes all along my thighs, up my stomach and my chest, all the way to my neck.

"Max, holy . . ." I trail off as his tongue swirls faster.

Even in my limited dating experience and the few serious

relationships I've had, I've always appreciated a guy who knows what to do with his mouth. But Max is head and shoulders above what I've experienced. He's clearly done this before. A LOT.

He hums against me and my knees buckle.

I tug him by the hair to look at me. "This feels incredible, but I'm not gonna be able to stand like this for much longer."

The smug smile he flashes up at me makes my heart flutter right in my chest. Whoa. I didn't think that sort of thing actually happened. I was wrong.

"Let's try this," he says.

With his hands on my hips, he helps me onto his bed, then slides me up so my head is nestled against his pillows.

He settles on his knees, between my legs. "Better?"

I grin and nod, and then he picks up where he left off until I'm panting and my legs are shaking once more.

The pleasure builds higher until my chest feels like it's going to explode. When I finally burst, I shake and shudder, I pant and moan. I attempt to count the seconds as a way to keep the time, but it's too much for my pleasure-riddled brain. I'm shattered in the best way, utterly annihilated by ecstasy.

As I come down, I slow-blink until the fuzzy stars in my vision dissipate. I lie back, limbs shaky and heavy, and take in the visual of Max wiping his mouth with the back of his hand and settling next to me in the bed.

He slides his massive arm under me and pulls me into his chest.

"You okay?" he asks with his lips pressed against my forehead.

"Hardly. But I love it."

I close my eyes and smile at the low rumble of his chuckle. For a few minutes we lie together, cuddled into each other. As good as that was and as sweet as it was that Max made our first time together all about me, I want more. I want to make him feel as good as he made me feel. This time some deep, primal part of me needs to touch Max at the same time as he touches me.

I pull out of his embrace and lean up on my knees, hovering over him.

His brow flies up. "Everything okay?"

"Yeah, just . . ." I climb on top of him and settle over his waist. "I want more."

A massive grin stretches his face. "I can get on board with that."

When I scoot down slightly, I feel his hardness against my thigh. "We're gonna need to do something about that. Do you have a condom?"

He smirks and reaches to his nightstand drawer at the side of the bed, then pulls one out. I snatch it from his hand and rip it open with my teeth.

"So wild. I love it," he says.

I put it on him with surprising speed, then move to lie on my back. I grab him by the waist and guide him over me, wrapping my leg around one of his. His eyes glimmer the slightest bit, as if he's shocked.

I chuckle. "What?"

"It's just . . . I wasn't expecting you to do that so . . . enthusiastically. You come off so shy and sweet and innocent."

I bite my lip. "I am. Until you get me into bed."

His eyes bulge. "Okay. Very, very hot."

I flush all over. When I start to feel him slide in, I gasp. I knew he was going to feel big—because he *is* big. I didn't know he'd feel this good, this quickly, though.

I close my eyes and savor the way he stretches me, the immediate intensity I feel. When he starts that slow slide, my mouth falls open.

Soon I'm clawing at the bedsheets like I'm crazed. I'm certain I'll go hoarse at the end of this, but I don't care. I could lose my voice for a year and it would be worth it, this feels so freaking incredible.

Max eases to a slower pace, then leans over me and kisses my shoulder.

"Damn it, Joelle. You are . . . god, you're . . ."

My eyes roll to the back of my head as I smile to myself. His inability to finish a sentence while inside me is the highest compliment. My vision focuses, and I take in just how gorgeous he is in this moment: eyes glazed over with arousal, jaw clenched, brow dotted with sweat, lips swollen from kissing me.

Seeing Max so turned on combined with just how good he feels has me tingling between my thighs once more. He digs his fingers into my hips and picks up the pace.

"Do you have any idea how long I've wanted to do this with you?" he growls.

I moan "No" and push my hips up higher.

"A long fucking time."

"Same," I rasp. "Same, same, same."

He goes harder and faster until my vision begins to go starry. And then he slips a hand between my legs and works the most sensitive part of me with the pads of his fingers. The intensity deepens until my legs start to shake. I reach around and grip a handful of his delectably rock-hard ass.

"I'm gonna need to get a good look at this up close very, very soon," I say.

He chuckles between pants. I babble that I'm close.

"Thank fuck."

And then Max puts it into some high gear I didn't know he was capable of. He goes harder and faster than I thought was humanly possible. It's enough, though. Because moments later I'm bursting once again. He isn't far behind. He tenses against me before shuddering, then grunting. He lightly bites the spot where my neck meets my shoulder. The soft scrape, so sweet and carnal at once, has me grinning in ecstasy.

We collapse on the bed, him on top of me, and stay that way for nearly a minute. I close my eyes and breathe in the mint-spice scent on his bedsheets, relishing the weight of his body on top of mine.

"Crap," Max mutters before he leans up. "I must feel so heavy on you."

He rolls off me and settles to my side. I immediately tuck into the crook of his chest and arm. "Yeah, but heavy in the best way. Like a sexy human weighted blanket."

He rumbles out a laugh, then slides out of my hold and off the bed to dart to the bathroom. I watch as he walks out, mesmerized not only by his exquisite ass but that massive back tattoo I got a quick glimpse of not long ago. I study that demon-skull and the words "Good Enough Alone" until he's out of sight. When he appears in the doorway thirty seconds later, I lean up on my elbows.

"Did you get a sufficient look at the goods back there?" he asks.

I nod and chuckle. He comes back to bed and tucks us both underneath the comforter. As I lie with my head on his chest, looking at nothing in particular, I work up the nerve to ask him what I've wondered for weeks.

"Hey. Can I ask you something?"

I press my eyes shut, annoyed at how awkward I sound.

The rumble of his chuckle echoes inside the room. "Shoot."

"That tattoo on your back is incredible."

"Thanks. That's not a question, though."

"Right." I scrunch my face against his chest. "I was wondering, what's the meaning behind it?"

When he doesn't say anything at first, I backtrack.

"Sorry, I'm sure you've been asked that a million times about your tattoos. It's probably so annoying, never mind."

"It's okay," he says softly. "You can ask me anything."

I smile into his chest.

"The meaning behind the image or the saying?" he asks.

"Both, if you're okay with it. They're both so beautiful."

He takes a few moments before he starts to speak. "It's a long story."

"I've got all day. We're playing hooky, remember?" I run my fingers along his chest, hoping that it sets him at ease.

After a few seconds, he lets out a breath. "I had kind of a rough upbringing."

I lean up to look at him. "I'm so sorry. I didn't meant to pry."

He tucks a chunk of my hair behind my ear. "It's okay."

I can tell by the way his gaze darts around my face that he's the tiniest bit nervous. So I settle my head back on his chest. Maybe if I don't look at him when he talks, it'll take some of the pressure off.

His body relaxes against mine.

"My dad died when I was a baby. And so it was just me and my mom, but she wasn't, um . . . very stable."

The hesitation in his voice as he speaks makes my throat ache. He's said so little, but there's so much pain in his tone.

"She was an alcoholic. She still is, last I heard."

After a beat of silence, I wonder if there's something I should say or do to comfort him, but then he starts to run his fingers slowly, softly up my spine. I practically purr at the sensation. And then I realize he must be doing that because he feels comfortable. With me.

So I stay quiet and let him speak when he's ready.

"She didn't really take care of me. I was kind of left to fend for myself a lot growing up."

He clears his throat, stammers, then stops himself. After a moment, he starts again.

"The last time I saw her in person was almost fourteen years ago. I was in high school. I hadn't seen her in months and heard that she was staying at someone's apartment. I went to visit her and when I walked in, she was passed out in the kitchen, in her own vomit. She had alcohol poisoning."

I hug tight against his chest.

"I called 911 and went to the hospital with her. When she came to, I begged her to quit drinking, to get help. She got mad and yelled at me for daring to tell her what to do. So I told her she wasn't my mom anymore and that I never wanted to see her again. And then I left."

My eyes water at the thought of Max experiencing something so traumatizing as a teenager, at the thought of him as a kid all alone, no one to count on or keep him safe.

"Max. I'm so sorry."

"It's okay."

I almost say that it's not okay ever for a parent to neglect their child. But I bite my tongue and keep the words from falling out. I'm sure he knows that. I'm sure he doesn't need me to go on about it right now. All he needs me to do in this moment is support him and listen.

"Before that day at the hospital, whenever my mom was too drunk to take care of me or was off on a bender, I'd stay with family friends or relatives."

"That must have been so hard," I say softly.

"It was." He pauses for a second. "I always felt like a burden. I mean, I know none of this was in my control. It's not like I wanted to impose on someone else's life and make them take care of me. But I didn't really have a choice—I was a kid. I just ended up wherever my mom felt like dumping me for weeks at a time. I remember some of her friends and relatives—my relatives—complaining about having to pay for things for me. So I tried not to ask them for money for lunch at school or clothes, stuff like that . . ."

When he trails off, I think back to when that kid Henry came to Max's store and tried to take a book, explaining that he didn't have enough money to pay for it, and how Max reassured him by saying he'd been in that position as a kid as well. This is what he meant.

"A few of the relatives and families I stayed with got sick of me after a while. And I could feel it, you know? Like, even though I was young, I could feel like I was bothering them, like I wasn't wanted."

My heart rips in half listening to him calmly tell me this wrenching memory. I snuggle deeper into his chest.

"Max, no. That's not—you were wanted. I promise you were wanted."

His heavy sigh gently rocks my head. "My grandparents wanted me. After that incident at the hospital, I lived with them until I turned eighteen, graduated high school, and ventured out on my own. They were loving and supportive. I was fortunate to have them. But that didn't erase the times before that when I stayed with other relatives or my mom's friends. And because I could feel that they didn't truly want me there, I acted out a bit. Gave them attitude, talked back, stayed out past curfew, that sort of thing.

"They'd yell at me for not listening to them. My uncle, who had kids of his own and clearly didn't want his drunk sister's latchkey and only took me in because my cousins liked me, started calling me 'little demon.' That became his nickname for me the year I lived with him, my first year of high school. I always hated it. But I never told him. Even after I stopped living with him, it stuck with me. So much that when I was nineteen and still struggling with myself, I decided to get a giant tattoo on my back of a demon skull as a 'fuck you' to my uncle. Like, fine, I'm a demon and proud of it."

I lean up to look at him.

He shakes his head. "It's silly, I know. And pretty damn petty. And immature. But there was a weird power I felt every time I went in for a session and got that tattoo on my back. Like, I was owning a part of me that he and so many other people in my life wrote off as something negative. Here I was embracing it, wearing it as a badge of pride."

"God, Max. That's . . . that's . . ." I make a noise that conveys a fraction of the disgust I feel on his behalf.

He cups a hand over my cheek, a sad smile on his face.

"Hey," he says. "It's okay."

"No, it's not. Max, he was your family. He should have welcomed you, his own nephew, with open arms. I can't . . . I can't even imagine my aunt ever treating me like that. She has two kids of her own who are older than me and live out of the country, but she's always treated me like her own daughter."

My chest tightens as sadness and anger converge inside me.

He kisses my forehead. "You have a loving and supportive family, Joelle. Some people don't, though. It's just the way the world is."

I shake my head. Again that sad smile pulls at his lips.

"And honestly? I don't think your reason for getting that tattoo is silly. At all," I say. "It's beautiful. You took a hurtful insult and turned it into your strength. That's admirable."

His smile turns tender. And then he pulls me to sit on top of him so that I'm straddling his midsection as he stays lying down. He tucks the blanket around my legs and waist.

"At my final session with the tattoo artist, I asked her to write 'Good Enough Alone' at the top, along the curve of my shoulders. At that time, I didn't think I needed anyone to feel whole or validated, especially not people who never wanted me in the first place."

When he swallows, there's a flash of pain in his eyes.

"I wanted a permanent reminder of that," he says quietly.

This time I'm the one cupping his face. "You're so strong, Max. You've done so much on your own, more than a lot of people could ever imagine doing. But I want you to know that you're not alone. As long as I'm around—as long as you want me around—I'm here for you. Always."

His stare turns glassy for the briefest moment. It almost looks like he has tears in his eyes, but then he blinks and it's gone.

He leans up and kisses me softly, saying a quiet "thank you" against my lips.

We shift so we're lying side by side again, me tucked into his chest, his arms wrapped around me, his chin resting gently on top of my head. It's barely noon, but my eyelids go heavy each time I blink. As Max glides his fingers up and down my back in that slow, soothing rhythm once more, I'm lulled into the most peaceful, satisfied sleep.

Chapter 15

Max

I glance around my kitchen, which is covered in flour. Just like I am.

What the hell was I thinking?

I let out a defeated chuckle before I dust my hands on my pants. But that doesn't make a difference because my jeans are covered too.

I don't know how the hell Joelle does this. Every damn day she's in that bakery hauling bags of flour, working and prepping dough nonstop. And bam, a few hours later, trays of delicious pastries appear.

And here I am, trying to make a single batch of croissants; I'm not even ten minutes into the recipe, and my kitchen looks like a giant bag of flour crashed into my house.

I shake my head at the mess and notice Doughnut perched in the corner, flour dusted over his forehead and nose.

I chuckle again, careful to keep my voice down so I don't wake Joelle. She's been sleeping for the past couple of hours, and

I thought it would be sweet to surprise her with some homemade croissants. But Jesus, are they complicated to make. I glance over at my laptop, which has the recipe on the screen . . . which is also covered in flour.

I grab the broom and dustpan and start to sweep all the flour I dumped on the floor when Muffin comes galloping in.

"No, Muffin!" I whisper-scream at her, but it's too late. She plops onto the floor and rolls over, now covered in flour too. Just like everything and everyone else in this kitchen.

The sound of footsteps softly padding down the hall grabs my attention. When I glance up and see Joelle wearing nothing but one of my T-shirts, I lose all the air in my lungs. If I weren't covered in flour, I'd walk up to her, wrap her in my arms, and kiss her until she's panting. Because holy shit does she look impossibly cute and sexy wearing my clothes, sleep still in her eyes, her hair falling over her shoulders.

Those big brown eyes do a slow scan of the space, of me and Doughnut and Muffin. Her mouth hangs open.

I tilt my head at her and shrug. "There was a minor situation."

"Looks like it." She laughs. "What happened?"

"I wanted to surprise you by baking some croissants."

The way her expression goes soft makes my heart thud extra hard.

"Max, that's so sweet."

I grab the broom and do a quick sweep of the floor. "Yeah, well, it's not happening. I don't think I have the proper skills to make an edible batch of croissants if I can't even handle the flour properly."

She walks over to me and I start to tell her to stay there so she doesn't get flour all over herself, but she ignores me. And then she tugs me by the shirt I'm wearing down to her mouth and plants a kiss on me that leaves me dizzy.

"It was so incredibly thoughtful of you to do that," she says. "And so, so cute to wake up and see you covered in flour."

I lean the broom next to the counter, pull her close to me, and kiss her again.

Both my breath and my heart go wild. This woman. God, this woman. I've never, ever felt like this before. Just seeing her, touching her, smelling her skin, turns me on. And at the same time I feel comfortable enough to tell her about my messed-up past and family history.

I've never told anyone what I told Joelle earlier today, about the meaning behind my tattoo, my mom's struggles with alcoholism, and how I was the unwanted kid in my extended family. Past girlfriends and even the few friends I have always got a sanitized version of the truth. Not because I don't trust them, but because I couldn't ever shake that on-edge feeling around them. They're all good people, I just never felt comfortable enough to be that raw with them.

Not the case with Joelle. She's the warmest, kindest, most understanding person I've ever met. And every time I'm around her, I feel at ease. Like I can be myself always and she'll never, ever judge me.

As long as I'm around—as long as you want me around—I'm here for you. Always.

The words she spoke to me earlier echo in my mind, leaving behind an ache in my chest. No one's ever made me feel that way, like they'd stand by me forever, no matter what, except Joelle. And it means more than I can even put into words right now.

She glances up at me, licks her lips, and flashes that scrunch-smile that always makes me weak. "Let's take a break from baking. Order pizza instead?"

I grin down at her. "Sounds perfect."

She offers to wipe down the counter while I get Muffin and Doughnut cleaned up. The sound of her phone ringing interrupts our cleaning session.

"Hey, Whitney. What's up?"

I recognize the name right away. Whitney is Joelle's tall and redheaded best friend who stops by the bakery all the time.

I'm just finishing toweling off Muffin when I hear Joelle start to stammer.

"Oh, um . . . crap, I . . ." She sighs. "I'm so sorry. I completely forgot. I got so busy at work with . . ."

She stammers, then sighs.

"Okay, I can't lie to you, Whit. I did actually forget about getting together for lunch, and for that I'm sorry. But it's not because of work . . . no, I actually haven't been to work at all today . . . it's a long story . . . yes, promise everything is fine . . . it's just that, well, I'm with Max right now. At his place."

I laugh when I hear Whitney shriek my name on the other line.

Joelle turns to me and shrugs. "Um, well, actually . . . we made up . . . yeah, he apologized. We both did . . . No, we're good . . . what do you mean?" Her eyes bulge. "Oh my god, Whitney."

Joelle's head falls back as she groans. "Okay, fine. Yeah. We did."

I smile to myself as I wash up at the kitchen sink.

"What? Whitney, no way am I doing that . . . because it's inappropriate!"

I twist around. "Everything okay?"

Joelle holds the phone away from her face. "Whitney wants to video chat. She wants to see us together."

"Sure."

"Really?"

"Yeah, why not."

With an exasperated smile tugging at those gorgeous rosy lips, Joelle presses a button on her phone screen. She walks over to stand next to me and holds her phone up. I crouch down a bit so we're both in frame.

"Okay, Whit. See? We're real."

I bite my lip to keep from laughing at how giddy Whitney looks as she takes us in.

"Holy shit. Are you wearing his T-shirt, Jojo?"

Joelle rolls her eyes.

I glance down at Joelle and nod approvingly. "I mean, she looks pretty damn good in my clothes, don't you think?"

Whitney giggles. "Okay. Let me just say for the record, I'm glad you two worked out your differences." A wide smile spreads across her face. "And I'm even more excited that you two are a thing. Finally! But dear lord, it took you two long enough. I mean, you worked side by side for over a year! And now look at how sexed up and—"

"Okay, Whit. Thanks so much, gotta go."

Joelle hangs up and we share a laugh.

"I like her," I say. "Very straightforward and says what's on her mind."

Joelle shakes her head, but the smile on her face tells me she loves her best friend. "That's definitely Whitney. It's why I love her."

I call in a delivery order for pizza and by the time we're done cleaning up the kitchen, it's at the door. Together we plop down on the couch and dig into the slices of bacon, corn, and arugula pizza on sourdough crust while I channel surf to find something to watch.

"Oh my gosh!" Joelle squeals. I turn to her as I chew and see she's picked up a thin paperback that was sitting on the side table. "You have *Revenge* by Yoko Ogawa?"

"Yeah. It's one of my favorite short story collections."

The look of pure joy on her face reminds me of a kid opening gifts on Christmas morning.

"I freaking love this book," she says. "It's one of my favorites, but no one I know has read it. I should have known you'd have it, Mr. Bookseller."

She dusts a kiss over my lips and gazes down at the cover, which depicts a tattered piece of paper. The word "revenge" appears like it's been slashed with a knife.

"I found that book by total accident at the library one day after school," I say. "The creepy cover sucked me in as a middle schooler in the mood to read something scary. You should have seen the look the librarian gave me when I checked it out."

Joelle beams at me. "You spent a lot of time at the library as a kid?"

I nod, my chest aching the slightest bit at all the memories that resurface. But then I focus on Joelle's gaze, how warm and tender it is. I know it's safe to tell her this—I know she'll understand.

"The library was a haven for me." When I say it, that pressure in my chest loosens. "First of all, it was free, which was great for a kid with next to no money. And being there, getting lost in all those stories and books, it felt like an escape from all the stuff happening with my mom and my family. I felt like a normal kid hanging out at the library."

"That makes so much sense," she says softly. "Is that what inspired you to open your own bookstore?"

I nod, and finish my slice of pizza, then offer her more. "When I was younger, it was my dream to have my own bookshop where I could always feel at home. And I wanted it to be an escape for customers too. That's part of the reason I started hosting book club. There's something comforting about seeing all those people convene every month and talk about books. Like, no matter what they've got going on in their lives, they can count on book club to be a fun and engaging time to spend with other people who love to read."

Joelle clasps my hand, lacing her fingers in mine. It's such a simple gesture, but it means so much. I can't remember the last time I held hands with someone—or the last time such simple skin-to-skin contact made me feel like my heart was going to shatter in the best way.

I swallow and take a breath, focusing on her gaze. She smiles, and it's like her gaze sparkles.

"You should read *Revenge* for book club one of these times," she says.

"I think that's a great idea."

She snuggles into my chest and for a few minutes we watch some show about twin brothers who renovate and sell houses together.

After a minute she looks up at me. "Thanks for the best day I've had in a long time."

"It was my pleasure—and the best for me too. I hope it's not the last time we do this. I really like you, Joelle."

When those perfect pink lips stretch into the biggest grin, I'm soaring.

"I like you too, Max. A lot."

Those are the last words we speak to each other for the next few hours. Because then she climbs on my lap and we go wild on each other with our mouths and hands. The only sounds we exchange are moans and pants.

Chapter 16

Joelle

B lack coffee today?"

Max smirks down at me as he stands in front of my counter. "I'm actually in the mood for an *ube* latte."

I wink at him. "You got it."

I can't stop grinning as I whip up his coffee order. It's been like this ever since that day almost a month ago when we skipped work in favor of lounging and fooling around at his house. We started officially dating right away, and every day since I've had a perma-smile on my face. Nothing can get me down, not even when Ivan told us at the beginning of July that the remodel was running a bit behind and it was likely going to be another month until our spaces were ready for us to move back into—not until early August. I grinned, shrugged, and cheerily said, "No problem!" at the news that now we'll likely be spending just over two months in the temporary shared space. Ivan was speechless, especially after receiving the same reaction from Max.

Right now, I'm too blissed out on orgasms from my insanely hot boyfriend to care about anything else. Even now, as much as I relish the fact that we're together, I have moments where I can hardly believe it.

Max Boyson is my boyfriend. The guy who looks like a sexy bad boy but has the heart of a cinnamon roll and runs the bookstore next to me is *my* boyfriend.

I think back to a week ago when he initiated the conversation about labels. I had been working up the nerve to broach that very same topic, but he beat me to it one day after we closed up the temporary space.

"Is it too soon to call you my girlfriend?" he had asked as I wiped down surfaces on my side of the space. My answer was to leap over the counter and into his arms, wrap my legs around his waist, and say, "Not too soon at all, boyfriend," before planting a kiss on him.

I bite my lip so I don't break into a clownish smile.

God, this feeling. It will never, ever get old.

Neither will seeing Max naked. Or feeling his body against mine. Or hearing him grunt my name as we're tangled together in each other's bedsheets.

I spin around and hand him his drink.

"How's Pumpkin?" he asks.

I glance over my shoulder to the built-in shelf along the back wall where I set her carrier. She chomps away on a baby carrot. "She's great. Happy to be back at work with me."

Max pulls a small packet of unsalted seeds from his pocket. "Thought she might like a snack."

I gasp softly, then lean up to kiss him.

I take the packet of seeds from him and set them to the side of the cage. "How are things going with Reggie?"

"So far, so good. He's a rock star."

A couple of weeks ago Max hired a part-time employee to help with the workload.

"Glad he's working out."

Max leans down so that he's closer to me. "Would you be able to get your family to help cover the bakery Sunday? I want to take you somewhere this weekend."

This time I actually let that clownish smile loose. "You want to go away together?"

"Yeah. And we're not really going that far." There's a glimmer in his eyes. "The rest is a surprise."

Just then Mom and Auntie pop up from where they're prepping and baking at the metal table behind the counter.

"*Anak*! You need to go."

"Yes, yes! You kids go have fun. We'll take care of the bakery on Sunday, no problem."

Their smiles are a blend of expectant and giddy.

"You sure it's okay? Mom, I thought you were taking that extra shift at the clinic."

"No, no. That's the weekend after."

"Auntie, what about your ankle?"

She slightly kicks her leg, which is fitted with a boot. "I feel great. I've been resting lots and I'm dying to get in more time here at the bakery. I'm so sick of sitting around at home."

I glance up at Max, who is observing with the most amused

look on his face. "I think you're all out of excuses. You're stuck with me this weekend."

I shake my head, laughing. "I can't wait."

When Max leads me through the lobby of the Paramount Hotel in downtown Portland, I'm elated. We just checked into our room and are walking to the restaurant.

"Are you ever going to tell me what the surprise is?" I say while I squeeze Max's hand.

"You're very impatient, you know that?" He side-eyes me.

"One of my few flaws."

When we walk into Swine Restaurant & Moonshine + Whiskey Bar, Max stops at the bar. He chats with the bartender, who's dressed like an extra out of *Peaky Blinders* with a tailored gray vest, white dress shirt, and gray dress pants. I take in the décor, which is clearly inspired by a Prohibition-era speakeasy. Dark mahogany is everywhere. It makes up the bar top, the tables, the flooring, and the massive wood structural beams dotted throughout the space. Brass lighting fixtures shine in the natural lighting that streams through the nearby floor-to-ceiling windows.

After a few seconds, the bartender looks past Max to smile at me, then leads us around the bar to the back where the kitchen is. It's a bustling space with a dozen people decked out in white chef's coats and hats rushing around hastily with plates and pans.

The bartender hollers at a guy in the back, who's hunched over a stovetop in a space that's semiseparated from the clamor of the main kitchen. I quickly recognize the equipment. The pastry workspace in this hotel kitchen looks like something out of my fantasies. There's a trio of ovens, a half-dozen metal multitiered racks to hold trays of baked goods, and two long metal tables. Every surface is stainless steel that shines so bright, it's almost blinding.

The bartender leaves just as the guy hustles over to us. I squint at him, noting that he looks familiar, but maybe that's just because he's super handsome. With his dark hair, ice-blue eyes, and square jawline, I'm sure he's mistaken for a TV chef often. He definitely has that look.

"Jacques, always good to see you." Max smiles at the man.

"Max, my boy!" he says. "You're finally here. This must be . . ."

"Joelle. My girlfriend."

My stomach dips when he says it. Yet another thing that will never, ever get old.

"She's the genius baker I was telling you about."

I flush at the thought that Max is telling people about me.

Jacques stretches his hand to me. I clasp it and go for a handshake, but instead he softly leads the back of my hand to his lips and presses a light kiss. "He neglected to mention how lovely you are."

I'm flushing hard-core now. "You're very kind."

"Just speaking the truth."

"Are you done hitting on my girlfriend?" Max says good-naturedly.

Jacques releases my hand and winks at me. "For now."

Max gives him a playful shove while I laugh.

"Jacques and I were roommates years ago when he first moved to Portland from Montreal. He's the head pastry chef here at the Paramount and sometimes goes on the morning news shows to do cooking segments."

My eyes go wide. *That's* where I've seen Jacques. I've watched him countless times on TV demonstrating how to make fancy pastries, like brioche French toast and cream puffs. He even did a segment on *Good Morning America* a few months ago.

"Holy crap. You're Jacques Kessler."

He beams and rests his hands on his hips. "In the flesh."

"My mom and auntie and grandma *love* you. They think you're so handsome." I immediately bite my tongue after I speak. I sound like a starstruck fangirl.

Jacques's charming smile doesn't budge. He's not the least bit bothered. "Clearly they have excellent taste."

I shove Max's arm. "Why did you never tell me that you're friends with Jacques Kessler?"

"Because he hits on anything with a pulse. I wanted to protect you." He knocks Jacques with his shoulder, but the chef simply shrugs.

We all laugh. Just then someone calls Jacques over to the back stove and he excuses himself.

"Just come over whenever you're ready," he says to me.

When I look back over at Max, his expression is tender.

"I thought you'd maybe like to bake together? Kind of like a private pastry lesson." He rubs the back of his neck as his eyes turn shy. "I know it's not the same as going to culinary school or getting to travel to Paris and visit all the best bakeries in person. But I just thought . . ."

I clutch my chest with my hand. My heart is beating out of control.

I reach up, pull Max to my mouth, and plant a kiss on him that's entirely too intimate for this upscale restaurant kitchen.

When I let him go, I'm vibrating with joy. "Max, this is honestly one of the most thoughtful things anyone has ever done for me. Thank you."

His chest rises with a breath, and then he beams. "So you're happy?"

"So freaking happy. I get a private pastry lesson with Jacques Kessler! My whole family and Whitney are going to flip out when I tell them."

The rumble of Max's laugh makes my heart soar.

"Have fun," he says. "I'm gonna go have a drink at the bar."

I nod excitedly, then run over to where Jacques is standing. He hands me an apron.

"Are you ready to get started?"

I tie on the apron. "So ready."

I look expectantly at Max as the server sets a white ceramic plate in front of him.

His eyes go wide at the two-inch-high puff pastry round topping the mug of lobster chowder that Jacques and I made this afternoon.

"Damn. You made that?"

I nod excitedly, then shift on my barstool next to him so I can reach over and move the plate and mug closer to him.

"Wait till you taste it."

For two unbelievable hours, Chef Jacques taught me loads of his secret techniques along with a few of his own recipes. It was a dream come true to work next to a renowned and talented chef, and I can't wait to use what I learned back at Lanie's.

I motion for Max to take the first bite. He drives his spoon through the tender puff pastry, which collapses into a million perfect little flakes right into the chowder. He blows on the steamy broth in his spoon, then tastes it. His green-brown eyes practically bulge from his head.

"Oh holy f—" He cuts himself off when a dad with his young daughter walk by us.

I cover my mouth as I giggle.

"Okay. That is honestly the best thing I've ever tasted."

"Eat up. There's more coming."

Jacques let me prepare a three-course meal to share with Max. First is a small cup of lobster chowder topped with puff pastry, followed by an entrée of beef Wellington with a mixed green salad, then finally peach cobbler for dessert.

I dig into my own serving of chowder. That first taste of the rich broth on my tongue has me rolling my eyes to the back of my head.

"Wow . . . just . . . wow," I mutter as I inhale the rest. "Jacques is incredible."

"So are you," Max says quickly. I notice his bowl is licked clean. "You cooked that too, you know."

I can feel the blush creep up my neck and cheeks as I gaze down at my chowder. "Yeah. I guess I am."

Max takes my hand in his. "Joelle. You are fucking brilliant. And talented. Own it."

I nod once. "I am fucking brilliant. And talented."

He beams at my affirmation. Then the bartender appears, a bottle of champagne in hand.

"Compliments of Chef Kessler. He wants to thank you both for dining as his guests this evening and offers his apologies that there weren't any open tables."

"It's no problem," we both say. But we're happy to indulge in the top-tier champagne.

As we sip, I glance around the space. The restaurant is bustling. Well-dressed patrons are seated at every single table. Servers dart around, ferrying plates in and out of the kitchen.

I glance down at the short black long-sleeve dress I packed and the rose-gold bangle on my wrist, glad that I took the time to run up to our room and change before sitting down to dinner with Max. I know he wouldn't have cared what I wore, but I hardly ever get to go to nice dinners like this. Taking the extra twenty minutes to swipe on some makeup and jewelry and wear something other than jeans and T-shirts caked in flour feels special.

"I can't remember the last time I've been out to a place like this—dressed like this," I tell Max in a soft voice.

"You look incredible," he rasps.

"This has been the most perfect day. Thank you."

Something about the look on his face has my heartbeat stuttering. The low mood lighting of the restaurant hits every beautiful angle of his face, making him look even more ruggedly handsome. But it's more than that. It's the way his expression is a perfect blend between wonder and contentment—at being here with me.

I catch myself hoping that he'll look at me like that forever.

Forever.

I quickly down some champagne and silently tell myself to focus on the moment, not anything more.

"It's nice to be able to get away for a bit," I say quickly. "I mean, I love my family, but living and working together is a lot sometimes."

Max nods like he understands. "Do you ever think about moving out?"

I'm jolted by the question, but only for a second. It makes sense for him to ask. He's thirty and lives alone, while I'm two years older and still technically living with my family, even though I'm in a separate apartment.

"Yeah. I do. I just . . . family means a lot to me. And they've been through a lot with their finances. I know I can't protect them from every bad thing that could possibly happen. But if I'm close to them—if I live with them, I can do little things. Like help around the house, help pay the bills, clean stuff, cook for them, take them to appointments, help them figure out their phones and the computer."

Max chuckles.

I shrug. "Maybe it sounds silly."

"It doesn't," he says with conviction in his tone. "If I had a family like yours, I would want to be as close as possible to them too."

His words land like a hug. So many people—so many guys I've dated—hear that I still live at home and think it's so pathetic. But they just don't get it. My family is all I have. And if I lose them, I lose everything.

But as I stare at the pastry crumbs on my plate, I can't deny that cooking with Jacques reminded me of what I thought I'd be doing all those years ago.

"I feel so guilty sometimes."

Max frowns at the words I only now realize I let slip.

"About what?" he asks.

I pull my lips into my mouth, nervous about how this is going to sound.

My gaze falls to my empty plate. "Sometimes a part of me still wishes that I hadn't given up my savings . . . that I had gone to culinary school and traveled to Paris, like I always wanted."

Even just speaking that turns the taste in my mouth bitter.

I shake my head. "God, I can't believe I said that."

"Hey." Max's hand rests softly on mine. When I muster the courage to look at him, I'm surprised by the soft look on his face. "Don't feel bad about that."

"But it's a horrible thing for me to think. It's so selfish."

"No, it's not. Joelle, you gave up your dream. That's so hard. And I bet it conjures up a lot of complicated emotions. No reasonable person would expect you to do something so selfless and be one hundred percent happy about it forever."

I take a moment and mull over his words. "That makes sense." I sip from my glass. "It's not that I regret doing it. I don't at all. If I had to go back in time and do it all over again, I would without hesitation. And I'm proud of the life I have now. I worked hard for my bakery and I love it. I just wonder sometimes what my life would be like had I been able to go to culinary school and travel like I planned."

"It's only natural to wonder about the choices we didn't make," he says. "We all do it."

I study his expression while I take in what he's said. The soft look on his face and in his eyes tells me that he's not judging me one bit. He doesn't think any less of me for what I've admitted. I can be myself around Max. I can be honest and real, and it doesn't change the way he feels about me. He still likes me. He still cares about me.

That thought turns my muscles loose and my skin tingly.

He lifts my hand to his mouth and presses it with a kiss. "You're the best person I know, Joelle. You could become a career criminal and I'd still think the world of you."

My head falls back as I laugh. Just then the server drops off two plates of beef Wellington in front of us. Max *ooohs* at the decadent dish before quickly picking up his utensils.

"I can't wait to see what you whip up at Lanie's after this," Max says as he slices his knife into the flaky pastry exterior.

"Definitely some variation of the chowder." I pause to savor a bite of beef Wellington, marveling at how tender and rich the meat is. "Not with lobster, though. That's too rich for my budget."

"So just regular chowder, then?"

I nod. "I've been trying to perfect my own chowder recipe ever since I had the most amazing clam chowder at this dive seafood shack near the Oregon coast on a road trip I took once with my aunt and Whitney. I've been trying to re-create it for years and failing miscrably."

I look up at Max, but he doesn't respond. He just takes a bite of his food, the look in his eyes wistful.

"Did you go on a lot of road trips with your family?" he asks.

"All the time growing up, especially during the summers when I was out of school. Usually just along the Oregon coast, nothing major. But it was a nice way to get out of the house and see some pretty scenery."

When he goes quiet, I don't say anything. I don't want to push him for whatever he's clearly working out in his brain.

"I've never been on a family road trip," he says after a while, his tone and expression the slightest bit embarrassed. "That sounds like it would be really fun."

There's a pull in my chest at the thought that Max didn't get to experience something so normal to me, a tradition that so many kids get to enjoy.

I set down my fork and knife and grab his hand. "Then let's do it. How about next weekend?"

His thick eyebrows lift the slightest bit. "Really?"

"Yeah. I wanna take the most epic road trip with you, Max Boyson."

The corner of his mouth hooks up into the most beautiful smile. "Okay."

We finish the meal, happy and satisfied. As we sip our champagne, Max leaves his credit card on the counter for the bartender, then hops up from his stool.

"I'm gonna say bye to Jacques really quick and then—"

I catch the sleeve of his dove-gray dress shirt and pull him close until his face is nearly touching mine.

"And then we'll go upstairs and have our real dessert?"

There's a flash in his eyes. "Screw Jacques, let's go upstairs now."

I laugh. "Say good-bye to your friend first. It'll just take a couple minutes."

He lets out a soft groan, which makes me laugh harder. When he leaves, I pull out my phone to make sure I didn't miss any calls from home. Not even a minute later Max is back, that wicked half smile on his face. He drops cash for a tip on the bar top. He scoops my hand into his and looks down at me. "Wanna get out of here?"

His eyes are alight once more. "Yeah."

When we get to our room, I walk straight to the window and open the curtains. We were lucky and got a room with a good view of the city. A million lights glitter in the distance as the soft hum of traffic echoes from below.

Max comes up behind me, places his hands on my waist, and presses his mouth against the side of my neck.

I close my eyes and sigh at the way the simple touch of his lips to my skin has me in goose bumps.

"So about that dessert," Max whispers against my skin.

He runs his fingers through my hair as he pushes it off my shoulder and away from my neck, giving it the slightest tug. A million goose bumps flash across my skin. Max lightly bites the spot where my neck meets my shoulder and slowly glides down the zipper of my dress. Then, hands on my waist, his insanely soft mouth dusts kisses down the exposed part of my back.

"No bra?" he growls against the midpoint of my spine.

I press my palms against the window and laugh. "Wasn't in the mood. Besides. Easier access."

He groans and slips a hand inside my dress and massages my breast. With his other hand he palms my ass. The whole time he keeps his mouth on the side of my neck, alternating between kisses and nipping bites.

There is most definitely going to be a mark there tomorrow. But I don't care. It's hot to think that someone could see the mark as proof of just how wild Max is for me.

I move to pull my glasses off and toss them on the chair next to us. My head goes dizzy at the mix of sensations from Max's lips and tongue and hands—the ache that spreads between my legs and up to my core, the goose bumps that dance across my skin, the tingles that flash through me when he teases my nipples between his fingertips, every time he squeezes my ass cheek.

I reach behind me and tug my hand through his hair, and then I turn my head and pull him into a kiss. It's a sloppy, filthy fight for control, but that makes it all the more fun. We're biting and sucking and teasing and licking, and I'm getting more rabid by the second.

I let go of his head and start to yank off the top part of my dress. He stops me with a hand on my arm.

"Do you really want to do this here?"

His cloudy gaze darts to the window, then to the street below. We're several stories up and the streets are so busy at this time on a Saturday evening that I'm certain no one cares enough to glance up and search the million little windows in the surrounding buildings.

But still. There's something so thrilling about the thought that people *could* see us, if only they look up.

I never would have thought to do something so wild with guys I've dated before, but being with Max brings out this uninhibited side of me I used to be too shy to explore.

"I want you right here, Max." I gasp into his mouth. "I want them to see. I want to show them I'm yours."

A bonfire erupts behind his eyes. His smile turns deviant in a way I've never seen. It makes my stomach flutter and that pulse between my legs throb even harder.

He yanks down my dress in a single move and I'm left in a lacy thong. Then he spins me around to face him, then lowers his mouth to my breasts. He takes his time teasing and licking and playing, just like he does every other time we're together. And like every other time, I fall apart so quickly, into gasps and curse words. His mouth just feels so insanely good on me every single time. As the seconds pass, my whole body aches in the best way, begging to explode.

When he finally lifts his head away, he blesses me with that naughty half smile. And then he starts to unbutton his shirt. I move to help him, taking the bottom buttons while he takes the top ones. In a few seconds the crisp cotton is gone from his torso. I yank down his pants, and soon he's in my favorite state of undress: naked, save for those snug boxer briefs.

But I don't get to admire him for long because soon he's slid them off and I'm gazing at an even more tantalizing image. My mouth waters as I glance down at him, waiting patiently as he fishes a condom from his wallet.

Once it's on him, it's like his animal side takes hold. His eyes are feral with lust and he grabs at me like he's dying for my skin on his skin, my mouth on his mouth.

He slides my panties off with a single move of his hand, and then he's back up to his full height. His eyebrow ticks up as he gazes down at me. Then he teases me with a kiss before pulling away and spinning me around to face the window once more, his hand on my back.

"Okay," he grunts in my ear. "Let's show them."

I plant my palms against the cold glass and stick out my backside farther. When he slides in, I press my eyes shut and groan. This is going to be so, so good.

His smooth, slow thrusts turn animalistic in a matter of minutes. All I can do is cry out as the pleasure consumes me from head to toe, gripping for dear life onto the glass.

My head is shrouded in a fog of arousal. I can't get out a single coherent thought other than more, harder, faster, *please*.

I tell Max exactly that. And he does it all.

When his sounds turn quick and desperate, when his fingers turn viselike against my hips, I slide one of my hands between my thighs and circle frantically in the spot I need it most. This is the wildest, most lustful thing I've ever done in my life. Never in a million years did I think I'd ever be the type of girl who wants to have sex against a window overlooking downtown Portland, but I've never been so turned on. I've never been so consumed with pleasure.

This is the effect Max Boyson has on me. Not only does he make me ooey-gooey on the inside with his thoughtful gestures, his sweet words, and the way he looks at me like I'm the only person in the room. But with a single teasing kiss and the touch of his hand on my skin, I turn sex-crazed. He makes me feel so sexy and comfortable all at once. I love love love all the sides this man brings out in me.

With a firm hand, he grips my jaw and turns my face to the side so he can plant a desperate kiss on my mouth. Soon I'm trembling as climax threatens to wreck me.

When it hits, that's exactly what happens. I groan-scream and come apart in Max's grip. My head goes foggy as pleasure annihilates me. It's a glorious end, though. I'm left quivering, barely able to stand, but Max holds me securely in his arms. It's the sweetest and hottest hug from behind: his entire body covers me while his open mouth rests against my shoulder, gasping and growling at once.

"Max."

"Joelle."

As we gasp in unison, I can feel the thud of his heartbeat against my back. It lands like a drumbeat, steady and powerful. I close my eyes and rest my palm against the center of my chest, smiling when I feel my own heart hammering away at the same frantic rhythm as his.

"I've never done that before," I say once my breath has steadied a bit. "Against a window, I mean."

His low chuckle rumbles behind me. "Me either. You must bring it out in me."

I spin around to look at him and bask in his stunning appearance: his heavy-lidded eyes that are drunk with pleasure, the sweat dotting his brow line, the crimson flush of his skin.

"You bring out a lot of things in me, Max."

With my palm on his stomach, I back him all the way to the bed. When the backs of his knees hit the edge, he falls onto the mattress. I climb onto his lap and push him flat on his back. He grins at my tiny show of strength as I lean down to kiss him. Before long he starts to harden underneath me.

This time when we do it, it's on the bed, just for us.

Chapter 17

Joelle

"Y ou're really not gonna tell me where we're going?" Max asks
from the passenger seat of my car.

"It's a surprise."

He fake-pouts, and I chuckle. It's day one of our weekend
road trip along the Oregon coast. This morning, we stopped at a
random lookout point near the ocean to eat the breakfast pastries I packed and just happened to see a humpback whale
breach the surface.

This afternoon we stopped in Lincoln City to check out the
coastal shops and stroll along a stretch of beach.

And now we're driving south along the 101 highway to my
favorite spot on all of the Oregon coast. My stomach leaps in
anticipation of Max's reaction.

I glance at him briefly. I can't see his eyes behind the black
lenses of his sunglasses, but his gaze is fixed on the crystal-blue
expanse of ocean in the distance. His stare has been directed
outside his window most of this drive except to chat with me,

and it makes my heart burst. I can tell that means he's enjoying this road trip. It means he's happy.

As I continue in the direction of Devil's Punch Bowl, I realize that Max's happiness is everything to me. It's why I was completely fine with leaving the bakery in the hands of Mom, Dad, and Auntie today and tomorrow—something that would have sent me into a spiral months ago. It's why I keep looking over at him to see his reaction. It's why seeing him smile makes my chest ache.

I'm falling hard for Max Boyson.

The lump that thought sends to my throat nearly causes me to cough, but I sip from my water bottle and it thankfully dissipates.

When I pull off the Oregon Coast Highway and turn toward the coastline, Max sits up in his seat. As I pull into the narrow parking area, he's full-on beaming.

"Holy shit," he mutters as he looks out toward Devil's Punch Bowl. That smile doesn't waver one bit.

We climb out of the car and walk up to the lookout point. Devil's Punch Bowl is quite literally that: a massive bowl shape in the coastal rock that's been naturally carved by the constant thrash of waves from the Pacific Ocean. Sea water violently churns, swirls, and foams against the rock.

Max swipes off his sunglasses and tucks them into the pocket of his jacket. The light reflecting off the white foam of the waves in front of us sparkles in his eyes. "Wow. That's . . ." He shakes his head, his gaze unmoving. "Incredible."

The wind picks up, blowing spray from the ocean all around us. I laugh as specks of salt water land on my glasses. I look over and see Max taking a million photos with his phone.

"Want me to take a pic of you?" I ask.

When he looks at me, my heart jumps. There's so much in that stare of his. Tenderness, affection, disbelief.

He shakes his head. "Nope."

And then he pulls me to stand next to him, wraps his arm around me, then takes a selfie of us. I'm grinning like a goober. Our first photo together as a couple. I bask in the joyful moment—this is everything I wanted for this trip and more.

After Max snaps more pictures, I tiptoe up and wrap my arms around his neck, then plant a kiss on his cheek.

We make our way down to the beach and check out a few of the tide pools. As we stroll along the shoreline, Max slows his long stride so my shorter legs can keep up. His worn leather boots are a stark contrast to the white sneakers I wear almost every day. I realize how we look so very opposite: a tatted-up bookseller clad in leather and the sweetie-pie baker in a puffer jacket and thick-rimmed glasses.

But when I look down at our clasped hands, my heart thunders yet again, like it has ever since the two of us got together. *We fit together perfectly.*

I stumble in the wet sand as the realization hits me.

I love Max.

He moves to help steady me. "You okay?"

I nod quickly. "Yeah, um, it's just really windy. And the sand. So wet. Makes it hard to walk."

I scrunch my face. Clunkiest recovery ever.

Max doesn't seem to notice, though. He just beams down at me. "This has been the perfect day. Thank you."

"It's not over yet. I could still screw it up," I joke, hoping that it covers up the nerves swirling through me.

He pushes his sunglasses to the top of his head, pinning me

with an intense stare that's also somehow so heartfelt. "You could never. I love it. So much."

As we make our way back up to the car, the word "love" spoken in Max's low growl echoes in my head. He loves this trip. Does that mean he could love me too?

I tuck away the thought for later as we head back to the car and drive to Newport, focused on giving Max the best road trip ever.

"I love this place already," Max says as he gazes at the flying saucer on top of the blue-and-coral-pink building that is South Beach Fish Market.

The hole-in-the-wall seafood joint is quirky for sure with the random artwork and sculptures all over the exterior. Giant cartoon renderings of fish and crustaceans in vivid colors adorn the outside, while the roof boasts a silver flying saucer and a lighthouse.

"Wait until you taste the food," I say.

It's a long wait in line, but I know once we get our meals and find a spot to sit down at one of the outdoor picnic tables, it'll be worth it.

As we sit down, I savor the clear summer weather with the sun shining bright above us, offering warmth against the brisk coastal breeze. When the aroma of spices, lemon, and batter his my nose, my stomach roars. I inhale my fish and chips before Max is even halfway done with his oysters and halibut.

"Damn," he says around a mouthful of food. "Sometimes I forget how monstrous your appetite is. I would have never guessed given your size. But every time I watch you eat, I'm reminded all over again."

I dig into my clam chowder. "Food is my life. I am not ashamed of it."

When the rich and creamy broth hits my tongue, I moan and roll my eyes. Max laughs. "That good?"

"So, so good. Here." I practically shove a spoonful into his mouth, dribbling a bit on his beard. I chuckle and wipe it with my napkin.

He smiles at first, but as he starts to chew and swallow, his eyes bulge. "Oh holy shit . . ."

A kid sitting nearby giggles as his mom gives Max a death glare.

"Sorry," he mutters before digging into more of the chowder. "Okay, yeah, that's way better than Jacques's lobster chowder."

I laugh and devour more of the chowder when Max passes the bowl back to me. "We can't tell him. It'll wreck his ego."

"It would take a lot more than that to wreck his ego, trust me. He's got the highest self-esteem of anyone I know," he jokes.

We finish dinner with our plates clean and our bellies full. I hop up to throw away our trash and run to the restroom to wash my hands. When I head back to our table, I spot an attractive woman standing next to our table, chatting with Max. All the telltale signs that she's flirting are there: she's smiling at him while leaning into his space and touching his arm every time she laughs.

I pause for a second, watching Max politely rebuff her by leaning away as he sits and not giving much eye contact.

The strangest thing? I'm not at all jealous. Because I don't blame that woman one bit for thinking Max is attractive and wanting to talk to him. I felt that way about him for a year and a half. At least she has the guts to do something about it.

I smile to myself. She's a bit too late, though.

As I walk over to them, I pick up part of their conversation.

". . . you should totally come by."

"Thanks, but I'm busy. I've got plans with my girlfriend."

"Aww, come on! Just one drink. On me, if you know what I mean."

She wags a perfectly shaped eyebrow at him. His smile turns to a wince as he looks away.

When I plant myself next to him, he twists around to look at me. I almost laugh at the relief in his expression.

"Hey," I say to the woman as I smile.

Her smile wavers the slightest bit. "Oh. Hi." She glances between us. "Oh! Sorry, I didn't realize . . ."

I climb onto Max's lap, straddling him with both legs wrapped around his waist. I snake my arms around his neck and then I gently bump my nose against his. Amusement flickers in his eyes as he gazes at me. And then I plant a kiss on his mouth.

When I'm done, I look back up at his admirer. "Sorry, were you saying something about a drink?"

Her jaw on the floor, she shakes her head. "Uh, no."

She mutters something unintelligible and then scurries away. Max squeezes my waist with his hands while the corner of his mouth quirks up. "That was pretty aggressive. I like it."

I chuckle. "I suppose that was a bit on the territorial side, but she sounded pretty adamant about getting you to go with her. She wasn't going down without a fight. I figured an obvious gesture was the best way to go."

I start to scoot off his lap, but he holds me in place. "I like it when you get a little territorial over me."

"Yet another thing you bring out in me."

Max's eyes smolder for just a moment. He gives my ass a light pat, then helps me slide off.

We head back to the car. After we buckle in, he glances at the back of my parents' SUV, which is packed with blankets, pillows, an air mattress pad, and other sleeping gear.

"You ever going to tell me what all that's for?"

I wink at him. "You'll see."

"Okay. Open your eyes."

Max lowers his hands from his face and turns around to look at the back of the SUV.

It's sunset and I've completed our car camp setup. The entire back is lined with the mattress, blankets, and pillows. I've Velcro-ed blackout panels along the windows for privacy, and there's one bottle of whiskey and one bottle of wine with a twist-off top waiting for Max and me to drink them.

As I sit in the front seat of the car, I gaze over at Max, waiting for him to say something. The neutral expression on his face sends a wave of nerves through me.

"I know this isn't ideal," I say quickly. "But because this trip was so last-minute, I couldn't find an open hotel or Airbnb that didn't cost hundreds of dollars a night. I'm sorry, I should have asked you first if you'd even be open to sleeping in the car—"

Max turns his head at me and grins. "This is fucking awesome."

Then he grabs my face with both of his hands and pulls me in for a kiss. When he lets me go, I have to gasp for air. Then he chatters excitedly about how he's always wanted to go car camping since he was a kid. I smile to myself, thrilled that he's happy.

He hops out of the passenger side and sheds his jacket, sweater, and jeans.

I glance around the area, relieved that this stretch of road we're parked on is remote. I took a side road off the highway that leads to a quiet bit of land overlooking the coastline.

"Max, what are you doing?" I giggle as I walk over to him.

"Getting undressed for bed." He says it like it's the most obvious answer in the world.

"Oh. Right." I shed my coat and sneakers but keep my yoga pants and long-sleeve shirt on. Even though it's the middle of July, this close to the ocean the temperatures rarely climb higher than midsixties in the summer, and it gets even chillier when the sun goes down.

We crawl back inside the car. While Max lies down in the back, I reach over the front seat and make sure the doors are locked. And then I pull my laptop along with the bottles of alcohol out from under the front seat and turn back to Max.

"Nightcap?"

He grins and nods.

"I forgot to pack cups, I'm—" I'm about to say sorry when he leans up and kisses me.

"Don't you dare apologize for another thing. Okay? This has been the most amazing day because of you. Thank you."

I smile at him and peck his lips, then hand him the bottles. He stacks the pillows so that he's in a half-sitting, half-lying-down position, then twists off the cap and takes a long swig of wine before handing it to me. We snuggle under the covers, tucked into each other, drinking and cuddling.

"I downloaded some shows and movies on my laptop," I say. "In case you were bored and want to watch something."

"I'm not even close to bored. I'm having the best time."

He sets the wine bottle off to the side. I look up and see the start of a grin tugging at his lips. "Actually."

I scoot to the side, giving him room to lean up all the way and reach for something in the front passenger seat. He grabs the backpack he brought with him, unzips the front pocket, and pulls out the steamy erotica book I sabotaged his most recent book club with.

"I brought this in case we wanted something to read," he says.

I notice there's a bookmark stuck in the pages, about two-thirds of the way through.

"You're reading it?" I elbow him.

He nods. "I had to find out what all the fuss was about." His eyebrow twitches as he looks up at me. "And I've gotta say, I definitely agree with the rest of the club. That threesome scene is hot."

I flash a smug smile at him. "It's one of my favorite books. I'm all about a descriptive and drawn-out love scene."

His grin turns sly. "Me too."

I snatch the book from his hands and thumb through the pages. "The writing is so realistic. Like, I've never read such an engrossing love scene before. Especially one involving three people. That felt so real, at least from my perspective. Well done to the author."

Max swigs more wine, then gazes at me. "Wait, have you . . . had a threesome before?"

I focus on the book, trying to appear as nonchalant as possible. "It was so long ago, I can barely remember." I love how he's so intrigued at what I'm saying.

The corners of his open mouth turn up and he looks away

from me, shaking his head. "Holy shit, really? I mean, that's pretty sexy . . ."

I burst out laughing. "I haven't. I was kidding."

"Oh." His cheeks flush fiery red.

I snuggle back into him. "Have you?"

Closing his eyes, he licks his lips, like he's relishing the feel of my breath that close to his skin. He twists his head to me and then opens his eyes. "Yeah. Once."

I gasp. "Really?"

He chuckles and nods, his eyes downcast, like he's slightly embarrassed.

"Well, come on now. Details!"

I squeeze his arm and he shakes his head. "No way in hell," he laughs.

I tilt my head at him. "Aww, come on. I don't mean, like, nitty-gritty stuff. Just if you enjoyed it. I'm curious. And very open-minded."

His eyes bulge slightly at my teasing. Then he reins in his expression. "It's not something I'm interested in doing again."

"That's totally fine."

"It was a long, long time ago. Like, ten years ago. It was fun and I don't regret it, but I don't have the desire to repeat it."

"Fair enough."

Admittedly the thought of sharing Max with another person isn't something I'm into. It would make me pretty jealous. But it's fun to tease him about it. And the fact that we can talk about past experiences so openly and comfortably endears me to him even more—and turns me on too. I've never felt that way with anyone before.

I maneuver so I'm lying on my left side facing him. I bite my lip and slide my hand up his shirt. "Okay, so this whole chat is turning me on, but we don't really have room in here to do a whole lot of . . . moving."

The vein that runs along the length of his throat pulses. He swallows and shifts slightly. I notice a bulge in his boxers. "Yeah, it's pretty unfortunate."

A naughty idea takes hold.

"Wait." Max looks at me expectantly.

I kick off the comforter to give myself enough room to take off my yoga pants and top. When I turn back to him wearing nothing but my bra and panties, his eyes turn to saucers.

"I'm liking where this is headed," he says.

I unhook my bra and toss it into the front seat, then I lock eyes with Max as I slip my hand down the front of my panties.

"We can do this instead." I bite my lip as my breath catches in my throat. "If you don't, um, think it's too weird."

Max lets out a sound that's somewhere between a grunt and a scoff, then rips off his boxers and his T-shirt in two seconds flat.

"Hell yeah," he growls as he tugs at the base of his length, his eyes on me.

I let out a breathy laugh, then slide off my panties the rest of the way.

"I hope that laugh wasn't directed at me." He smiles slightly before that concentrated look of arousal takes over his expression.

"I just . . ." I close my eyes, groaning softly as I slowly work myself with my fingers. "You got undressed so fast. I'm impressed."

I move quicker, savoring the ache between my legs as it slowly intensifies. When I open my eyes, he leans so close to my face, I can feel the hot breath from his mouth coat my lips.

"I can do a lot of things quickly if I'm tempted. And you, Joelle . . ." He shudders as he works himself in his hand, his eyes never leaving mine. "Seeing you touch yourself is the ultimate temptation."

My mouth is on him instantly. With my free hand, I claw at his hair, and we kiss each other breathless. Soon we're moaning into each other's mouths. Max's hand is on my waist, and then he slides down to squeeze my ass.

Something inside me takes hold. I grab his hand and push it between my legs to take over.

"Please," I whine. "I know we can't have each other the way we want right now, but I just . . . I need you to touch me."

He nods at me, jaw clenched, like he's determined to take this task and run with it. And run with it he does. His massive hand works me into a tizzy, and soon all of the muscles in my body are tense with pleasure.

"Joelle," he rasps against my mouth. "I want you any way I can have you. Always."

Even though I'm lying down on my side, I'm dizzy with arousal. God, even just his words are enough to send me over the edge. I clutch his bulging arm as the ache inside me builds. When I burst, he's right there to absorb it all: my screams with his mouth, my thrashing body with his own.

When I finally come down, I set my sights on what's between his legs. I reach down and take my time with him, relishing his ragged breaths and growls, how his muscles go tense, how his eyes focus when he breaks apart, and how shy his gaze turns when he's finished.

I press a kiss to his lips, then lean up to grab napkins from the center console to help him clean up. When we're through, we're a sweaty, panting mess, and the inside of the car feels ten degrees warmer.

"So much for all those extra blankets I brought."

Max chuckles, then pulls me against his chest and kisses the top of my head.

When I start to drift off, I hear the low rumble of Max's voice. "It's perfect. *You're* perfect."

I mumble, "So are you," before I fall asleep.

"Okay, first things first. When we get back to Portland, I've got to steam-clean the back of this car."

Max barks out a laugh from the driver's seat as we drive back to the city. "Oh come on. It's not that bad."

I twist around to look at the pile of blankets I didn't bother to fold sitting in the back.

"I need to. I can't stand the thought that my parents will be driving around in their vehicle, which you and I defiled, leaving behind God knows what—"

Max is howling. "Okay, okay. Fair point. Just the thought of your parents knowing what we got up to back there freaks me out. We'll get it cleaned up." He reaches over and scoops my hand up, then kisses my knuckles. "Promise."

As we drive home from the most amazing road trip ever, I'm floating. This was technically our first getaway outside the city and it couldn't have gone better. And it's a promising sign for us as a couple, because it doesn't seem like the setting affects our compatibility. Whether we're cramped in our shared workspace, holed up at Max's house, at a luxurious hotel, or spending the night in my parents' car, it's always the same. We have the best time together, whether we're laughing or sitting in contented silence or cuddling or screwing each other's brains out.

I know how rare that is. I'm through-the-roof giddy that I've found someone whom I can go anywhere with, do anything with, and we'll have the greatest time, always.

My head lolls on the headrest as the joy courses through me. I gaze over at Max, who's focused on the road ahead. There's a pulse that aches inside my chest at just the sight of him. I can barely swallow, it's so strong.

You're in love with him.

I nod my head in quiet acknowledgment, wondering just how long I can keep this to myself before it bursts from me.

The sound of his phone blaring is a welcome distraction. He pulls it from his jacket pocket and scowls at the screen.

"Everything okay?" I ask. "You can pull over and answer it, it's totally fine."

"Uh, just . . ."

I wait for him to finish speaking, but he doesn't. He just keeps looking between the road and his phone. Finally, he silences the ringer.

"You can answer it, Max. We're in no rush to get back."

"It's fine," he barks, then tosses his phone on the dashboard with a smack.

I go quiet instantly. Max snapped at me loads of times in the first weeks that we shared our current workspace, but we weren't a couple then, and I was giving it as much as I was getting it from him. Yeah, fighting sucked back then, but there's something different about being on the receiving end of his anger and irritation as his girlfriend. Before it stung; now it cuts.

"Sorry." The word falls out as a heavy sigh from his lips. "I didn't mean to snap at you."

I soften the slightest bit. "It's okay."

"It's not."

He stares ahead at the road and pulls his lips into his mouth. Like he's trying to decide if he wants to say more.

"That was my mom calling," he says after a minute of silence.

"Oh." And then I go quiet, clueless as to what else to say. He's only mentioned his mom once before, and the little bit he told me about her was upsetting.

"Why is she calling you?" I ask gently.

"She's sick. She has liver disease."

His curt, emotionless tone throws me. He says it like he's reading from a cue card.

"Oh my god. Max, I'm so sorry."

When he shrugs, I almost jolt. That's a hell of a nonreaction. Almost like he's unbothered.

His focused gaze doesn't budge from the road ahead as I stare at him and wait for him to say more.

"I can take over driving if you'd like to sit for a bit before you call her back," I finally say after a long stretch of silence.

"I'm not calling her back."

"Why not?"

I know this isn't my business, but I can't help my curiosity. The way Max's mom abandoned him is unforgivable. But it sounds like she's seriously ill and wants to get in touch with her son. Wouldn't that warrant at least a phone call?

When another long silence stretches between us, I speak.

"Max, I know it's not my place to say, but I bet it would mean a lot to your mom if you got in touch with her."

The corners of his mouth curve up in a bitter smirk. "Yeah, well, it would have meant a lot if she had been a halfway decent parent to me as a kid, but we don't always get what we want." As he sighs, it fades away.

I stammer for a second at his response. "Of course. I get that, Max. But have a heart. She's sick. I'm not saying you have to run and be by her side, but maybe just answer her phone call."

He shakes his head as he tightens his grip on the steering wheel. "You don't get it, Joelle."

"You're right. I don't. And I don't mean to tell you what to do, and I'm sorry if this is coming off that way. But will you just think about it? You don't have to make any decisions now, but it seems a little severe to cut her out completely. Maybe she's changed. Maybe she wants to make amends. Maybe she—"

"Don't defend her."

There's a bluntness to his tone that hits so hard, I fall into the back of my seat.

"Max, I'm not defending her. What she did to you was horrible. There's no excuse for it. But someday you might look back on this and regret not reaching out to her. I just know that I'd regret it forever if I fell out with a family member and rebuffed their attempt to reconcile. You never know what—"

"Joelle. Stop."

The way he spits my name pinches deep into the hollow of my chest, where my heart is. It carries the pain and bitterness of a curse word. I never thought my own name could sound so brutal.

"You don't know what you're talking about." For the split second he turns his eyes from the road onto me, I'm frozen. Despite the low volume of his voice, the disgust and anger are clear as the blue sky above us.

"Not every family is like yours, okay? Don't compare your experience to mine. We're nothing alike. Not even close."

Pain radiates from the center of my chest at the quiet anger and resentment emanating from him. I'm stunned by how, in the space of minutes, he swung from affectionate to so detached.

For the rest of the drive back to Portland, I don't speak another word. I just stare straight ahead at the road.

Chapter 18

Max

When I pull into my driveway, the tension between Joelle and me hasn't dissipated at all.

We haven't spoken a word to each other since my mom's unanswered call. Joelle hasn't even so much as looked at me. I don't blame her.

The way I spoke to her before we went silent on each other was harsh to say the least. And honestly, if someone had spoken like that to me, I would have been pissed. I might have even gone off on them. The fact that she's choosing simply not to speak is pretty kind of her, all things considered.

I just wish there were a way to explain exactly how I feel whenever I see my mother's phone number pop up on my screen—"anger" doesn't cover it. It's more like a cocktail of rage, pain, frustration, and bitterness, all mixed together with the heartbreak that's lingered over me like a thick fog ever since I was a kid. It wouldn't matter to me if my mom did a complete one-eighty this very second and transformed into the most selfless, giving person in the world. It wouldn't erase how she abandoned me as a child, when I needed her most.

How do I explain that, though? How do I tell Joelle all of this without sounding like a heartless jerk? Family means everything to her. And I get why she's so adamant about me considering getting back in touch with my mom. If she were in my position, I know without a doubt she would reach out. She'd give my mom the second chance she doesn't deserve—she's *that* kindhearted.

I just can't get there. I can't will myself to pick up when my mom calls. The most I could do was call her doctor back weeks ago in June when he left another voice mail telling me about her deteriorating health. I was so consumed with shock that it took days to process it all. It's why I was such a jerk at work, why I snapped at Joelle so often, which led to a lot of our fights at the time. It threw me for a loop that I was even on my mom's emergency contact list after not talking to her for years, and especially after what I said to her the last time we saw each other in person . . .

You're not my mom anymore. I don't ever want to see you again.

I notice Joelle fidgeting as she sits in the passenger seat, clearly waiting for me to make the first move.

When I twist to fully look at her, something inside me shatters. Her face. Even when her expression is neutral, there's still a joy about her. It's in the lightness of her eyes, the gentle way the corners of her mouth curve up the slightest bit, like she's on the verge of a smile, always.

But right now, she's hurting. I can tell. Her gaze is tinged in sadness and worry. And it's because of me.

"You wanna come inside for a bit?" I say gently, the first time either of us has spoken in a while. "My neighbor has been looking after Muffin and Doughnut while I was gone, but I know they'd love to say hi to you."

She nods and follows me inside. When Muffin gallops up to Joelle and licks her hands as she pets her, she smiles. I'm grateful that Muffin could lift her mood a little after everything I've done to bash it.

I grab her a glass of water from the kitchen as she settles on the couch with Muffin. When I sit down next to her, I notice she stiffens slightly before scooting away. Damn. That hurts. I deserve it, though.

Joelle's delicate fingers scratch behind Muffin's ears. I almost laugh at the dopey look in Muffin's eyes, she's so content. It's clear she's fallen hard for Joelle—just like I have.

I gently grab her hand in mine and wait for her to look at me.

It takes a few seconds, but after studying our interlaced fingers, she finally looks up at me.

"I'm so sorry for how I acted in the car," I say. "I had no right to go off on you like that. You were just trying to help."

I pull her hand to my mouth and kiss the back of her knuckles softly. Her eyes flutter the slightest bit.

"It's okay," she says softly. "I was overstepping by pushing for you to do something you're clearly not comfortable with."

"Yeah, but I could have told you how I felt in a nicer way. There was no excuse for me to be a dick."

She nods, but judging by the faraway look in her eyes, there's still something on her mind.

"Tell me what you're thinking," I say gently.

She hesitates for a moment. "I'm so sorry for what you're going through right now. And I'm sorry to hear about your mom." She bites her lip, like she wants to say more. "I just wish I knew what to say to make you feel better, to help somehow. But I feel like sometimes I say the wrong thing and make things worse. I mean, remember that day I tried to ask you out and babbled sexual things about bone marrow instead?"

I squeak out a weak chuckle.

She swallows and shakes her head, her expression back to serious. It's like she's frustrated with herself. "And now *I* feel like the jerk because here I am making this moment about me when you're the one who's going through all this—you're the one who deserves support."

"Joelle, no." I clutch her hand to my chest. "It's not like that at all. You've been here for me, supporting me so much. I can't even tell you how much it means."

Her eyes light up the slightest bit when I say that.

"You make me so happy," I say. "Happier than I've ever been."

The corner of her mouth quirks up, and it feels like fireworks going off inside me.

"I'd be a disaster without you," I say.

With that, she pulls her hand from my chest. For a split second I panic at the loss of contact, but then she scoots toward me and hugs my chest.

"I'm here for you, Max. Always."

Those words. Every time she says them, they land like an arrow to my heart. They're a reminder that I've got her in my corner. And I want her to know that I'll be there for her too. Always.

"I'm here for you too, Joelle. Always, no matter what."

The way she melts into my body softens me. I'm head over heels for this woman, and I fucking love it.

Love.

The word echoes in my mind.

I wrap my arms around her and kiss the top of her head. For a quiet minute we just hold each other. I close my eyes and relish the feel of her against me.

Without her I'd . . .

The thought cuts off in my head.

Without Joelle.

Just imagining that scenario has me panicking.

Love.

An unfamiliar ache claims my throat as my heart races.

Love.

It rings louder in my head until it's the only word I know.

Love.

I glance down at Joelle, cuddled into my chest, blinking slowly, her delicate shoulders rising with each breath she takes. And that's when it hits me. I don't ever want to know a life without Joelle. Because I'm in love with her.

The thought lands like a brick to the head, but in the best way. Because the impact of that realization leaves me in a daze. It's like I'm floating. The most thoughtful, beautiful, kind, funny, and loyal person I've ever met—and she's with me.

And I love her.

I open my mouth to say it but stop myself. What shitty timing that would be, while we're in the middle of an emotional conversation about my damaged relationship with my mom.

I take a beat, swallow, and refocus. I run my fingers through that wavy black hair, close my eyes, and breathe in. That flowery fruity smell I've come to crave coats the insides of my lungs.

I'll tell her soon. Just not now.

"I don't know how to navigate this mess with my mom," I say after a minute.

"It's okay that you don't," Joelle says. "It's a complicated situation, and you're entitled to all of your feelings. I'm sorry that I didn't say that sooner. I should have. And I'm sorry that I tried to oversimplify it in the car. That was insensitive of me."

"Hey." I sit up and maneuver her in my arms so that she's turned to me. With my hand hooked under her chin, I gently tilt her face to me. "Stop apologizing, okay? This is my own mess and I'll admit, I don't have the slightest clue how to handle it. But I am going to spend more time thinking about what I need to do. You've helped me realize that I shouldn't be so dismissive."

The tiniest smile pulls at her mouth.

"But I need you to know this, Joelle. None of this is your fault. You have no reason to say you're sorry for anything. You've got the biggest heart of anyone I know. The way you approach every person and every situation with kindness, without any agenda whatsoever, blows me away. I love that about you."

The word "love" lingers on my tongue, just like the taste of her after a kiss. She smiles softly and the hesitation in those beautiful brown eyes melts, leaving behind tenderness.

"You really mean that?"

"I do. I love that about you, Joelle," I repeat. "So much."

She dusts a kiss to my lips. It feels a lot like a question, like she's asking me if in this moment, after everything that's happened between us, I'd be up for more.

Yes. With her, I'll always want more.

I return a slow, teasing kiss of my own. Things amp up and I pull her onto my lap. Soon she's straddling me with no shirt on,

I've lost my beanie and my own shirt, and we're groping each other.

I stand up, keeping hold of her. She wraps her legs around my waist, and I walk us slowly down the hall.

"Mmm, wait," she whines against my mouth. "I haven't showered. I'm so gross, and I don't . . ."

She trails off as I turn into my bathroom, then set her down. She shuffles her bare feet against the gray stone tile, an inquisitive look on her face as she looks around the narrow space bathed in neutral hues.

I push open the glass door and turn on the shower. Water cascades from the waterfall showerhead.

"Oh," she says as she grins and bites her bottom lip.

By the time we've helped each other out of our clothes, the water's warm. I help her in first, then step in. And then, under the hot stream of water, we resume our dirty kissing and grabbing.

"Wait, wait." She presses a hand against my chest, then reaches for the shampoo bottle on the ledge. "I do need to get clean first."

I laugh and follow her lead by shampooing my own hair and doing a quick rinse with body wash. She holds her hand out for the loofah, but I shake my head. "Let me?"

A devilish smirk tugs at her perfect mouth. When she nods and licks her lips, I have to take a second. God, this woman. The way she's sweet and filthy all at once is enough to make me lose it right here. But I refuse. Not before she gets what I'm dying to give her.

I work up a lather and run the loofah all over her body. I take my time, paying attention to every part of her. Those beautifully curved hips, the fullness of her thighs, the gentle curve of her waist, her arms, her hands, the swell of her boobs. And then I lather up my hands and slowly work between her legs.

She clutches both hands around my biceps, and her toes curl against the earthen-hued river rock that lines the shower floor. Her eyes go wide and pleading as she looks up at me.

I lean down to kiss her. "Tell me what you want."

"You. Just you. Please."

With her breathy request, I'm ready to burst. Not yet, though.

She reaches down to palm me, but I gently push her hand away. I want this to be one hundred percent about her.

When she presses her mouth against my shoulder and her sounds go louder and more frantic, I work my hand faster. She's panting, pleading, shouting. When I feel the sting of her teeth against my skin, I grin. Fuck yeah, my girl is rough when she loses it and I love it.

I love her.

She explodes against my palm, the weight of her body shuddering against me. I've got her, though.

I've always, always got you.

When she starts to ease back down, she lets out a breathy laugh. "Oh my god."

I nod down at her, which only makes her laugh harder. Then she glances down at what I'm sporting between my legs and flashes a naughty smirk. "Let's do something about that."

Soon it's me at the mercy of her hands. My head spins at the pleasure she delivers so confidently, like she knows every single one of my buttons to push.

When I lose it, I'm shuddering and grunting. For a few seconds, my vision's blurry. She's that incredible.

Soon she comes back into focus. The flicker in her eyes, the most angelic smile, pure tenderness and joy in her expression as she gazes up at me. I'm toast. I've lost all my words except for one.

Love.

I ache to say it as water rains around us, creating the most surreal shield. Nothing and no one can penetrate this bubble we've created for ourselves.

But before I can utter a word, she places her hands on my shoulders and pulls me down to her mouth. Another slow, long, teasing kiss. It goes on for more seconds than I can count, until all I can hear is the thud of my heartbeat in my ears and the sound of our pants. And then I decide that *this* is a perfect moment on its own, these seconds where there are zero words exchanged between us, where it's just our bodies expressing what we feel for each other.

I tuck that four-letter word away for later on, when we're not making up after an argument—when we've been dating longer than a month. I'd probably sound like a lovesick teenager saying it now. It's probably better to wait a little bit longer.

I can't stop thinking it, though. I think it as we spend the next few minutes in our shower bubble kissing and grabbing. I think it as we dry off and get dressed. I think it as we steam-clean the car. I think it as we cook dinner together in my kitchen. I think it as we snuggle on the couch and watch TV. I think it as we go wild on each other in my bed that night. I think it before we drift off to sleep, cuddled in each other's arms.

Chapter 19

Joelle

"You've been in such a good mood lately, *anak*. What's the occasion?" Mom wags her eyebrow at me as she rolls out croissant dough.

"Oh! Well, um . . ."

I can't help the blush painting my cheeks. Even in the dull shine of the metal refrigerator I'm standing next to, it's visible. Ever since Max and I got back from our weekend road trip along the Oregon coast just a few days ago, I've been giddy. I've been basking in the realization that I love him.

I didn't have the guts to tell him. The closest I got was when we were in the shower together at his place right after driving back. Looking into his brown-green eyes, clutching his wet skin, my heart racing, feeling his breath against my mouth and my skin, I was vibrating with the urge to say those three words that had been bouncing around in my head all weekend.

But I stopped myself. Instead, I grabbed him and kissed him. I decided I didn't want to come off like a lovesick schoolgirl, saying "I love you" to Max after just a month of being together. He'd probably freak out.

But I gushed my feelings for Max to Whitney as soon as I made it home, and ever since then, I've been glowing, vibrating with the joy of being in love with the most amazing man . . . and silently wondering when will be the perfect time for me to tell him.

Even though I haven't told Max, I can sense a change in me ever since realizing my feelings for him. The air feels crisper when I breathe. The sky looks bluer. Food tastes better. Stuff like songs and the sound of birds chirping hits differently. It's like I'm hearing something extra in the melodies, something that makes my ears perk up in a way they never did before.

I shrug at Mom, fully aware of the cheesy grin I'm sporting. "Just had a really nice weekend away with Max, that's all."

"Oh, I bet," Auntie Elba says as she twists around from the stovetop, where she's finishing up the *ube* glaze I started for the batch of croissants Mom is rolling out. "Two days alone with that hunk? I'd be smiling too."

Mom and Auntie share a chuckle as I narrow my eyes at them both. Then I dart my gaze to Max, who thankfully hasn't heard them from his side of the space. He's busy showing his part-timer Reggie something on his laptop.

"So! When are you two going away again?" Mom asks as she dusts the metal table with a fresh sprinkling of flour. "You both work so much. You deserve some romantic time off."

I've been wondering that myself. I'm already dying to go on another getaway with Max, but things have been so busy for both of us at work, it's hard to justify taking time away again.

"Maybe you should hire someone to help out here at the bakery, like Max hired someone to help him at the bookstore," Auntie says. "That way it's easy to leave for a bit when you want to."

I don't miss the look that passes between her and Mom.

"That's a great point, *manang*," Mom says pointedly. I wonder if they rehearsed this. It sounds like it. "When Ivan is finished renovating, your bakery will have more space. It would be nice to have extra help, don't you think?"

"Oh, um. Yeah. Maybe. I haven't really thought about it."

That's not entirely true. Hiring part-time help was a pipe dream for the first two years that Lanie's was in business. I didn't have the budget for it, and with the family pitching in to help almost every day, I could make do.

But when I ran the numbers for my budget last quarter, I noticed that I was making enough to hire some part-time help a couple times a week. I just haven't been brave enough to pull the trigger. And I know why.

Just the thought of changing any part of the business, even a minor adjustment, sends me into hives. Even though hiring help is a small step in the grand scheme of things, it still marks a shift: my business would be growing. And when you grow, there's a risk that it could all come crashing down.

And I know what it's like to dream big and have it all implode. I remember the devastation I felt when I was eighteen and realized that I'd never be able to make my dream of going to culinary school and jetting to Europe come true, not if I wanted my family to survive financially.

The bigger Lanie's gets, the more there is to lose if for some reason it doesn't work out. I've got a firm handle on the way things are now: a small bakery that I can run on my own most days with the help of my family.

But if I build up my dream bakery with a staff of people and then something happens to ruin it all? I don't know how I'd cope.

"You know, we can pitch in and help you hire someone," Mom says in that same matter-of-fact tone.

Auntie starts to say something about how they've been saving a bit more money too that they can give to me, but I shake my head. "Nope. Not necessary. Thanks, though."

The slight curtness in my tone signals the end of that discussion. No way am I taking money from anyone in my family, especially after what they've been through.

"Speaking of the renovation," Mom says to Auntie, a clear attempt at changing the subject. "Have you noticed that the crew hasn't been in yet today?"

"Huh. That's strange," Auntie says as she vigorously stirs the glaze.

"Maybe it's a bank holiday. Or maybe they took the day off," I say.

A few customers walk in and I run over to the register to help them. When I look up from the register, a smiling Whitney waltzes in. She drops her purse onto a nearby chair and darts behind the counter to give me a hug before hugging Mom and Auntie. Then Auntie asks her to taste the glaze.

Whitney gives her an enthusiastic thumbs-up while making "mmm" noises as she licks her lips. "Oh, that's really yummy. It's so creamy. And wow, did you add something extra? Normally the *ube* glaze you make tastes like a nutty vanilla, but this batch almost tastes coconutty."

Auntie claps her hands as she beams. "You've got a good palate on you, Whitney. That's exactly what I added."

She and Whitney high-five before Whitney turns to me. "You're looking especially blissed out today, Jojo." She winks.

"Just feeling a bit loved up, that's all."

Just then Max stands up and aims a sexy smile at me. Mom, Auntie, and Whitney all wave at him. He and I laugh. Then he turns away to answer a phone call.

Whitney turns to me. "Have you told him yet?"

I bite my lip. "Not yet. I want to wait for the right time."

"Told who what?" Mom asks.

"The right time for what, *anak*?" Auntie inquires.

I refrain from openly rolling my eyes. My family is as nosy as they are loving.

"Joelle is in love with Max," Whitney whispers to them. "She's trying to figure out when to tell him."

Mom and Auntie squeal and clap. I shoot them a look and they quiet instantly. Max and Reggie look over at us, clearly confused by the noise. I shake my head at them to ignore the spectacle.

I groan softly. "Whit, really?"

She flashes an apologetic smile. "Oh come on, Jojo. It's so obvious you're in love. Your family was going to figure it out eventually."

I stammer, reluctantly accepting that she's right.

"Oh, *anak*. I remember when your dad first told me he loved me." Mom rests her hands on her chest, a wistful look on her face. "We had just shared a passionate night away at—"

I hold up a hand as Whitney's eyes widen. "Mom, please don't say another word." As much as I adore that my parents are still madly in love with each other, I don't want to hear any of the dirty details.

Auntie shakes her head at Mom. "My gosh. Keep it PG, will you?"

They start to bicker in Ilocano about something else, and I breathe out a sigh of relief that we don't have to hear my mom describe the physical passion between her and Dad.

I chat with Whitney, and she fills me in on how well that coding internship is working out at her company.

"They're expanding it so we can admit more students into the program."

"Whit, that's amazing!"

Max walks over to the counter. He leans over to me, and I tiptoe up to peck him lightly on the mouth.

"This is the first time you've had the chance to come over and say hi all day. Are you getting sick of me already?" I tease.

"Not even close." He tucks my hair behind my ear before tracing his finger softly along my cheek and ending at the bottom of my chin. Then he tilts my face up before dotting another light kiss on my lips. "We've just been slammed. Business is booming, thankfully."

"Yay."

"Aww, you two," Whitney teases before she walks over to help Mom lift a bag of flour.

Auntie darts over and hands Max a fresh croissant with *ube* glaze.

"Thank you, Elba. I've been dying for one of these."

"They're my specialty," Auntie says as she turns back to the stove. "No one makes them like I do. Sorry, *anak*, but it's true."

I chuckle. "It's okay, I'm well aware."

"Hey, did you see Ivan earlier when he stopped by?" Max asks. "He looked a little stressed."

"I didn't get a chance to talk to him during the morning rush."

"He seemed really all over the place," Max says. "Hope everything's okay."

I wave a hand. "I'm sure it is."

A week later, I'm eating my words. Clearly things with Ivan and the renovation are not okay.

It's the end of July and for a solid week, the renovation crew hasn't shown up to do any work. For the first couple of days, I didn't even think twice about it. Construction work schedules can be sporadic even at the best of times.

But yesterday marked a full week of the crew no-showing. And we haven't seen Ivan in days. When we've called him for a status update, he's never picked up. All of our voice mails have gone unanswered.

So today after work, we finally said screw it and walked over to the front of the building to see the situation for ourselves.

And now, as I stand next to Max in the middle of what was supposed to be the eventual new and improved Lanie's, I'm panicking. The schedule was already a month behind, but when Ivan broke the news about that weeks ago, I didn't care about a month. I was hooking up with Max and nothing could faze me.

But now, I'm faced with the very real prospect of losing my business space. Judging by the state of things, the crew isn't going to make the beginning-of-August deadline Ivan gave us—that's just days away. Which means Max and I won't be moving back into our store spaces anytime soon.

Panic settles like a sharp cramp in the pit of my stomach. I do another slow gaze around the bakery, which looks like a disaster. Butcher paper covers the new hardwood flooring, which seems to be the only part of the interior that's completely finished. Part of the ceiling has been removed, revealing metal ducts and wires. A stack of lumber sits in the corner, along with two brand-new windowpanes. Sawdust coats almost every surface.

When we make our way to Max's bookshop, it's a similar scene. Half of the wood flooring has been replaced, while the other half has merely been torn up. The ceiling is intact, but there's a giant hole in one of the walls that separates the actual store from his office.

Max gazes at it, a dazed and concerned look in his eyes. "What the hell were they even trying to do?"

I shake my head in disbelief. What does this mean for our businesses? Are we even more behind schedule now? Did Ivan have some sort of emergency, and is that why he's been MIA? Did he fall out with the crew?

A million scenarios flit through my mind, like a stack of papers fluttering around in a windstorm.

"Why won't Ivan just call us back?" I say, as I trip over an errant power drill.

Max reaches his hand out to steady me. Then he clenches his jaw and tugs at his hair. "I wish I knew, sweetie."

I wrap my arms around his waist and press into him. Just the sound of my pet name from him eases the panic spiraling inside me the tiniest bit.

His muscled arms squeeze me back. And then he sighs and lets go. "I gotta get home and feed Doughnut and Muffin, then take Muffin for a walk."

"I'll wrap up here and meet you there soon."

"Don't take too long, okay?" The hint of mischief in his gaze is enough to make me smile in this uncertain moment.

"I won't."

He pulls me in for another hug. "We'll figure all this out. Promise."

I close my eyes and breathe in his spice-mint scent, hoping that what he says is true.

After he leaves, I head back to the shared space to finish closing up. As I round the corner to the entrance, I spot Ivan walking up while glancing down at his phone.

"Ivan. Hey."

His eyes go wide as he stops dead in his tracks. "Hey, Joelle. I, uh, I didn't know you'd still be here."

The way he fidgets before shoving his hands in his pockets throws me.

I ignore his odd body language and decide that now's as good a time as any to ask him directly what's going on. "Max and I have been worried about the state of the renovation since we noticed the crew never showed up this week. And we never got a heads-up from you, so . . ."

I trail off as I take in the twist in his expression. He looks like he's in pain. He opens his mouth but hesitates. And that's when I notice the bags under his eyes and how pale his complexion looks. His dress shirt and pants are rumpled to hell, almost like he slept in them. Even his glasses are askew.

"Ivan. What's going on?" I try to sound as gentle as I can even though I'm stressed as hell about the situation.

He shoves both of his hands in his mahogany-brown hair. His

lips quiver. "Joelle, I'm so sorry. I'm so damn sorry for leaving you and Max hanging this past week, I just . . ."

His voice breaks and that's when the tears come. As sobs rack Ivan's body, I stand there, speechless.

"It's okay," I finally say after watching him cry for several seconds.

I rest a gentle hand on his arm, quietly observing how thin he feels in my hold. Ivan's a slight guy to begin with, but he's lost weight. What is going on with him?

I lead him slowly into the shared space and coax him to sit down. He rests his elbows on his knees and cries quietly, his face in his hands. I dart over to grab him a handful of napkins and bottle of water from the refrigerator on the bakery side.

"Here, drink this," I say as I hand him the water.

He mutters what sounds like a "thanks" through a whimper.

I crouch next to him. "Just breathe. It'll all be okay."

He takes three deep breaths, then a long gulp of water. I hand him some napkins. He dabs at his face as he shudders out an exhale.

Even though I'm dying to know what's going on, I don't push him. Ivan is clearly distraught and peppering him with questions will likely make him feel worse.

A couple of minutes pass, and I pull up a chair to sit next to him.

"Are you okay? Do you need me to call anyone to come help you?"

Ivan shakes his head, and a dejected expression settles across his face. "I didn't know you'd be here." He repeats what he said to me when I ran into him minutes ago.

He's not looking at me as he speaks. His gaze is fixed on some random spot on the floor.

"Well, I'm here. And I want to help you. What's going on?"

He finally looks at me. "I'm sorry, Joelle. I'm so fucking sorry." When his voice starts to break, he swallows. "The renovation . . . I don't . . . I mean, I think . . ." He lets out a breath. He sounds like someone just kicked him in the stomach. He scrubs a hand over his face. "It's a mess, Joelle. And I don't know how to fix it."

My brain struggles to make sense of the fragments he's said. "What are you talking about?"

"The renovation is over."

"Clearly it's not. Max and I walked over there a bit ago and they're maybe halfway done . . ."

I stop speaking when I realize I've misunderstood Ivan.

"I don't have the money anymore. It's gone."

My mouth hangs open as I struggle to process how in the world that can be true.

"What? Ivan, what do you mean you don't have the money? You said you've been thinking about this renovation, planning it, all that. I mean, yeah, it was a surprise to Max and me when you sprang it on us, but—"

He shakes his head. "Listen. I fucked this up. I fucked this up big-time. And I can't keep it from you guys anymore."

Dread takes hold of me, like a fist twisting through my lungs.

"Tell me," I say in a weirdly calm voice.

"Remember my dad? He was with me the day I told you and Max about the renovation."

It takes a second for me to pull up the memory.

"Yeah, I remember."

"We've been estranged for a while, but he came back into my life this past year." He winces. "God, I know how that sounds, but he's been in and out of my life since I was a kid. I guess I always kind of idolized him. Typical son, wanting to impress his dad . . . though he himself was never really all that impressive, now that I think about it."

He mentions something about how his dad would chat about all these mystery business ventures that he didn't understand because he was too young.

"He always had money," Ivan says. "I thought it was all okay . . ."

I'm unnerved. It feels like a therapy session with the way he's spilling his guts, but nothing is making sense to me.

"He started helping me manage my properties last year. I thought he was turning a corner. No more disappearing on zero notice and then popping up unannounced like he did my whole life. I mean, a whole year. He was good for a whole year."

Ivan's eyes fill with tears. I reach over and pat his arm. He nods a thanks and sniffles.

"A couple months ago, he came to me with this idea to go in on a renovation together. He did the research and ran the numbers, showed me how it would increase the building value and then I could refinance. He even convinced me to open a bank account together. It all looked and sounded good."

Ivan glances off to the side and closes his eyes for a moment. "I was so stupid to believe him. So, so stupid." He lets out a breath. "He took off with the money for the renovation. It's all gone. And I don't have enough in my savings to pay the crew to finish it. And I—I have no idea what to do now."

It's a struggle to make out what else he says. I'm too shocked. All I can focus on is that fact that my bakery and Max's bookshop are in shambles and could very well stay that way—and there's nothing I can do about it.

"Joelle? Joelle, are you okay?"

I realize that I've just been staring at Ivan and not speaking.

"Wait, what are you saying?" I sputter. "Are you saying that the building is just going to stay this way? That Lanie's and Stacked won't ever reopen?"

"I don't know," he says, his voice laden with fatigue and sadness. "I've been scrambling this whole week to figure this out. At first I tried to track down my dad, but he's disappeared without a trace. And when I realized that looking for him would be a lost cause, I tried to figure out a way to dig myself out of this hole. I've considered getting a loan to cover the rest of the renovation, but what I qualify for wouldn't be enough. I looked into liquidating some assets, too, but I don't have much. I pleaded with the construction crew to give me more time to figure it out, but they walked. I don't blame them. I mean, I can't expect them to work for free."

I nod to show that I understand, even though I'm the one on the verge of tears now.

"I—I even thought about selling the building to a buyer with enough money to finish the renovation as a last resort, but I don't know if that would work out. There's no guarantee the new owner would keep you and Max in the building. Once they buy it, they might raise the rent crazy high or kick you out. And I don't want to do that to you guys on top of what I've already done to you."

Ivan glances down at my lap and I realize I'm digging my nails into the tops of my thighs. My bakery, my business, my livelihood . . . it's so close to being over.

"I'm sorry, Joelle." Again Ivan holds his head in his hands, his bony elbows balanced on top of his knees. "I know this is the worst news I could ever give you. And I know that you must hate me—"

"I don't hate you, Ivan."

The shocked look on his face would make me laugh if the current circumstances weren't so dire.

But it's the truth. As devastated and freaked-out as I am about the uncertainty that lies ahead for me and Max, it's not Ivan's fault. His father is to blame. He cruelly took advantage of Ivan's kindness and love and betrayed him. Sure, it's Ivan's mistake and it's likely going to screw us over, but I don't have it in me to lash out at him. He trusted someone he loved—he trusted his father, one of the people you're supposed to be able to trust above everyone else. And his father made the choice to ruin everything for all of us.

"I could never hate you," I say in a quieter tone. "Your dad, on the other hand? I hate him a lot right now."

"Me too," he mumbles.

He downs the rest of his water. I hop up and swipe the bottle of whiskey Max keeps in the drawer of his console table, grab two paper cups, and hand one to Ivan.

He stares at me as I pour, like he's unsure of what to do or say.

"I think we could both use something stronger than water right now," I say.

He nods and takes a swig at the same time I do. We both wince as we swallow.

"I kind of know what you're going through," I say after a second. Ivan whips his head up to me, and I immediately regret my wording because technically I don't. I've never had one of my parents hurt me like this.

"What I mean is, I know what it's like to plan for something—to dream about something big and have it taken from you in the worst way. It's devastating. But I can't even imagine how traumatic it must also feel when the reason it didn't work out was because your own parent screwed you over."

Ivan blinks at me, like he can't make sense of what I'm saying. So I explain what happened to my family when I was eighteen and how their financial ruin led me to give up culinary school. The whole time he listens intently.

After a few seconds and another swig of whiskey, Ivan speaks. "I'm sorry that happened to your family, Joelle. And I'm sorry you had to give up your dream to help them."

"It's okay. I had my family. I've always known without a doubt that I could rely on them. Even when we had no money and were struggling, I never questioned their love for me. And I knew that they would always do what they could to help me, even if it was at their expense. Always. I'm sorry you never had that."

A weird sense of calm washes over me. Maybe it's part numbness because I'm still processing the shock of everything. But part of me really is calm. Because even if this is the end of my bakery, I'll still have my family. They'll help me in whatever way they can. They'll love me always. And I know beyond a shadow of a doubt that they would never, ever do something so hurtful to me. They'd rather endure the worst pain in the world than see a single horrible thing happen to me. That's something I've taken for granted my whole life. It's not something everyone has. Ivan doesn't. Neither does Max.

Max. I take another swig of whiskey when I think about Max and how devastated he'll be when he finds out about this.

A few minutes pass, and Ivan stands up.

"Where are you going?"

He runs a hand through his dark wavy hair. Even blinking seems to take an extra second for him given that he looks wrecked with exhaustion.

"Not sure," he says. "But I need to do something. I don't know what yet, but I promise you I'm going to try."

"Look, I'm not gonna lie, Ivan. I'm freaked-out right now. My brain is a jumbled mess and I have no idea what the right thing to do is," I say. "But whatever you decide to do, whatever ends up happening, please keep Max and me in the loop. Don't ice us out. We're your tenants, and we don't deserve to be left out to dry like this past week."

A sheepish expression clouds Ivan's face. "You're right. I'm sorry I did that to you. I won't do that again."

"If Max or I call you, please answer your phone. Even if there ends up being nothing you can do, we still deserve to know."

"I will. I promise I will."

For a second, I stay sitting while he stays standing, both of us saying nothing.

He starts to turn to leave, then stops himself and turns back to me.

"I know you have no reason to trust or believe me after what I let happen, Joelle. But I promise I'm going to find a way to fix this. Maybe it ends with me selling the building, and you never see me again. But I'm going to do everything I can to make sure you keep your space. I'm going to try my hardest to make this right."

I believe him. Maybe it's the conviction in his stare and his tone. He was so broken minutes ago. He couldn't speak, he was crying so hard. Maybe it's the way that he's standing now—tall and confident, like he's bracing himself for battle.

Or maybe it's simply because I can tell he means what he says. I know he's going to try like hell. Just like somehow he knew three years ago that I meant it when I swore to him that if he leased me the space for Lanie's—if he took a chance on me, an ambitious stranger with zero experience running a business or a bakery—that I would try my hardest to make it a success.

He believed me then, and I believe him now.

That doesn't mean it'll all work out. It just means he's going to try with everything in him. And that's enough for me.

So I say to him what he said to me then. "I have faith in you, Ivan."

His mouth curves up in the smallest smile.

"Thanks, Joelle."

When he leaves, I grab my things and head for Max's place.

Chapter 20

Joelle

When I knock on Max's front door, I can barely stand up straight.

My arms and legs are as heavy as cement. It's weird how physically exhausting it is to have an emotional conversation. As hopeful as I am that Ivan will figure out a way to save the renovation and the building, doubt lingers in the back of my mind. There are so many ways for this to go wrong.

The door opens to reveal Max's grinning face, interrupting my thoughts.

"Hey. I was just about to call you." He steps aside to let me in.

"I guess I did take a while."

Either my defeated tone or the fact that I can barely smile at Muffin as she greets me tips Max off that something's wrong.

He pulls Muffin off me by her collar, then tells her to go sit on her bed, which is at the far side of the living room. She trots away and he turns back to me and reaches out to gently grab my hand.

"Is everything okay?"

I shake my head. He starts to press, and I lead us to sit on the couch.

"Ivan came to the building after you left."

Max's brow furrows. "What happened?"

I take a breath and tell him the entire disaster story. About how the renovation has halted due to Ivan's dad stealing the money they pooled together to pay for it. About how devastated Ivan is, how he was sobbing inconsolably for minutes. About how he's scrambling, thinking of everything to figure out a way to fix this potentially unfixable mess.

The whole time Max listens quietly. The only indication that he's upset is the way his eyes widen slightly and the clench of his jaw.

When I finish, I reach over and take Max's hand. "I'm sorry."

He frowns at me, and I know what he's going to say—that I don't need to apologize when I didn't do anything wrong.

But then the look on his face softens. And then he just nods, like he appreciates my empathy in this moment.

Despite what a dumpster fire this situation is, I relish the silence we share while holding each other. There's nothing we can do right now, but at least we have each other.

After a minute, he lets go of my hand and stands up, then walks over to the kitchen and swipes his phone off the counter.

I sit up. "What are you doing?"

Instead of answering me, he quickly dials a number and walks off to the side of the kitchen so I can't see him.

"Hey, Reggie. It's Max. Can you call me back please when you get the chance? It's urgent."

I relax against the couch, realizing he's calling his employee, probably to keep him informed of what's going on. And then I deflate slightly when I realize that I'll have to tell my family too when I go home.

When Max walks back out into the living room, I expect him to sit back down with me, but instead he stares at his phone, his finger flying across the screen as he paces around the space. Muffin pops her head up, her inquisitive eyes following Max as he strides back and forth. Doughnut, who's curled up on his bed under the nearby side table, barely glances up at him before yawning and falling back to sleep.

"Max, why don't you sit down?"

Just watching him stomp back and forth exhausts me.

"I can't just sit here and do nothing, Joelle."

I frown at the dismissiveness in his tone. "What's that supposed to mean?"

He stops walking, then looks up at me. "Nothing. Sorry."

But the way he clenches his jaw even harder makes it difficult to believe him.

I stand up and look at him. "Look, there's not a lot we can do right now, okay? Why don't we just take the rest of the evening to process everything and—"

"And what? Leave it all to Ivan to sort out?" He tugs off his beanie and tosses it onto the nearby armchair. "What a great idea. That's worked out well so far."

I catch the start of an eye roll. But before I can call him out, his phone rings. He answers it immediately.

"Hey, Reggie. Thanks for calling me back."

I start to turn back to the couch, but Max says something that causes me to stop midstep.

"Your sister is an investigator, right? Would she know how I can go about tracking someone down who's just stolen a large amount of money?"

My jaw falls open as I listen to Max's end of the conversation.

"Can you give her my info and tell her to call me as soon as she can? Thanks, man."

When he hangs up, I'm speechless. "Are you seriously calling an investigator on Ivan and his dad?"

Max looks up from his phone, his expression incredulous. "Why wouldn't I? They're on the verge of ruining us."

"Ivan didn't do this, his dad did."

"Fine. I'll explain that to the investigator when they get hold of me. Maybe we can talk to Ivan and get him to give us info on his dad so they can track him down more easily. Maybe then we can go to the police too. It'll be easier to arrest him and start sorting out this shit show the more information we have."

I hold up a hand. "Whoa, hold on a minute. That's not really our place to demand that of Ivan, at least not right now. He's just started to sort through all this. Max, he's emotionally distraught over what's happened."

"Yeah, and I'm pretty distraught over possibly losing the storefront for my business," he spits. I don't respond.

After a second, he throws his hands up. "You can't seriously think that the best thing for us to do is just sit back and do nothing?"

"I never said that we should do nothing. I just said that it might be best for us to take tonight to gather our thoughts."

He tilts his head to the side as he looks at me, like he can't believe I've said that.

"Besides, Ivan said he was going to try his best to figure out a way to fix this," I say. "Can't we just give him a bit of time?"

"God, Joelle." A bitter laugh falls from Max's lips as his gaze flits off to the side, like it's taking too much effort to even look at me. "I know you want to see the good in everyone around you, but sometimes people are absolute pieces of shit, and they'll fucking ruin you if you let them, family or not. And if we just sit here and wait for Ivan to figure this all out, I promise you, we'll be beyond fucked."

I've heard Max swear plenty before, but not like this. Not in such an angry tone lobbed right at me. Not while he's insulting my character.

"Wow. That's a low blow." I stumble back.

His hard expression eases the slightest bit, like he's just now realizing what he said.

He holds up his hand at me. "I know you mean well, but please think rationally about this."

I swallow fury at his patronizing tone and even more patronizing words.

"Max, Ivan is a good person. Yeah, he made a mistake with his dad, and I'm just as pissed about it as you are. I've worked so damn hard to establish Lanie's. To see it like this—halfway torn down and on the verge of ruin—kills me. But Ivan didn't mean to do this. We can give him a bit more time before we sic the FBI on him or whoever you think is gonna swoop in and solve this problem. Look, we have the shared space still. In the meantime, we can keep working there until we find out more."

Max scoffs and rolls his eyes in full view of me. I bite down hard so I don't scream.

"Is that honestly what you want to do, Joelle? Keep working in that cramped hellhole on the off chance that Ivan is going to get his shit together, track his dad down, magically procure the money that went missing, and then finish the renovation? Then what? We'll just move back into our storefronts and pretend like this bullshit never happened? Please for the love of god tell me you're not that naïve."

A strangled noise escapes my lips. Who the hell is this guy? This man who clearly thinks I'm an idiot who has no clue how to handle a crisis? How the hell is this the same guy who's made me melt with the sweetness of his words, who baby-talks to his rescue dog and cat?

I step toward him. "Don't you dare speak to me like I don't know anything. I've worked in that building longer than you have. I've known Ivan longer than you have too. He gave me a chance when he first leased that space to me. When no one else would, he did. He hasn't charged us rent ever since we started working in the shared space. The least I could do—the least *we* could do—is wait longer than an hour after he breaks the news to us before losing our shit on him."

Another joyless chuckle falls from Max's lips. He starts to turn to walk away from me, but I catch him by the wrist and make him face me.

"Ivan just got the devastating news that his dad betrayed him. Don't you get how traumatizing that is? God, just give it a minute before you go on some vigilante hunt, will you?"

He jerks his hand out of my hold and scowls down at me. Suddenly I feel so tiny and insignificant. I've never felt that way around Max before. Ever.

"Are you always gonna do this, Joelle? Make excuses for people and their shitty families even when they don't deserve it? I get that family means everything to you, but if you keep that attitude up, you're never going to get past where you are."

"Um, excuse me? Where exactly am I, Max?"

He inhales, then closes his mouth, like he knows he shouldn't be thinking what he's about to say.

"Tell me." I'm so loud, Muffin whines from her bed.

"You're a pushover, Joelle. You let people walk all over you and you don't even know it. All those free pastries you give out to Clarence and whoever else you see who's down on their luck? How you let random teenagers and elderly people stay in your bakery for hours after buying only one thing? How you barely put up a fight when Ivan first proposed the idea for the renovation? That costs you money, Joelle. You can't afford to be so weak forever, okay? If you don't do something to change that about yourself, it's going to cost you everything someday."

His words land like a rock chucked at my face. I have to bite the inside of my cheek to keep from crying. I can't believe the man I love thinks so little of me.

"I'm not a fucking pushover." I jab my finger at his chest. He doesn't budge. Annoyed, I drop my hand back to my side. "I just understand where Ivan is coming from. I'm not some unfeeling robot who lives to wage war on everyone who wrongs me. And it's ten times harder when the person who wrongs you is your family."

"Is it? I wouldn't know." Max's sarcastic tone breaks the last of my resolve.

I blink and a tear falls down my cheek. It doesn't faze him, though. His expression remains stony as he glares down at me.

"Of course, you wouldn't understand how messy family can be. I don't expect *you*, someone who's never been part of a family in his entire life, to know anything about that."

Max's scowl melts from his face the instant those words fall from my mouth. And when I realize what I've said, I lose all the air in my lungs. "Harsh" doesn't begin to describe it.

I can tell by the way his mouth parts open slightly, the way his brow hits his hairline, like he's still absorbing the shock of my insult, that I've landed an insanely painful blow.

I fall back a step, then clench both hands into fists. Even the sharp pain of my fingernails digging into my skin does little to ease the dread washing through me right now.

I say his name, but he spins away, shoulders hunched, and walks into the kitchen.

"Just leave, Joelle."

His mutter is without spite or spirit or anything resembling the energy that coursed through him just seconds ago.

I stare at his broad back, shaken at how slumped over and defeated he is.

"Max, I—"

"Leave."

I give Muffin one last pat on the head and Doughnut a scratch under the chin. Then I grab my purse, stumble out of Max's house, and sob the entire drive home.

When I get into child's pose, the urge to cry hits. Again. Damn it.

I close my eyes and try to breathe. Over and over I force air into my lungs, then back out again. It does nothing to ease the pressure in my chest or the burn in my eyes.

When I feel a hand on my shoulder, I open my eyes and twist my head to the side. There's Whitney, concern marring her otherwise cheery face. Her eyes water as she stares at me.

"I'm sorry," she mouths quietly as the instructor of our yoga class quietly paces around the dim room, reminding us to gently breathe in and out as we wait for the sun to rise.

A hot tear falls down my face, landing on the pink cushy material of my mat. I scrunch my mouth to keep from bursting into full-blown sobs.

Going to yoga today was a terrible idea.

But I get why Whitney pushed for it. I'd been holed up in my apartment crying in the week since Max and I fought and broke up. I only ventured out once—the morning after our fight, to go to work. Even though I had spent the night crying, I was hopeful then. I hadn't reached out to call or text Max, thinking that it would be best to give us the night away from each other, then we'd see each other at work and talk things out.

Because of those words—that promise we made to each other all those weeks ago.

Here for you. Always.

I meant it every time I've said it to Max. And I believed that he meant it when he said it to me. Yeah, we had a horrible argument, but my promise still held true. No matter what, I want to support him through anything. And I thought we'd be there for each other and figure out a way to get through this mess.

But when I arrived at work, Max wasn't there. When I asked his part-timer Reggie where he was, he said that Max decided to take some personal time away from work and would be gone for the foreseeable future.

I was stunned and confused at first. I immediately called and texted Max, hoping with everything in me that he'd pick up, we'd apologize to each other, and work this whole thing out. But my calls went straight to voice mail, and my texts went unanswered.

Max couldn't have made it any clearer. He was done with me.

I've been existing in a heartbroken stupor since then. The whole time Whitney has watched me cry nonstop and barely leave my bed. And, like the amazing best friend she is, she took off work and covered for me at the bakery, kept it running along with the rest of my family since I'm too heartbroken to function.

So when she walked into my apartment this morning suggesting that I venture outside for the first time in days, I figured I owed her.

I didn't want to, though. I wasn't even close to being ready to go out into the world again. I would have been just fine staying in bed, wearing that same pair of pajamas I've been wearing for days, refusing to shower, and padding around my apartment.

But I made myself. Because I knew it meant a lot to Whitney.

But now, as I curl into a ball on my yoga mat and give in to the sobs, it's clear I made the wrong choice.

I close my eyes to keep the tears from pouring. They do anyway. I cup a hand over my mouth to muffle the sounds I'm making. It's no use.

I hear Whitney quickly shuffling to sit up and scoot over next to me, and then footsteps from my other side.

"Oh, honey, are you all right?" the instructor asks.

I nod yes, even though I'm quietly sobbing. Least convincing gesture ever.

Whitney links her arm in mine and helps me up, quickly explaining that I'm going through a breakup. Even through my tear-soaked vision, I can see all the heads pop up in the dim studio, nodding their understanding.

She leads me out of the room, and together we scurry out of the studio and to her car.

"Oh, Jojo," she says after she buckles me into the passenger seat. "I'm so, so sorry."

She digs out a handful of fast-food napkins from the center console and hands them to me.

I wipe my face, blow my nose, and shake my head at her. "It's okay," I say, voice breaking. "I knew I wasn't ready to go out yet. I just wanted to make you happy. You've done so much for me this past week."

"Remember all the breakups you've helped me through? It's what being a best friend is all about."

When my face is halfway cleaned up, I look over at her. Her pitying expression makes my eyes burn with tears yet again.

"I'm just such a mess." I sniffle. "I know it's been a week, but I still can't believe things are over between me and Max."

She offers a sympathetic nod.

"I can't . . . I can't believe I said such a hurtful thing to him." Tears tumble down my cheeks. "After what he's been through. After everything he told me about his life growing up."

I battle the urge to sob by clamping my mouth shut. I stare out the window to spare Whitney from having to look at me in such a pathetic state. My chin trembles so hard, it hurts.

Just then she rests her hand on my leg. "Jojo, look at me."

When I finally turn to her, she takes a long breath. "What you said to Max was hurtful, sure. But he said some terrible things to you too. Don't give him a pass on that and then be so hard on yourself. It's not fair."

"Yeah, but . . ."

I can't fight her on that. It's true. We're both guilty of hurling insults at each other.

"But just because he said mean things too doesn't make what

I did okay," I say. "His family life and childhood were terrible. Traumatizing. And I used that against him. That's unforgivable. And clearly what I said cut him deep."

"Joelle, I know you're heartbroken. And I'm so, so sorry for the pain you're going through. You're my best friend and I hate seeing you so torn up." Whitney's eyes shine with unshed tears. "But you can't keep going like this. You have to figure out a way to move on."

Just the thought has my head spinning.

I throw up a hand. "Whitney, I can't. I don't know how, okay? I'm probably going to lose the building where I run my bakery. And I already lost my boyfriend. I haven't heard from Max since he took off and had Reggie take over at Stacked. I haven't heard from Ivan in just as long. I'm sitting in this weird limbo where I technically still have a space to work, but who knows for how long? I have no idea what to do to even start to move on. I just . . ."

My throat aches and I swallow.

"It feels like I lost everything. Again." I let out a soft cry. I drift back to the day I discovered my family's financial ruin, and how that night after I decided to forgo school and Europe in order to help them, I sobbed quietly in my bedroom.

"Joelle. Joelle, listen to me." Whitney grabs my hand to get me to look at her once more. "You absolutely haven't lost everything."

The certainty in her tone throws me. She sounds almost mad.

"I have, though. Whit, how can you look at my situation and think it's anything other than screwed?"

When she sighs, her shoulders slump. Then she turns to the steering wheel, starts her car, and drives me back to my house. I don't say a word when I climb out of the car and stomp up to my apartment above the garage. If I do, I'll burst into tears, and Whitney's seen me cry enough.

I walk straight to my bed, toss my glasses onto the nightstand, fall face-first into my sheets, and pass out.

"Wake up, Joelle."

The sound of Whitney's voice jolts me out of my groggy stupor, but I keep my eyes closed. When I don't get up right away, she gently shakes my arm.

"Joelle. Come on. Please."

Her pleading, tired tone compels me to open my eyes. She's sitting next to me on my bed, her angelic face pulled into a frown.

"Let's go."

"Go where?" I mutter, swiping at my glasses.

"It's a surprise."

I squint at the indigo sky through the nearby window. Crap, it's nighttime? How long was I asleep? Has she been here the whole time?

My bladder is screaming at me, so I run to the bathroom. When I come back out, Whitney gestures for me to follow her out of my apartment, which I do, my head in a fog. I owe her an apology for how I acted earlier today. I shouldn't have just walked out on her like that.

When she leads me to the living room of my parents' house and I see my entire family sitting there, expectant looks on their faces as they stare at me, I'm floored. Clearly this was planned.

"*Anak*, come sit." Mom pats the middle of the sofa.

When I fall onto the faux-velvet cushion between her and Dad, they wrap their arms around me and kiss me on each cheek.

"Is this some sort of intervention?" I mumble.

"Kind of," Whitney says as she takes the armchair across from the couch.

I glance up and see Apong Celeste gazing at me from her plush recliner, her eyes misty. Auntie Elba sits on the ottoman next to her, her pained gaze trained on me too. I feel like an animal at the zoo.

"We're so sorry to hear that you and Max hit a snag," Mom says.

I open my mouth to correct her overly optimistic take on our breakup, but she holds up a hand.

"But that has nothing to do with why we wanted to see you. We're sorry you're sad, but it's time to start focusing on other matters."

"Like what?"

Dad pats my leg. "Like your bakery—your business and what you'd like to do with it. Future planning sort of stuff."

"Um . . ."

Five expectant faces gaze at me.

"Honestly, guys, I think it's silly to even think about planning anything right now," I say. "I'm in a holding pattern until we get word from Ivan on what's going on or what he's planning to do next."

Inside I deflate. I held so much hope for Ivan to figure out a way to salvage things. But clearly, that's not going to happen. It's the beginning of August and I haven't heard from him since I ran into him at the building a week ago and he told me about his dad stealing his money and halting the renovation. If I weren't currently nursing the worst heartbreak of my life, I'd be calling him to get a status update, but that wouldn't make much of a difference. He'd probably just tell me what I already know: that the renovation is a lost cause, he can't fix it, and he'll have to sell to someone. Then I'll be at the mercy of a totally new landlord who will likely kick me out so they can finish the renovation and charge an insane amount of rent money to the new tenant.

"It's not looking good," I mutter. "And I don't know if I have the energy to come up with a new plan right now."

It's weird how adamant my family is about this. They know what a mess it all is.

I notice Apong's and Auntie's expressions flinch slightly, and a pang of guilt hits me. They've been working so hard for me this past week and I haven't even told them thank you.

"Thank you all for what you're doing to keep the bakery going," I say softly. "But I have a feeling this may be the end soon."

Mom and Auntie scoff, catching me off guard.

"No. No, no, no. Not the end, *anak*." Auntie sits up straighter. "Yes, this building and renovation nonsense isn't ideal. But if you think this is the end of your beautiful bakery, you're mistaken."

Mom nods along. "We're going to help you. Whether you like it or not."

"Um, what?"

Dad clears his throat, and I turn to him. "No matter what happens—if you have to move to a new building and start fresh somewhere else or if you can stay in the building and have to contend with higher rent, whatever it is. We're going to support you."

I start to groan. "You guys, I appreciate that. But you know I'm not taking money from you to finance my business."

"Too bad," Dad says.

His hazel eyes shine with a familiar gleam. I recognize it from when I was a kid and he'd listen intently while I told him the same stories and jokes over and over, always laughing like it was the first time he heard them.

"You helped us when we needed it most," Mom says. "You gave up your dream to keep us from falling into squalor. And now it's finally our turn to help you. If you let us."

"We have money set aside to help you, no matter what you decide to do."

My head twists back and forth between Mom and Dad as they speak. "What? How?"

Dad tilts his head at me. "Honey, do you really think we didn't learn something from our biggest mistake?"

He twists and grabs a folder from the side table and hands it to me. When I open it, I see a printout of an online bank account statement. At the bottom a figure is highlighted in yellow.

My eyes bulge at the figure. "What the . . ."

"That's yours!" Auntie says cheerily.

My head snaps up at her. "What do you mean, that's mine? Auntie, that's tens of thousands of dollars . . ."

She nods excitedly as she beams. "Yes. And it belongs to you."

"But . . . how?"

Mom explains that ever since their bad investment, she, Dad, and Auntie started researching more about saving and investing. The three of them started attending a monthly free personal finance workshop for senior citizens at the local library that offers classes on budgeting, saving for retirement, and investing. When they started getting back on their feet financially a handful of years ago, they and Apong all started putting aside small amounts of money every month in an account for me. Dad mentions too that every year he and Mom receive bonuses at their work and they've been setting aside a portion of that money for me.

"We've been trying to figure out a way to tell you about the account so we can hand it off to you," Dad says. "But we knew you'd fight us."

"You never take money from us," Mom says. "Even when we insist."

"But you deserve this," Apong says. "You did so much for us, Joelle. You still do."

"You saved us all those years ago when you gave up your college fund to help replenish what we all lost. And when you worked to help us financially," Auntie says. "This is our way of thanking you."

"It's not as much as was in your college fund," Dad says. "I wish more than anything that we could have given you every penny of that back."

Mom nods along, squeezing my hand.

"But this is the best we can do," he says. "And now's as good a time as any to hand it off to you, when you're facing a potentially big shift in your work life."

My gaze flits between all of them as they speak. Then I hold up both of my hands so I can have a second to process it all.

"Wait a minute. You guys socked away money for me for the past several years?"

They all nod. Auntie mentions that her son and daughter, who travel abroad for their jobs most of the year, sent some money to give to me too.

My eyes bulge. "Auntie, I'm not taking money from my own cousins—"

She holds up a hand. "They insisted, *anak*. I'd be living with one of them if they didn't travel so much for their jobs, but I just can't handle the constant moving from country to country at my age. They're grateful for the stability you've helped give me and this is their way of thanking you for it."

I stammer for a few seconds as my brain struggles to process all of this. "Whitney pitched in some too."

I whip my head at Whitney.

"Jojo, you know I have the money. I'm a programmer and my company pays way too much."

"But that doesn't mean you have to give me money."

"I know I don't have to. I *want* to. Remember how many times you've helped me out by catering work events?"

"Yeah, but your company always pays me."

"And all those times you let me stop by the bakery and snack on pastries. All those dinners you've cooked for me over the years because you know better than anyone just how dangerous I am in the kitchen."

I gawk once more at the highlighted figure on the bottom of the paper before looking up. "Whitney, even if I were to add all that up, it's not worth what you contributed."

"It's worth it to me, Jojo." Her tone hits me square in the chest. "You're my best friend, and I want to do this for you. Let me."

I stammer some more, then turn back to my parents.

"But . . . what about you? Your savings, your retirement—"

"We have money saved, honey. We all do," Dad says.

"Yeah, but it's not enough—it's not the amount that it should be by now."

"But that's not for you to worry about, sweetie."

He says it gently, but I don't miss the pointedness in his tone.

I straighten up and turn to him. "Dad, if you think I'm going to take that much money from you when my own family is in need—"

He grabs my hand gently. "We're not in need. Okay, yes, we're still a few years behind where we should be in our savings and retirement. But that's expected given the financial disaster we were in years ago. But we've been diligent about planning, budgeting, and saving for the past several years, and we've made up a lot. Mom and I will be able to fully retire in five years. Yeah, that's not where we wanted to be, but really, that's not that far off from where the target was in the grand scheme of things. We'll get our full social security benefits then too. That'll help a lot."

Auntie pipes in and says she'll be able to get her full social security benefits at the end of next year.

I turn to Apong.

"I'm okay too, *anak*," she says. "The fact that we all live together makes such a difference. Less expenses, sharing the burden, all that. It helps my retirement savings go a long way. That and all the money I win whenever I gamble with my friends."

I chuckle softly, still in disbelief.

"You don't have to worry about us so much," Mom says gently. "We have it all worked out. It's not what we initially planned, but that's what happens sometimes. And yeah, we'll probably run into some bumps here and there. But that's life. You figure it out as you go. We'll be okay."

I look at all of them, speechless.

Mom pats the papers, which are still sitting on my lap. "This way, you have some money to help you figure out the next steps for your bakery. Or if you want to move out to your own place."

"You want me to move out?"

"Oh, no! We want you to stay as long as you want. We love having you so close," she says. "But we know you're not a kid anymore. We know you want your own space too. And we also know that part of the reason why you're still at home is that you want to be nearby in case we need your help. But you've spent enough time helping us. It's time for you to do something for yourself."

This time when I tear up, it's not because my heart is broken. It's because it's swelling with the love I have for my family.

"You did all of this for me."

"Of course we did." Auntie hops up and sits on the coffee table in front of me, then grabs my hand. "You did a selfless thing for us when you were barely eighteen. You deserve every good thing that comes your way."

I open my mouth to thank them, but instead I burst into tears. As I cover my face with my hands, I feel the warmth of my family surrounding me. It's an awkward group hug, but I adore it.

When they release me, I look up and see that they're all teary-eyed and sniffling. Even Whitney is smiling as she looks on, her gaze misty.

"I can't believe it. Thank you all so much."

They all nod and tell me how much they love me.

I stand up to give Whitney a hug.

"I know this doesn't help with the whole heartbreak problem," she says.

I let out a soft, snotty laugh.

"But it's something good at least," she says. "Something else to focus on."

When we break apart, I hold her by the arms and look up at her. "It's not just good. It's amazing. Thank you."

I turn back to my family just as my phone starts to ring. I dig it out of my pocket and my eyes go wide.

"Who is it?" Whitney asks.

I hold up the phone to her and her eyes widen. I gaze down at the name on my screen as my ringtone blares. I didn't think he'd ever call.

I force myself to take a breath and then answer.

Chapter 21

Max

What the hell am I doing here?

As I walk through the hallways of this hospital, my hands are shaking. I ball them into loose fists over and over, but that doesn't seem to help. A cold sweat breaks out along the back of my neck. I reach up and rip off my beanie and tuck it in the back pocket of my jeans. Why the hell did I even bother to wear it? This is Phoenix, Arizona, in August. It's hot as hell.

I stop for a moment and step off to the side to catch my breath. I'm nervous as shit and it shows.

I spot a drinking fountain a few feet away, walk over, and gulp until I'm breathless. And then I lean against the wall and take a few moments to just breathe.

I'm here to see my mother.

That's a phrase I never thought I'd utter. Ever. But I said it when I checked in with the reception desk on this floor.

Now I have to actually do it—I have to see her.

Despite the slow, deep breath I take, I can still feel my heart.

It's racing like I've just taken a hit of speed. It's honestly sad that I feel this way. Normal people don't have a near breakdown when they visit their parents.

I'm not normal, though.

Joelle's words from last week ring in my memory, like an earworm I can't get rid of.

Of course, you wouldn't understand how messy family can be. I don't expect you, someone who's never been part of a family in his entire life, to know anything about that.

Even now, just the memory of her trembling voice speaking those words slices me. I didn't know that someone as sweet as Joelle could be so cutting.

Let's not rewrite history. She said it because you hurt her first, remember?

I rub my face with my hand and wince as I think back on all the shit I said. How I called her weak. How I lobbed insult after insult at her because she wanted to give Ivan some time to figure out our mess of a work situation instead of going after him and his dad, like I insisted.

I remember the tears streaming down her face. I remember the pain in her voice as she tried to reason with me. I remember how broken she looked when she walked out of my house.

Yeah, she hurt me with what she said. But she only said it because of how I hurt her.

And because it's true.

Even though it was one of the worst things anyone has ever said to me, Joelle was right. I was just so pissed in the moment after finding out about what Ivan's dad did. Stacked isn't just a business for me—it's years of hard work, it's my dream come true, it's what makes me happy. Just the thought that I could lose the storefront I'd spent so long building up killed me. Sure, I could move to a new building and start over. But that place is a second home to me. And to know that I could lose it because of some conniving, thieving prick had me seeing red.

But when I gave myself a few days to think about it, to let that haze of rage dissipate, I felt bad for Ivan too. That must have destroyed him, trusting his dad and having him screw him over like that.

It's not far off from what I've experienced with my mom.

A heavy sigh sinks my shoulders. I pull my phone out of my pocket and pull up Joelle's name for the millionth time. She's probably worried that I haven't shown up for work in a week. Or maybe she's pissed that I haven't called her or messaged her in just as long. She's probably destroyed that I deserted her at the worst possible time, that I went back on my word to her.

Here for you. Always.

Knowing that I'm doing the exact opposite of what I promised her sends a shooting pain through my throat and chest.

My thumb aches to tap it so I can call her and tell her sorry for leaving without saying good-bye, to explain to her that I just needed some time away to untangle the mess of thoughts and emotions inside me and that's why I've silenced all calls and messages on my phone, to beg her to give me another chance so we can work this out.

To tell her that I love her.

But I can't, not yet.

Her words were harsh, but they pointed out something I didn't realize until then.

No, I don't know what it's like to be part of a family. But I want to. Someday I want to have a family of my own—with Joelle, if she'll take me back. And to do that, I need to see my mom. I need to talk to her and figure out what the hell went wrong with us, so I don't make that same mistake with my own family.

I focus on the hallway in front of me. Her room is at the end of it. All I have to do is walk there.

So I do. I will each leg forward until I'm at her open doorway. And then I force myself to step inside.

I stop at the foot of her hospital bed and lose all the air in my lungs.

She's tucked under stark white bedsheets, a blue gown draped over her bony shoulders, eyes closed, skin pale, mouth open, her chest rising and falling with each labored breath she takes. Even her hair looks tired and spent. It used to be thick and wavy and blond. Now it's thin and dull.

Her right arm dangles at the edge of the bed. She's hooked up to a million machines. There's an IV, a monitor making a steady beeping noise, another monitor, and another machine.

"Mom," I say softly. She doesn't budge.

The word lingers on my tongue. It sounds so weird. So unnatural. I haven't said it in years.

"Mom." I say it louder. This time she stirs for a moment before moaning.

Then she blinks a few times before her eyes go wide as she looks at me.

And then she smiles. "My baby."

Her words land like a punch to my gut.

"Max," I say curtly. "Call me Max."

Her smile fades and she nods. "Max."

She moves to sit up slightly. I can tell she's holding back a wince as she adjusts her position. When the urge to help her hits, I'm thrown. It lands almost like an instinct. Like when I see a kid or older person struggle with their footing and I rush over to help them.

But I force myself to stay put.

"I'm so happy you came," she says. "Here, sit."

She points to the chair next to her. I sit down and rest my hands on the tops of my legs. I don't know if she was expecting a hug or a kiss. I don't know why she would after all that's happened.

But as I look over at her, I notice the pain in her eyes. She's hurt that I didn't move to embrace her.

I ignore the squeeze in my chest and clear my throat.

"It's really good to see you." She smiles once more.

"How are you?"

Terrible question, I know. But I don't know what else to say. We haven't seen each other in fourteen years. She's akin to a stranger to me.

Only she's not. She's your blood, whether you like it or not. And you came to see her for a reason.

She shrugs. "I've been better."

A chuckle escapes me, which makes her smile widen.

"How bad is it?" I ask after a moment.

Her mouth slowly turns down into a straight line as she looks around at the machines surrounding her bed. "I've got liver disease."

I already know this. When I finally called her doctor back, he explained her diagnosis and everything it entailed. But hearing her say it, seeing her, watching as her body slowly gives out after years of alcohol abuse hits so much harder. It's raw. It's real. And it's gut-wrenching.

The ache in my chest deepens until I feel something inside me crack.

"I'm sorry," I say softly.

"I did it to myself." She shakes her head and sighs. "I quit drinking last year, but I don't think that's going to make much of a difference at this point."

I nod, despite how heavy my head feels.

Just then she pats her hands on her lap and flashes a small smile. "But enough about me. Tell me about you. I wanna hear everything."

I hesitate for a second. But then I push against every urge that tells me to run out of the room and never look back, and I talk to her.

"I live in Portland. I run a bookstore."

Her smile goes wide. "I'm so proud of you. I knew you'd do something like that. You were always reading when you were a kid. My smart little guy. Do you remember how you read the most books out of anyone in your class when you were in fifth grade? No idea where you got that from. All the reading I do is skimming the covers of magazines when I stand in line at the grocery store."

I scrunch my lips in lieu of a smile and nod.

"I think you got it from your dad," she says softly, tentatively, like she's not sure if she should mention this at all. "He liked to read."

"I never knew that."

I swallow and go quiet, reminded that I know next to nothing about my father.

Her eyes fall to her lap and she fumbles with her bedsheets, like she regrets what she's said. The silence between us stretches until it's screaming in my ears. I shift in my chair and then start talking again just to break it.

I tell her about Muffin and Doughnut, about the house I bought a handful of years ago. I tell her that I run a book club at my store. I tell her that I got really into trail running and weight-lifting in my twenties. I tell her I'm a terrible cook.

The whole time she listens with a smile. And then her gaze glides to my forearm. "Well. Look at that."

It takes a second before I realize she's talking about my sleeve tattoo.

"Yeah. You were never a fan, I know."

"It suits you, though."

This time when she smiles at me, I return one of my own.

"So. Tell me. Does my handsome and brilliant son have anyone special in his life?"

I don't know why I didn't expect this question. It's a question that parents ask their kids all the time. It's also a question that makes my stomach churn and my eyes burn. I clear my throat to stave off the urge to cry as my gaze falls to the floor. I've done that plenty since Joelle and I split.

"I see," she says after a minute. "Girl problems?"

I hesitate, and her eyes go wide.

"Or, um, boy problems? Sorry, I guess I'm not sure, and I really shouldn't assume."

I make a weak chuckle sound. "It's okay. Her name's Joelle. And yeah, I guess you could say we're going through a rough patch. Actually, I think we're technically broken up."

Even though neither of us said the words "We're done," that's pretty much the overall sentiment of how we left things. I told her to get out of my house after we argued, and I disappeared on her after that. She's probably so hurt and upset that I did that—she's probably done with me.

"Well, rough patch or breakup or whatever, tell me about her."

I tell her that Joelle runs the bakery next to me, that I had a crush on her the entire time we worked side by side. I tell her she's the most beautiful, giving, thoughtful, sweet, and funny person I've ever met.

The whole time she listens intently, barely even blinking.

"She sounds like a doll. What happened?"

"Um, well, it's complicated."

I give her an abbreviated version of the mess currently happening with our building, with Ivan and his dad. I tell her how Joelle and I argued about how to handle it.

"Let me guess. You wanted to go rogue on the son of a bitch, and Joelle didn't think that was such a good idea."

"Pretty much, yeah."

"Gotta say, I like her already."

I smile softly and glance down at my boots before looking back at her. "We said some hurtful things to each other. And I just . . ."

It feels like there are a million tiny needles jabbing all over my skin as I try to get this out. It's the most unnatural thing in the world to have a heart-to-heart conversation with my mother. But I want to—I *need* to do this.

"Family means everything to Joelle. She's really close with hers. And she tried to get me to see that I should cut Ivan some slack because it was his dad who screwed him over, and that it must be so jarring to be betrayed by family like that. But I didn't care. Because family never meant that much to me."

She nods, like she knows exactly what I mean.

"I called her weak," I say softly. "Told her she was too soft for her own good and that one day it would ruin her."

Her eyes widen.

"Yeah, I know," I mumble. "And she told me I'd never be able to understand what she or Ivan or anyone else goes through because I've never been part of a family before."

For a few seconds we go quiet, the beeping of the medical machines the only sound between us.

"That part is all my fault," she finally says. "If I had been a better mother to you, you'd have a family, Max. And for that I'm sorry." Her eyes water and her mouth wobbles. "I'm so, so sorry for what I put you through. For how I abandoned you, left you to fend for yourself, then passed you off to whoever would take you. If I could go back and do it all over again, I would in a heartbeat." Her voice shakes. "I'd get help and try to kick that horrible addiction so I could be a halfway decent mother to you."

Tears plummet down her sunken-in cheeks. I grab the tissue box from the nearby table and hand it to her.

"I'd hate to think that my mistake could cost you your happiness, honey. That it could cost you a shot at your own family someday."

This time when the lump hits my throat, I can't swallow it back. It stays lodged, until my eyes start burning.

"I do want a family," I say after a minute. "I just don't want to mess it up like . . . I mean . . ."

"Like I messed it up."

Even though it's the truth, it still cuts deep to hear her say the words. She knows how badly she hurt me. It's obvious in her pained gaze, in the way she was desperate to reach out to me, in how she's treated this entire wrenching interaction between us like it's the most special visit in the world.

Then without warning, she sits up and reaches to touch her hand to my arm. "Listen to me, Max. You won't mess it up, not like I did. You're my good boy. You always were. Even with all the chaos and pain I brought into your life, you made it out intact. You grew up into a good person. You've always had the strength of character to do what was right even when it cost you so much. I couldn't be prouder of you."

I blink and a tear falls. I quickly wipe it away.

"Go to Joelle and apologize to her. Tell her you love her. You love her, don't you?"

I nod. "More than I've ever loved anyone before."

"Tell her that. And then tell her the truth. That you were wrong and that you're so sorry for hurting her. That you'll figure out the mess at work. That nothing is as important as her. That you want a life with her, a family, babies, all that."

I nod, and she gives my hand one more pat before letting me go.

"You make it sound so simple," I say through a sad chuckle as I wipe my eyes.

"It's not. But it'll be worth it."

We sit quietly together as I soak in everything she's said. And then I gaze up at my mother and look at her in a whole new light. Sick yet recovering from her addiction. Insightful in a way I've never observed her to be before.

She was a terrible parent to me when I was a kid. But she's different now, and I'm different now too. And the person she is currently is somebody I actually want to be around.

An overwhelming crushing sensation lands at the center of my chest.

"I'm sorry, Mom. For waiting this long to come see you. For

being angry at you for so many years. For refusing to speak to you."

She shakes her head. "You don't need to be sorry, Max. I deserved that after what I did to you."

"It doesn't make this situation any better."

She follows my gaze as I glance at the machines she's hooked onto.

"No, it doesn't," she says. "But I'm grateful that I get to see you right now. I'm grateful that you're talking to me. After everything I've done to hurt you, it's more than I deserve."

When I reach my hand out to her, it takes a second for her to realize what I'm doing. But when she places her hand in mine and I wrap my fingers around hers, she smiles so big.

"My baby," she says in a shaky voice.

I can't speak or I'll lose it. So I just nod and give her hand a gentle squeeze.

Chapter 22

Joelle

When I walk into the shared space, I glance around. It's well after we've closed. Maybe that's why Ivan asked to meet here.

I'm a few minutes early, but I planned it that way. When Ivan called me earlier to tell me that he wanted to update me on the status of his search for his dad and what that means for the renovation, I was stunned. He sounded so breathless on the phone that I had no idea what to think. All he said was that he needed to meet me at the building now because he needed to tell me something important.

I have no idea if that's good news or bad news. If it's bad news, it could mean that I'll have to leave this building. So that's why I'm pacing around the small shared space, taking it all in. The appliances in the back, the metal table where I've prepped a million pastries, the counter where I chat and laugh with customers.

And then I glance over to Max's side and take in the towering bookshelves, the console table he somehow folds his tall self behind whenever he's checking out customers or doing office work.

My throat starts to ache. If this is the end, I'm going to miss it so, so much.

I miss you so much, Max.

I pull out my phone, pull up his number, and fight the ache in my fingers to tap his name and call him. I have no right to reach out to him, not after this many days without contact from him. He clearly doesn't want to talk to me.

But I can't help the ache in my chest whenever I picture his face or replay his voice in my head or recall his taste on the tip of my tongue. I'd give anything to have him back, to redo that moment when I hurled those insults at him.

The door swings open and in walks a breathless Ivan, his button-up as wrinkled as a crumpled-up piece of paper and his hair a greasy mess.

"Joelle. Hi."

He heaves a breath and falls into a nearby chair. I grab a bottle of water from the fridge and walk over to him.

"Are you okay?"

He nods and thanks me as he accepts the bottle. As he chugs the water, I study him. Sweat drenches his brow, his upper lip, the bridge of his nose, all over his neck. It's August in Portland, so that means almost every day is sunny with highs in the mideighties. Definitely warm for this temperate city where not everyone has AC. But Ivan is perspiring like an interrogated criminal. His expression is so flustered and fatigued it's hard to read him. Is he about to give me terrible news?

He swallows, gasps, and looks up at me. And then he breaks

into a smile. "I found my dad. I got most of the money back. It's all going to be okay."

My jaw drops. And then I let out a cry-scream that makes Ivan jump. A second later I tackle him in a hug.

"Oh my god, Ivan! Are you serious?"

He lets out a muffled noise against my shoulder and I quickly release him.

He straightens his glasses and lets out a laugh. "I'm serious. It's a long story, but I promise you it's all going to be okay."

He babbles something about driving to the middle of nowhere, Nevada, with zero cell service, sleeping in his car, regaining legal control of some bank account, contacting the remodeling crew, and a bunch of other things I won't remember because the only thing I can focus on in this moment is the fact that my bakery and Max's bookstore are going to be okay.

We're going to be okay.

It's not until I notice the look on Ivan's face that I realize his tone has gone sad and nervous.

"I decided to press charges against my dad. For stealing the money. He's been taken into custody."

"Oh my gosh. I'm sorry, Ivan. That must have been such a difficult decision to make."

He nods sadly as he looks at the ground. "It was. But it's the right thing to do. I found out he's conned multiple people before me." He shakes his head like he's in disbelief. "I don't want him to do this to another person. It was a nightmare to go through."

He mentions what a struggle it was to track down the people and the businesses that his dad had made purchases from with the stolen money. Some luxury condo lease and a couple of cars.

He had to explain to them that the money was stolen, and thankfully they reversed the purchases to avoid getting involved in the legal claim Ivan had filed.

"I'm still several grand out, though. Dad decided that a weekend in Vegas would be fun and went nuts with the gambling," he says, his shoulders hunched. "I won't ever recover that money, but I'm thankful I was able to get most of it back."

I rest a hand on his shoulder. "The fact that you've been so measured and rational when it comes to dealing with your own family member in such emotionally charged circumstances shows what a good person you are."

He smiles slightly, but his eyes still read sad. "I appreciate that."

I pull up a chair and sit next to him. For several seconds we sit quietly, and I try to settle from the shock.

"His arraignment is next Tuesday morning," Ivan says in a weak voice. "I don't know if I should go."

"Do you want to?"

He doesn't answer right away. "Yeah, I do. It's just weird, you know? Going to my dad's arraignment for a crime he committed against me. How messed up."

"It's not your fault, Ivan. You're doing the right thing. The ethical thing. You should be proud of yourself."

He nods even though the expression on his face reads unsure.

"I can come with you if you want. For moral support."

His brow lifts in surprise. "I can't ask you to do that."

"You're not asking. I'm offering."

"You'd do that?"

"Of course I would."

A weak smile appears on his tired face. "Thanks, Joelle."

He stands up to leave but then turns back to me. "Oh, and I

tried calling Max, but no answer. I called the bookstore and Reggie says he's out of town."

"Oh. Um, yeah. I'm not sure where he is. Or what he's doing."

"I hope he comes back soon," Ivan says. "I want to tell him the good news."

"I can try to call him."

Ivan pats my arm. "You're the best, Joelle. Really."

When he leaves, I pick up my phone and dial Max. I still have a million things to say to him, the first of them being an apology, but hopefully this news about the building will lift his mood.

But there's no answer. I'll have to leave a voice mail.

"Hey. It's me. Can you please call me? There's so much I want to say to you, and I can't do it on a voice mail. Oh, and I have news too . . . really, really good news. So just . . . please call me back, okay? I'm here for you, Max. Always. I miss you and I hope you're okay."

And then I hang up and hope with everything in me that Max calls me back.

Chapter 23

Max

"You sure you've got everything you need?"

My mom smiles at my question. It's the fifth time I've asked this ever since I took her home from the hospital.

"Yes, I'm sure." She glances at the kitchen in her apartment. "I've got a fully stocked fridge thanks to you. I'm good to go."

"And you're sure you listed all of your meds for the pharmaceutical delivery service?"

"Yup. I'm happy I don't have to go to the pharmacy ever again."

"You double-checked your next doctor's appointment?"

She sighs, but her smile doesn't budge. "Yes, honey. I'm good."

I nod and shuffle my feet as I stand in the entryway of her apartment. I've been with her two weeks, and she's been discharged after regaining a bit of her strength. Even though she's still in serious condition due to her liver disease, her doctor explained that as long as she takes her medication, abstains from alcohol, and lives a healthy lifestyle, she can expect a decent quality of life.

She gazes at me, like she's looking at me for the first time.

"As much as I love having you here, you've got a long drive ahead of you," she says. "And you've got a special someone to see."

"Yeah. I do." Just the thought of Joelle has me giddy and racked with nerves all at once. I should have reached out to her days ago, but I've been busy visiting Mom in the hospital and trying to get her set up after she was discharged.

But now that I'm about to head back to Portland, I've got to switch my focus. I can't wait to tell Joelle about visiting my mom. She's going to be so happy for me.

If she forgives you for what you said.

That thought lights a fire under me. God, I hope she does, I'm aching to call her on the drive back. I've let enough days of silence pass between us. As soon as I leave here, I need to reach out to her to let her know she's been on my mind this entire time and that she's the first person I plan on seeing once I'm back in Portland.

I walk over to Mom. "Call me if you need anything, okay?"

She wraps her arms around me. It takes a second before I slide my arms around her and hug back.

"I will. Thank you, honey. For everything."

I close my eyes and squeeze her gently. Things between us aren't magically fixed, not by a long shot. But we're better than we were. I'm actually on speaking terms with my mother, and we're hugging. That's more than I ever thought would happen.

I head for the door, but before I even reach for the knob she stops me.

"You think I can meet Joelle sometime?"

Her eyes are shy and her tone is hesitant. She knows it's a hell of an ask given everything we've been through—and given the state of her health.

I nod anyway. "If I'm lucky enough that she takes me back, yeah. I know she'd love to meet you."

She flashes a smile and waves good-bye. I dart down the stairwell of her apartment building, then jog to my car.

When I take my phone out of do-not-disturb mode, dozens of missed calls and texts pop up. My voice mail is full too.

"Jesus."

Maybe ignoring my calls and texts for two weeks wasn't the smartest thing in the world to do given everything going on with Joelle and the building. But I've been so focused on my mom that I didn't want to be distracted by anything else.

I start to thumb through the missed messages but quickly lose patience. It'll take forever to get caught up with everything. There's even a missed call from Ivan, but I ignore it for now. I don't have the energy to deal with whatever news he has. I need to hit the road.

And call Joelle.

Apologizing over the phone isn't nearly good enough after what I've done, I know that. She deserves for me to grovel to her face-to-face—and I'm planning on doing that as soon as I get back. But I hate to think of having even more time pass between us before I can even try to make things right.

So I dial her number, then pull out onto the road and merge onto the freeway. It goes to right to voice mail. My heart sinks. That means either her phone is off . . . or she's blocked me.

I listen to a few voice mails on speaker as I drive, deleting messages from vendors about canceled deliveries for the store. My brain is scattered as I try to think of what to do next. If only I could just talk to her, to let her know that I reconciled with my mom and that I've been thinking about her this whole time . . .

The sound of Joelle's voice emanating from my phone jolts me.

"Hey. It's me. Can you please call me? There's so much I want to say to you, and I can't do it on a voice mail. Oh, and I have news too . . . really, really good news. So just . . . please call me back, okay? I'm here for you, Max. Always. I miss you and I hope you're okay."

I swallow past the squeeze in my throat. Her voice sounds so raw, like she's been crying—but hopeful too.

I'm here for you, Max. Always.

The impact of her words feels somewhere between a punch to the gut and a warm hug. Because after everything that's happened between us, she still wants to be with me, just like she promised. Just like I promised I'd be with her always, through anything . . . and then I broke it as soon as we fought, and I left with zero notice, then cut off all contact.

"Damn it."

I tap her number, hoping that this time she'll answer. But just like before it goes straight to voice mail. My anxiety spikes and I force out a breath, then breathe in again. I stomp the gas pedal, hitting ten over the speed limit as I weave between slower-moving cars along the interstate. I've already wasted too much time. I need to get back to Joelle. I need to explain what happened, why I left the way I did, why I went no-contact, and why it was all a horrible mistake. I need to make it to her as quickly as I can to show her that I meant what I said—I want to be there for her through anything, always and forever.

I try calling her two more times even though I know she won't pick up. But I need to keep trying. My mind races. How the hell am I going to get in touch with her when I've got a twenty-plus-hour drive ahead of me?

Then I have an idea.

I call the one person who just might be able to help me.

When Whitney picks up on the third ring, I'm as relieved as I am nervous. She's Joelle's best friend, and I'm certain she's told her everything that's happened between us . . . including the hurtful things I said and did.

"Well. Look who it is."

I grimace at the irritation in her tone.

"Hey, Whitney. I'm so sorry to bother you. I know I'm the last person in the world you want to hear from—"

"Nah, that would actually be my cheating ex-boyfriend," she says. "But yeah, after him, you're next."

"I guess I deserved that."

"Damn right you do. Do you know how heartbroken Joelle has been over you, Max? I've never seen her like that over anyone. Ever."

"I-I'm . . ."

"She cried the entire week after you left town and ghosted her. Did you realize that?"

A gut-punch sensation wallops me. I have to hold extra tight on the steering wheel. Christ, I hurt her. I hurt her so bad.

"Whitney, I—"

"She was inconsolable. Absolutely wrecked. She couldn't even get out of bed until I forced her to."

My heart shatters inside my chest. It feels like a thousand pieces of glass are cutting it open.

"Shit."

A sigh is the only response she gives me. I stay quiet, waiting for her to speak first. There's nothing I can say to make this better right now.

"Look, I'm Joelle's best friend, so she tells me everything," Whitney finally says. "That means I know what you two said to each other when you fought—I know she said hurtful things to you too, and she feels terrible about it. But Max, you really did a number on her by icing her out like this."

"I know. And I'm so, so sorry for that," I say quickly. I start to explain the reason why I left, how after our fight it made me realize that I needed to work on the issues I had with my mom, which prompted me to travel to her.

"I know I went about this in the worst way, I know I have to explain all of this to Joelle, but . . ." I huff out a shaky breath. "I love her. I have so much to apologize for, so much to tell her. But she didn't answer her phone the times I tried to call her just now and I'm terrified that means she's done with me, so that's why I called you—to beg you to help me figure out a way to get in touch with her." I stammer as I struggle to find the right words. "I . . . I know I messed up big-time. I wasn't around when she needed me the most. I know that's awful, but I want to make this right. I want to be by her side from now on, for everything, forever. Will you help me figure out a way to get her back? Please?"

A long silence follows. At first when I don't hear anything, I assume she hung up on me, but then I hear the sound of her exhaling.

"You love her?"

"So much. More than I've loved anyone."

Another long pause.

"Good. Because she loves you too."

I almost choke. "She does?"

"Yes. She is head over heels in love with you, Max. She told me after the weekend you two went to the coast."

The pieces of my heart slowly meld back together. "Th-that's when I realized I loved her too."

The chuckle Whitney lets out throws me off. "God, you two. So cute. You make me sick."

"Sorry?"

"Never mind. Listen. I wouldn't normally offer to help the guy who trampled on my best friend's heart, but you're different, Max. She loves you so much. And even though you both hurt each other, hearing you explain yourself makes me think you two can work through this."

I release the breath I've been holding.

"You really want to get her back?"

"Yes. More than anything. I'll do whatever it takes."

"Okay. Good."

I'm heartened at the lift in Whitney's voice.

"I have an idea," she says. "It'll require groveling."

"Of course."

"And you're gonna need to make it to the courthouse in downtown Portland by Tuesday morning."

I pause. That's random as hell.

"What? Why?"

"It's the perfect opportunity for a grand gesture. Don't you have romance novels at your store? To get the girl you have to do some groveling."

"Oh. Um . . ." I'm a little thrown, but there's no doubt in my mind that I want to get back to Joelle as quickly as I can. "I'm ready. Whatever it is, I'll do it."

Chapter 24

Joelle

"Hey. Are you okay?" I whisper to Ivan as I sit next to him in the courtroom.

He swallows and takes a second before answering. "Yeah. I think so."

His eyes are glued to his dad, who stands handcuffed just a dozen feet ahead of us. Next to him is a tall woman in a suit—his lawyer, I assume. The entire courtroom is silent as the judge recites a laundry list of charges. I forget them as soon as he says them. I'm not at all versed in legal jargon, but it's more than just that. It's the fact that everyone here seems bored with the proceedings. The tone of voice the judge uses sounds like he's reading an instruction manual. The lawyers offer quick and short answers. The bailiff standing at the front of the courtroom yawns like he's about to fall asleep standing up.

I guess it makes sense. This is their job. They do this every day, week after week, month after month, for years.

It's still astounding, though. There's so much at stake in this minutes-long hearing. Ivan's dad's fate. Restitution for the people he swindled. Ivan's well-being. And none of it garners more than a passing glance from almost everyone in this room.

But then my ears perk up at the next thing the judge says. "Mr. Mercer, how do you plead?"

I notice that Ivan frowns slightly, like he's bracing for what his dad's about to say.

"Guilty, Your Honor."

I can only see the back of Mr. Mercer's head. I vaguely remember what he looks like. I only saw him one time earlier this summer and it was only for a few seconds. He was smiling then. But now there's a hunch in his shoulders and defeat in his tone. Maybe now that his freedom and livelihood are in jeopardy, he finally realizes what he did wrong.

When I look over at Ivan, he's frowning slightly. This must be a nightmare, seeing his own dad locked up for committing a crime against him.

The arraignment ends, and we stand up. I expect Ivan to turn and look at his dad before he's led away, but he doesn't. He files out of the courtroom without a second glance behind him.

When I look back over at where his dad stands, he turns and I see his face. His expression is twisted into something that looks a lot like anguish. I wonder if he wanted to look at Ivan one last time.

I follow Ivan outside onto the steps of the courthouse. Now that it's the middle of August, morning temperatures in Portland sometimes hover around the fifties and sixties. Ivan shivers slightly, but I can't tell if it's because he feels cold or he's just that distraught at the situation with his dad.

He lingers on the steps for a second, then squats in his suit to sit, rests his elbows on his knees, and shoves his hands in his hair.

I walk up to him. "Hey."

"Hey." He doesn't bother to look up.

"You doing okay?"

He shakes his head, and I sit next to him.

"It's weird," he says after a few moments. "I thought he would plead not guilty. He's never been the kind of guy to own up to his mistakes. I figured this would be no different."

"Maybe when you're staring at a decade in jail, you rethink things."

He lets out a sad laugh.

"Or maybe he realized what he did wrong and truly wanted to own up to it," I say.

"Yeah. Maybe."

"I'm sorry that you're going through all this, Ivan."

"Me too." He sits up and his arms fall to his sides. "Thanks for coming with me."

"I don't know if I was much help."

"You were, Joelle. You made me feel so much less alone. That means more than you know."

This whole morning he's been so quiet and sullen, I wondered if it even made a difference that I was with him. To hear him say this is a relief and a comfort.

"No one should have to go through a tough moment like this on their own." I pat his knee, and together we sit and stare as an endless stream of people walks up and down the courthouse steps.

My mind drifts to Max. I wish he were here right now, sitting next to me, holding my hand. Even though this morning's hearing was about Ivan, I'm still reeling from the days of uncertainty that led up to today. Having Max with me would have been such a support.

"You heard from Max?" Ivan asks out of the blue.

"Oh, um. No. I haven't."

I slump forward and skim the hem of my skirt. Max never returned my message. I finally turned my phone off after waiting for him to reply. It just got to be too upsetting hoping to see his name flash across the screen every time it buzzed or rang, then seeing it was never him. It's clear as ever that he wants nothing to do with me.

As much as that kills, there's nothing else I can do other than accept the fact that we're done and move on—even though that's going to be tough. Ivan was able to reach out to the contracting team, sort out payment, and set up a new schedule. They're due to finish everything by the end of September. That means Max and I have just over a month to work together in that cramped shared space—which is going to be a whole new level of uncomfortable given the fact that we're no longer together.

Just the thought of working so close to him—seeing him every day, catching glimpses of his smile, hearing his laughter—while knowing that we're over is going to destroy me. I'll be a barely functioning, heartbroken mess crying into my croissant dough. Even just thinking about it now has me fighting back tears.

"Well, hopefully whatever personal stuff Max is sorting out gets resolved soon," Ivan says, pulling me back to the moment. "It'll be nice for him to come back to some good news about the building, I think."

I clear my throat and force a smile. "Yeah. Hopefully."

The sudden screech of tires jerks both of our heads up and we look toward the street. My eyes go wide. That's Max's car, double-parked right in front of us.

The driver's-side door flies open and out hops Max, looking the most disheveled I've ever seen him. His head pivots from left to right, the look in his eyes desperate and searching. When he spots me a second later, he beams. My heart leaps in my chest.

As he runs toward me, I slowly stand.

"Joelle, I—"

"Yo, buddy! It's illegal to double-park on the street. Don't you know that?"

Max growls and throws his head back, then twists around. "I know that!" he shouts back at the stranger standing on the side-walk. "Would you just give me two minutes to win back my girl-friend? Then I promise I'll move."

My mouth falls open as a handful of people passing by laugh and whistle. But Max doesn't hear them. All he seems to register is me. His stare is focused and intent, like I'm the only thing he can even see.

When he's this close to me, I notice that his features are racked with fatigue. His hair is matted and floppy, like he hasn't bothered to wash or comb it in days. He looks like he hasn't slept in days either. His clothes are rumpled, and there are bags resting under those mesmerizing green-brown eyes of his.

"Joelle." He takes my hand in his. "I am so, so sorry for leav-ing you after we fought—for disappearing after promising you that I'd be there for you. You promised you'd be there for me, and I'm the biggest jerk for not showing you that same support. And I'm so sorry I took off without calling or texting you. I needed some time to myself to figure out the mess in my head after our fight, but I should have never just ignored you like that. I promise I'll never, ever do that again. You mean everything to me." His chest heaves as he takes a breath. "And I'm sorry for the hurtful things I said to you. I didn't mean any of them. I was pissed at the situation with the building and took it out on you. I love that you're so kind and generous and empathetic and that you put family first. You're the best person I know. You're a ray of sunshine and I love that about you. I still can't believe you ever wanted to be with me."

A woman passing by makes an "aww" sound.

He pauses, the look in his eyes turning intense and tender all at once. "I love you. I didn't know I could be so happy until I met you."

I go breathless. "You love me?"

"So goddamn much."

My eyes well up and my trembling lips curve up in a shaky smile. "I love you too, Max."

That half smile I adore so much appears. And then he closes his eyes for a long second, as if he's savoring my words. He looks back down at me. "God, it feels so good to hear you say that."

I step closer to him. "I love you."

I'm about to pull him into a hug, but I stop myself when I remember that I owe him an apology too.

"I'm so sorry, Max. That awful thing I said about you not ever being part of a family? I didn't mean it, I swear. I wish I could take it back. I was just so upset and hurt and drained and worried about the building renovation, and we were fighting . . ."

He shakes his head. "It's okay. I said some horrible things to you too, remember?"

"We both did."

He laces his fingers in mine. "I went to see my mom."

"You did?"

He nods. "I want to tell you all about it. You were right. She's changed. A lot. She apologized for neglecting me as a kid. We're not magically better, but we're better than we were. We're talking now. We even hugged. That's a start. And I realized that I want her in my life again. I would have never gotten to this point without you."

I smile, tears pooling in my eyes that Max was able to reconnect with his mom.

"For the longest time I learned to live without a family, and I thought I was okay. And I was for a while," he says. "But meeting you made me realize just how amazing it can feel to share your life with someone. You showed me how important family is, and you helped me realize how much I want a family of my own someday. With you."

I huff out a snotty laugh-cry.

He tugs a hand through his hair. "That must sound insane. We've only been together for not even two months."

"It doesn't. At all. And really, we've known each other for a lot longer than that. We've been working side by side for almost two years. It just took us a while to admit our feelings. But I think they were there a lot longer than we realized."

He flashes a flustered smile. "You're right."

"I want the same things you want, Max. Kids, a family, a life with you. Everything."

I'm barely able to get that last word out before he grabs my face with his hands and kisses me.

"I love you," he murmurs against my mouth.

"I love you," I murmur back.

Around us there's clapping and cheering. When we pull apart, we see two police officers leading a guy in an orange jumpsuit and handcuffs up the stairs near us.

"Woo-hoo!" he yells. The officers roll their eyes, but Max and I chuckle.

"You two are together?"

We look down at Ivan, still sitting on the steps a few feet away, gawking at us.

"Oh, um, yeah." I laugh while Max nods.

Ivan's face lights up as he hops to his feet. "What? I had no idea!"

"Yeah, it kind of just happened," Max says before glancing at me. I scrunch-smile at him.

Ivan pats us on the arms, then looks at Max. "Oh hey, you missed some exciting news about the renovation and the building while you were gone."

"I already know. I'm so glad to hear the renovation is back on and that the building's gonna stay in your hands, Ivan."

"Wait, how did you find out?" I ask, now wondering too how he knew to find me at the courthouse if he's been away with his mom this whole time.

"I tried calling you on my drive back to Portland, but you didn't answer. So I called Whitney and begged her to help me get in touch with you so I could apologize and start to make things right with you. She filled me in on everything that happened while I was gone. She told me about the hearing today and how you were showing up to support Ivan. I drove as fast as I could without getting pulled over so I could make it here. I've already missed so much while I was away. I want to be there for you from this moment on, Joelle. Forever."

I tear up once more.

"Whitney also suggested I grovel. A lot."

I chuckle. "Of course she did."

He pulls me close to him once more. "She also told me you deserve to be with someone who's willing to say 'I love you,' no matter if we're blissfully happy or fighting like cats and dogs—and mean it just the same."

I think back to when I spoke those words to her as we were ranting about decent men. Whitney is the absolute best.

Max swallows, his eyes sparkling with emotion. "I want to be that guy for you, Joelle. More than anything."

"You are, Max. You're it for me."

"Hey, lover boy. You mind moving your car?"

Max releases me and flashes a thumbs-up to the stranger hollering at him. He starts to lead us toward his car, but I turn back to Ivan. "You okay to get home?"

He smiles softly while looking between the two of us. "Yeah, I'm good. Congrats, you two."

We wave good-bye, then climb in Max's car. As he speeds in the direction of his house, he clasps my hand in his.

"God, I missed you." He presses a kiss to my hand.

"I missed you too."

When we stop at a traffic light, he turns to look at me. "I'm sorry I didn't call you. I was so focused on things with my mom, I pretty much ignored my phone the whole time I was gone."

"It's okay, Max. I understand. I'm just so glad you got to see her. And I'm so glad you're back."

He hesitates for a moment. "I told my mom about you. She wants to meet you someday. If you're okay with that."

I squeeze his hand in mine. "I would love to meet her."

I lean over to kiss him. The car behind us honks their horn and we break apart, realizing the light is green. Max waves "sorry," then pulls ahead.

When we arrive at his house, I greet Muffin with loads of pets and scratch Doughnut under the chin as he lazes on the back of the couch.

And then I turn to Max. He grabs me by the waist, presses me against him, and leads me in a sensual kiss.

"I have some exciting news of my own." I snake my arms around his neck. "I'm moving out of my apartment."

"Oh wow, really?"

I nod. "I think it's time. My family's a lot more stable than I realized. I don't think they need me nearby as much as I thought they did."

"You'll always be close to them, no matter where you live."

I smile up at Max, grateful that I'm with someone who understands just how much my family means to me.

He wags an eyebrow at me. "Does this mean you're looking for a place to live?"

I grin wide. "Maybe."

"May I suggest the Boyson residence?" He glances around the room. "It's rather cozy if I do say so myself. The owner is a heck of a guy who will make sure your every whim is catered to."

When he wiggles his eyebrows, I burst out laughing.

"And he's got two cute pets who already adore you and would love for you to move in."

"That does sound enticing. But only if I can bring Pumpkin along with me."

"Obviously."

We fall into a familiar rhythm of filthy kisses and eager hands. Soon we're shedding our clothing onto the floor.

"Mmm, shower," Max mutters against my lips. "I need a shower. I'm so dirty right now."

I lean away, playfully pulling out of his hold, and walk down the hallway to stand by the bathroom door.

"You know, if I'm gonna move in, first I think I'd like a tour of the bathroom, specifically the shower. I need to know what kind of water pressure this place has before I commit to anything."

A mischievous gleam flashes in his eyes. "You've been in that shower once or twice before. And you seemed to enjoy your time in there, if I remember correctly."

"True, but I think I need to test it out one more time. Just to be sure I know what I'm getting."

That half smile I love so much appears. As I stand there, I soak in the bliss of this moment. Max and I are together. After eighteen months of harboring secret crushes on each other, a million friendly conversations—and a few super-awkward ones—and all the conflict and work upheaval and family struggles, we're here. Together. Back in each other's arms and crazy in love.

The motion of his muscled, beautifully tattooed arm yanking off his shirt pulls me back to the very hot moment unfolding. He walks over to me and hoists me over his shoulder. I squeal before falling into a fit of giggles.

"Allow me to give you an up-close-and-personal grand tour of the shower," he says.

"And the bedroom after that?"

"Absolutely."

And for the next few hours, Max Boyson gives me one hell of a grand tour.

Epilogue

Max

W hat'll it be today? Black coffee or *ube* latte?"
The smile Joelle greets me with as I order at her bakery counter slays me. It always does.

I do a quick look around, happy that there's no one else in line right now so we can have a moment to ourselves. Then I rest my palms on the counter, lean over, and press a quick kiss to her lips.

"Both. I need all the caffeine."

She chuckles, then glances lovingly at my chest. "I do too."

She leans down and gives our baby boy a kiss on the top of his head. "Someone was fussy last night."

She shakes her head, chuckling before turning around to pour coffee and whip up my *ube* latte.

I straighten up and cradle my hand around little Roan's head as he snoozes away in the baby carrier I'm wearing. When I feel the softness of his skin and that fuzzy mass of brown hair against my palm, my chest swells. Our little guy. It's like my heart is about to burst in my chest.

Having a baby is the single hardest thing I've ever done. It's also the absolute best. We're only three months into parenthood and we've endured sleepless nights, endless diapers, and one fever so far. I can't complain too much, though. Joelle is nursing him and is up with him multiple times a night to feed him. I do as much as I can with diaper changes, burping him, taking him on walks, and carrying him around with me while I work at Stacked, and then take care of everything around the house. But it's nowhere near what she does. She carried him and gave birth to him, after all. Nothing I could ever do will ever compare to that, and I tell her every day how in awe of her I am.

She made me a dad—the greatest thing I could ever imagine being. Every time Roan smiles up at me, there's an explosion of joy inside me. Feeling his tiny, chunky hand wrap around my finger will never, ever get old. I didn't think I could love another human as much as I love our son. And I didn't think I could ever feel as happy or complete as I do with Joelle and this little family we've created together.

"You two are killing me with your cuteness."

I glance up at Joelle, who's beaming at us, her heart in her eyes. She slides two cups to me and practically awws as she takes in the visual of me cradling our son.

"You know you're at maximum attractiveness with our baby strapped to your chest, don't you?" she teases.

I start to ask what in the world she's talking about, but then she nods to the lobby of her bakery. I spot a handful of people looking at us.

"They're checking you out," she says softly as she wiggles her eyebrows at me. "I don't blame them. You're definitely a hot dad."

I chuckle before taking a sip. "Well, that works out well because you're pretty hot yourself."

Her full cheeks blush as she looks up at me. It's the truth. My wife is a stunner. And every day that I get to wake up next to her and our son feels like a gift.

I still can't believe this is my life. I'm the luckiest guy in the world.

I glance around the remodeled space and take it all in. When Ivan presented the completed renovation to Joelle and me, there was a caveat: the contractor had mistakenly taken down the wall between our two shops, essentially making it a shared space. But Joelle and I were thrilled. It meant that we could continue working together in one space, which we loved. No, I didn't love the cramped quarters of our temporary shared space in the back, but I loved working in the same area as her. And now we could keep doing that.

When customers walk into the open-concept space, Lanie's is on one side and Stacked is on the other. They can go back and forth between browsing books and chowing down on pastries. Books and baked goods. It's the perfect match.

Just then Joelle's mom, Ramona, and Auntie Elba pop out from the kitchen.

Joelle flips around. "What are you doing here?"

"We just wanted to drop by and see if you needed any help with the baby," Ramona says.

Joelle laughs. "Of course you did."

Ever since Elba retired, she's been helping out at the bakery almost full-time. With the money Joelle's family and Whitney gave her and the increased business we've been getting ever since the renovation, she was able to hire one full-time employee and one part-time employee to help at the bakery in addition to Elba. The rest of Joelle's family still drop in during the week when they have free time. That's been a huge help since Joelle is technically still on maternity leave, even though she pops into the bakery to check on things regularly.

Ramona and Elba walk over to me and give Roan kisses and snuggles.

"You're sure you don't need us to take him?" Ramona says to me, an eager look on her face.

"We're sure, Mom." Joelle laughs. "You're taking him this weekend, remember? Let him have some time with Daddy today."

Ramona and Elba nod their understanding.

Elba smooths her palm over his head. "Cutest baby ever. I can't tell if he looks more like you, *anak*, or you, Max."

"He's all Joelle," I say. "Even my mom says so."

It's hard to believe that after that years-long rift between us, things between my mom and me are good. Her health is still touch and go, but she felt well enough to come to our wedding last year and visit us last month to see the baby. We're not as close as Joelle's family, but we're in a good place. We call each other regularly and she, Joelle, and I are in a group text chat to share pictures of the baby. I'm genuinely happy that she's part of my life now.

I glance between Joelle and Roan. "All that dark hair and those deep brown eyes. He's got her nose too. Lucky kid."

She scrunches her face at me. God, I love it when she does that.

"Babies' looks change a lot, though, as they grow," Ramona says. "He could end up looking a lot like you as he gets older, Max."

"He'll definitely be as tall," Elba says. "Look at how long he is already. And just three months old."

Ramona and Elba fawn over his impressive size before reaching up to give me quick hugs. Ramona heads into the kitchen while Elba shoos us off to the side to have a minute to ourselves while she takes over the register.

"You feeling okay?" I ask Joelle.

She nods. "Tired like always. But so, so happy."

"Story of my life."

She chuckles. When I gently grab her waist and pull her into me, careful not to crush Roan, she goes quiet. Her eyes dart around the space.

"We're in public."

"Don't care." I wag my eyebrow at her before planting a kiss on her mouth. It's nowhere near as filthy as I prefer and lasts only a couple of seconds, but she brings up a good point. We *are* in public.

When we break apart, I gaze down at her. "Tired and happy and wouldn't want it any other way."

She grins up at me. "Same."

Joelle

That kiss is just what I needed.

As I gaze up at Max, my stomach flips. Even after almost two years together, just one kiss from Max Boyson has me in a tizzy. And I freaking love it.

I give our baby boy another snuggle and kiss, then take in the sight of the two of them. How did I get so lucky? I have the most wonderful husband, a perfect baby, a supportive family, and a thriving business.

And then I decide it doesn't matter how. All that matters is it's happening, and I should relish every moment.

Roan's eyes flutter open and for a second, he fusses. Both Max and I freeze as we look at him. Typical new-parent move, holding our breath to see if our baby will cry while hoping he falls back to sleep.

Thankfully he's back to snoozing instantly. Max and I smile at each other.

"Good job, Roan," Max whispers. "Stay asleep for as long as you can, buddy."

"Can you believe we named our son after a random song we heard at a bar?"

Max chuckles. "I absolutely can since we couldn't agree on a name and were desperate by that point."

Right after our honeymoon in Europe, I got pregnant, which we were ecstatic about. We wanted to start trying for kids right away and I was shocked and thrilled when it happened so quickly.

But then came the name selection process. We couldn't agree on anything—every name I liked Max hated and every name he liked, I loathed.

But one night when I was eight months along, we were out at a pub and grill for dinner. It was open mic night and one of the singers performed an acoustic version of the song "Whiskey to My Soul" by Roan Ash. It didn't sound like the country version— it was more folksy and bluesy. And it was so beautiful and brought up a memory I hadn't thought about in months.

As the lyrics echoed around us, I looked at Max.

"Whiskey," he whispered. I could tell by the look in his eyes that he was thinking about it too.

Of that random afternoon two years ago in his office when we shared a few glasses of whiskey and everything started.

When the song ended, the singer announced the name of the original artist. Our gazes locked.

"Roan," I whispered.

"I like it," Max said.

I rested my hand on my belly and spoke the name softly to our son. "Roan. That's your name, baby."

Max leans down to kiss the top of his head. And then the door swings open and in walks Whitney.

She stops in her tracks and scrunches her face as she places a hand on her chest. "Cutest family ever."

"You always say that," I say with a laugh.

"Well, it's true."

Whitney coos at Roan and gives Max a hug. He glances over at his bookshop on the other side of the space.

"Reggie and Henry have got a line at the register. Better go help."

"You sure you're okay to take Roan with you while you do that?"

He tilts his head at me. "Of course. You rest for a while. I've got this."

He winks at me, flashes that half smile, and I go gooey inside as I watch him walk away.

I turn to Whitney. "What's up?"

"I came to take you out to a manicure and pedicure. You deserve to be pampered."

I could cry, I'm so happy. But then I check the time. "None of the nail salons are open yet."

"I made special arrangements for the salon down the street to open early for us."

I pull her into a hug so fast, she lets out an "oof" noise.

"You're the most amazing friend, Whit. Thank you."

"You deserve it, Jojo. You do so much every single day. Besides, a trip to the salon is the least I owe you after you introduced me to Jacques. That guy. Oh my goodness." Her stare turns dreamy.

At our wedding, I introduced Max's friend Jacques to Whitney after noticing how his eyes practically popped out of his head when he saw her. They've been dating ever since.

"You hooked me up with a handsome celebrity chef, I'll never have to cook again in my life. For that, I'll love you forever, Jojo."

We giggle as I grab my purse. I tell Whitney I'm going to let Max know where we're headed. When I tell him, he nods excitedly.

"Go, have the best time."

I press a kiss to his mouth, then give Roan a kiss. Before I turn to leave, I take a moment and look at the two of them. My heart thunders in my chest at the sight of my husband and our baby.

My boys.

My whole world, right in front of me.

Max smiles at me. "All good?"

I kiss both of them again. "Yup. I just can't resist my bookstore boys."

Acknowledgments

This book was an off-the-cuff idea that I didn't think would end up as an actual book, but it did and I'm so beyond happy because It's my favorite thing I've ever written, and I've got a load of people to thank for that.

To Stefanie Simpson, thank you for letting Doughnut make a cameo. You are a gem and I love you.

Sandy Lim, thank you for beta reading this book and for some of the most meaningful feedback I've ever received. I'm lucky to call you my friend.

Skye McDonald and Sonia Palermo, thank you for being the wonderfully supportive friends I've always dreamed of having.

Thank you, Rachel Lukas, for letting Pumpkin be part of this story.

To my amazing editors, Sarah Blumenstock and Liz Sellers, thank you for loving Max and Joelle as much as I do and for all the work you put into this book.

So many thanks to Vikki Chu for designing a truly breathtaking cover that I still can't stop staring at.

Thank you to my agent, Sarah Younger, and Nancy Yost Literary Agency for supporting me.

To my husband, my family, and my friends, thank you for loving me and being proud of me always. Thank you to Salem for being the best cuddle buddy.

And to everyone who reads this book, thank you so, so much. I know I say this all the time, but it's true: you're the reason I do this. Just knowing that you enjoy reading the stories I write means more than I'll ever be able to express.

Sarah Echavarre Smith is a copywriter turned author who wants to make the world a lovelier place, one kissing story at a time. Her love of romance began when she was eight and she discovered her auntie's stash of romance novels. She's been hooked ever since. When she's not writing, you can find her hiking, eating chocolate, and perfecting her *lumpia* recipe. She lives in Bend, Oregon, with her husband and her adorable cat, Salem.

CONNECT ONLINE

SarahSmithBooks.com

🐦 AuthorSarahS

📷 AuthorSarahS

Ready to find
your next great read?

Let us help.

Visit prh.com/nextread

Penguin
Random
House